COPPER APOCALYPSE

A Novel by

Richard Griffin

Acknowledgements

To Patsy,
for her encouragement and support

COPPER APOCALYPSE

Grace Point Publishing

This is a work of fiction. Names, characters, places, organizations, events and incidents either are the product of the author's imagination, or are used fictitiously. Quoted items are in the public domain, or used per the fair use rule of copyright.

Edited by
Kyle Griffin

ISBN: 978-0-9835496-1-1

Copper Apocalypse

Prologue

If you gaze into the night sky from anywhere on Earth, the Moon won't look any different now than it has for the past 6,000 years. Changes to the Moon's surface, an impact crater for example, even a particularly large one, would not be noticed from the ground without the aid of some man-made device. And yet, the winds of change were reaching out through time and space, to sweep across this barren orb that has fascinated mankind since he first glanced skyward at its wonder. Incredibly, man had been to the Moon and left his mark. Decades later he would return, not just to further space travel, but out of need. This time his goal was to reach the mineral rich planet of Mars.

Chapter One

"O wonder! How many goodly creatures are there here!
How beauteous mankind is!
O brave new world that has such creatures in it!"
The Tempest – William Shakespeare

Five years after the lunar drilling accident, Richard Phelps was up on a ladder splashing flat tan paint on the shining outer skin of his AeroStream camper. He was attempting to camouflage its presence among the thousands of dead tree trunks high on the bluff when he heard the dog signal her subdued alarm. Roo Roo hadn't been prompted to bark, or growl at anything for nearly two years. There had been no need, as no human had ever visited the compound and all of the forest animals were dead. Yet, there she was standing erect, focused on the creek nearly a third of a mile below, hair bristling from neck to tail, emitting a low, but menacing growl.

Phelps grabbed his M4 carbine with its 12 power scope and sprinted to where the little dog was standing. "Shhhhh." he commanded his pet, giving a pat on her shoulder, thankful he had a dog for a time like this. Laying on the flat rock surface, he peered through the lens of the scope. It was about mid day and bright out, brighter than it had been for a long time, due to the now constantly thinning cloud cover. The toast colored mini Dachshund stuck her cold wet nose in his left ear to welcome him, then returned her attention to the creek. 'People!' Phelps thought with some excitement. Survivors! Then reality jolted him. *Intruders!*

~~~~

Emma Cross stood nervously waiting to be transported to the launch platform. She had never flown before, yet she was waiting with fifty-nine other people to board a space vehicle on its way to the Moon. Through the thick tempered glass of the terminal's windows that glistened blue silver, she could see the ship she would be boarding and the launch superstructure, radiantly awash in floodlights against the night sky.

The craft designation was BN-ESV-3, or ESV for short. It was a sleek, streamlined, self-contained spaceship vastly superior to its predecessors. Its hull significantly reduced drag and narrowed the ship's shockwave thereby lowering the energy requirements needed to reach Earth's escape velocity of 1.48/ mps, the minimum speed required to leave orbit and travel freely into space.

The ESV's innovative hull design had allowed engineers to rethink the propulsion system generally reserved for rocket powered space shuttles. Early space vehicles used cryogenic propellants in which the fuel and oxidizer were in the form of very cold, liquefied gases. The fuel and oxidizer were stored in separate tanks and fed through a system of pipes, valves, and pumps into a combustion chamber where they combined and were ignited by sparks to produce thrust. The engine could be throttled, stopped, or restarted similar to that of a car engine.

Solid propellant motors, on the other hand, are a much simpler design. They consist of a steel casing filled with a mixture of solid compounds which burn quickly, expelling gases from a nozzle to produce thrust. A disadvantage with solid propellant rockets is that they cannot be shut down. Once ignited, they burn until all the propellant is gone.

It was precisely that difference in combustion control that caused engineers to select a solid propellant propulsion system for the ESV's launch delivery system, totally removing the liquid component. Due to advances in chemistry, solid composite propellants could now be used to power heavier spacecraft using a single booster rocket to reach escape velocity. They were also less expensive, safer and easy to produce.

The real beauty of the ESV was not in its elegant design, nor sophisticated drive, but in its ability operate as a conventional airframe, and in particular, to perform like a jump jet. It could virtually land almost anywhere. And though that was of small importance to Emma at the moment, it would become vitally important in a way she couldn't yet imagine. Large enough to transport 60 passengers and crew, and a whole lot of cargo, the ESV was quite evolved from the space shuttles of the late 20th and early 21st centuries.

The ESV also had a radical launch delivery system influenced by the Russian aircraft carrier Kuznetsov. It looked very much like a giant amusement ride. The Kuznetsov was a 67,000 ton aircraft carrier that had a unique ramp on its bow causing it to be called the 'ski jump carrier'. When Ronald Reagan Jump Port was first conceived, it was based on the idea that traditional vertical launch facilities would be replaced with a new design, specifically for ESVs, that eliminated the vertical gantry and bulky tri tube configured launch vehicle. The new system incorporated maglev technology employed in high speed trains, a hydraulic steam catapult similar to those used on modern day aircraft carriers, and a curved ramp design borrowed from the Kuznetsov.

Emma was adjusting her NPD, or 'negative pressure device', which was worn over her GPATT issued space fatigues. NPDs had replaced the old 'G' suits early astronauts wore. They were lightweight, comfortable and could be donned, or removed almost as easily as a pair of slippers.

"First time?" said a voice softly from behind her.

She turned quickly to see a young man in uniform who was also wearing an NPD.

"I beg your pardon?"

"Looks like you are having some trouble with your NPD."

"Um, yes, and no." she responded in an attempt to answer both of his questions.

"I see." he said with a smile. He nodded toward the sleek craft. "Quite a sight, isn't it?"

Emma looked out through the glass wall at the ESV now positioned at the boarding platform, shining brilliantly in the bath of floodlights. Theirs was a panoramic view of the long superstructure that ended in an upward curl which guided the craft through its unconventional takeoff from horizontal to vertical.

It was a very efficient system. After cargo and baggage were loaded into its hold, the ESV would be towed onto a track where it would rest on magnetic elevation, or MAGLEV, rails. From below ground the single rocket booster would be elevated and attached to its underside. Once secured, the ESV would travel a short distance along the rails to an embarkation platform where passengers and crew would board. It would then move a short distance to the launch preparation area where it was connected to a catapult while a blast shield was raised.

In combination the catapult, maglev system and rocket booster would propel the ESV down the tubular construction superstructure and then thrust it skyward where the rocket motor and the ESV's engines would carry it into space. The RJP had the most energy efficient space vehicle launch system in the world.

Known by the acronym RJP, Ronald Reagan Jump Port was located in southern Texas between Route 77 and Laguna Madre, just east of Armstrong. There was no space available to expand the facility at Cape Canaveral, and virtually every other tract of land along the US coast line was either too small, too close to civilization, or had serious environmental impact issues. There were numerous private sites available, but none were close enough to open water.

The site search committee wanted the location to be remote for safety, security and low environmental impact. Any prospective site had to be minimally intrusive on the human population, and it had to be relatively close to water for safety in the event of a malfunction, and for efficient recovery of the rocket motor. The Armstrong site had it all.

"Impressive." Emma responded.

"One thing they don't tell you in training." he continued.

"Oh, what's that?"

"Cross your hands on your chest, like this, during takeoff." he encouraged, making an 'X' with his arms over his chest. "It's a bit more comfortable that way."

"You've done this before, I take it?"

"Yeah, that's my bus." he spoke softly, nodding toward the ESV. "I'm the driver, Adam G. Pickett, at your service. Enjoy the ride." he intoned cheerfully, and then quickly departed.

Commander Adam Pickett loved to make the EP3 shuttle run because it frequently provided him with the opportunity to see the Turbine Line, the name given to the nearly 10,000 wind turbine generators which were planted in the continental shelf along the eastern seaboard of the United States, through the eastern Caribbean islands, and down the coast of South America to Rio de Janeiro. The view was impressive from high above the Earth, especially after sunset when the glow from the tower lights illuminated a thin gently curving contour that neatly paralleled the continental coastlines. When high atmospheric pressure allowed an unobstructed view, passengers and crew alike were in for a treat, and they usually remained conspicuously quiet absorbed with the display that this impressive feat of engineering provided.

Connected to land based transmission facilities by large diameter pure copper cables, these giant windmills produced clean cheap electricity for coastal cities and towns. First utilized on land, wind turbines were somewhat limited in use due to location, space and aesthetics. In open water not only were aesthetics greatly enhanced, the wind turbine proved to be reliable, productive and low maintenance. The wind turbine also had minimal environmental impact and was beneficial to sea-life because its tower base configuration attracted fish the way a reef does.

Several factors contributed to the overall pleasing aesthetic of wind turbine generators in open water, which included a 12 mile minimum distance from land with reasonable accommodation to that restriction to conform to aesthetics. The towers had identical exterior high luminescent, or HILUME lighting arrays, a 1,000 foot tower height based on mean high water depth, min-max distance parameters between the towers, and rigid manufacturing guidelines regarding color, structural shape and size of the towers, turbine housing and rotor blades; they all had to be identical regardless of manufacturer. Made from a copper alloy these monolithic structures were impressive to behold at water level, and though there were windmill farms all over the globe, the sight of the Turbine Line on route to outer space was stunning. The show was over in moments, though, as the ESV made its way one revolution around the Earth before linking up with Orbiting Earth Platform #3, or EP3 as it was universally referred to.

Emma's first space stop, EP3, was one of three large geosynchronous space stations in high Earth orbit. It served as the transfer point for ESVs on route to the Moon. Once docked with EP3, ESV crews would change out for the approximately nineteen hour continuing flight to Orbiting Lunar Platform #1, or LP1. Each leg of the tour had its own unique challenges and required skills.

Coupled with the inhospitable environment of space, Government and Private Aerospace Transportation Technologies (GPATT), pronounced "gee pat", believed it paramount fresh crews take over at the start of every sortie, despite the fact all ESV crews trained for and rotated through all legs of the flight to the Moon. Tours were a complex rotation of sorties to and from the Earth, the Moon and orbiting platforms that usually lasted approximately six days ending in a return trip to Earth. During rotation, each crew could fly only one sortie within a 24 hour period. Shuttle runs to an OEP were usually short, but they offered the best scenic views, which is why Commander Pickett enjoyed them so much.

A transport vehicle ferried Emma, along with the other passengers and crew, to the embarkation platform where they boarded the craft in much the same way one would a commercial passenger plane. The cockpit had no barrier walls separating it from the passengers like commercial airliners. In other aspects, it had many of the amenities one might expect to find on an international flight, but those were usually reserved for the nineteen hour voyage to the Moon.

One innovation to traveling and living in space was Mag Lon, a thin magnetized cloth-like material which incorporated a micro hook and loop attachment system similar to Velcro. One half of the system, known as ML-A was permanently attached to walls, ceilings, floors and countertops, while the other half of the system, ML-B, was attached to shoes, boots, clothes and the exterior surfaces of whatever else needed to be temporarily secured. ML-A covered 80 percent of the internal surface area of EP3 and the other space platforms. If an object had ML-B on it, you could literally stick it just about anywhere. Mag Lon was particularly effective for walking about in a microgravity environment.

Emma boarded the vessel and was escorted to her assigned seat. Although they were designed to help the body deal with 'G' forces, the seats of an ESV were surprisingly comfortable and about the size of those found on first class air travel. As Emma waited for the ship to finish boarding she found herself remembering the training she and her fellow space travelers received. It was far less physically rigorous than what earlier astronauts received because so much more information had been obtained regarding the effects space travel had on the human body. In fact, the success of the GPATT program was probably responsible for leading the public into believing space travel had few associated risks. Nothing could have been further from the truth. But unlike the astronauts of the space shuttle era, ESV space travelers were spared some of the discomforts earlier astronauts were subjected to.

The first issue Emma's training dealt with was space adaptation sickness (SAS). The symptoms are similar to being seasick.

The second issue dealt with acceleration and deceleration forces. These forces are expressed in terms of 'G', with 1-G representing the normal gravity experienced on Earth. As G-force increases, the body begins to feel heavier. It becomes more difficult to move and blood circulation lessens as the heart must work harder to pump blood through the body. This impaired circulation can lead to a loss of consciousness, which normally does not occur until around 4 or 5 'G's, particularly for someone who hasn't undergone the proper training.

But even with training, high 'G'-levels can lead to serious problems such as the inability to breathe and diminished blood circulation. Fortunately, ESVs rarely exceeded 3 'G's which is quite tolerable for humans.

The majority of Emma's training dealt with reducing the adverse effects living in space has on the human body. Space is usually referred to as a zero gravity environment, but in reality it is a microgravity environment. Regardless, little to no gravity in space has interesting effects on the human body.

For example, in low gravity muscles atrophy and become less resistant to fatigue. This can cause muscles and ligaments to tear under stresses that would ordinarily not be a problem on Earth. Over time the body loses calcium and bone mass because the load against the body's skeletal structure is reduced. Many adverse affects can be countered and even reversed with regular rigorous exercise, good nutrition, vitamins and proper hydration. The orbiting Earth and Lunar Platforms owed a significant part of their construction to a large rotating tube which simulated partial gravity, thereby helping to counteract some of the negative effects long term forays into space have on the body.

"Must be nerves." she whispered softly, trying to convince herself was the reason for thinking about all this right before takeoff. Suddenly, she was startled out of her daydream by a voice over the ship's intercom.

"Ladies and gentlemen, welcome aboard GPATT ESV, Bluewing. I am Systems Officer Lance Hartwell. This is pre-flight check. The screen in front of you should be displaying our pre-flight check list. All lines must change from red to green, or we cannot launch. Pre-flight check will be exactly the same as your training. I will be monitoring your station from my command screen. If anything does not connect, I'll know about it." Pausing between each instruction he continued, "Item one. Please connect the green pressure line at your seat to port 'A' on your NPD, now. This provides pressure to the suit which will automatically increase and decrease with 'G' forces. Item two. Connect the white cable to port 'B' on your NPD. This allows us to monitor your vital signs. Item three. Lock your feet into the base plate. Simply insert the toe and press down with your heel. Item four. You should recall that every seat has its own built in communication device. All you have to do is say "Comm One", and this will initiate communication between your seat and mine. You must do this before each transmission in order to speak to me. Remember, the comm system is not for idle conversation. Use it only if you have a problem. Everyone, please say "Comm One" now for a communications check." Almost in unison the passengers complied.

"Item five, and last on the list, secure your safety restraint system by gently pulling on the overhead bar. This will cause it to engage and lock itself into place. Remember, the emergency release handle is in the front of your seat base. Please leave the safety restraint system engaged. It will release after we dock with EP3. Please also keep your utility bag with you at all times. SAS can strike without warning, and in a micro-gravity environment, you don't want that floating around. Trust me."

Monitoring his command screen the Systems Officer confirmed all seat positions were in fact, glowing green. "This is Comm one. I am showing green for all stations. Are there any questions?" After a moment of silence signaling there were none, he added, "One final note. For your listening pleasure we will be piping in radio communication between launch control and Bluewing during launch prep and docking. Enjoy the flight."

Through the tiny but powerful speakers in each seat back Emma and her fellow spacefarers heard,

"Commander, this is Comm One. We are green across the board."

"Roger, Comm One. Control this is ESV Bluewing. We are 'green' for launch. I repeat, ESV Bluewing is 'green' for launch."

"Roger that, Bluewing. You may proceed to LC."

Commander Pickett engaged the MAGLEV system allowing Bluewing to be towed along the rails to what was known as the 'jump pit'. There the ESV was hooked to the catapult and handed over to Launch Command for take-off. The process took only five minutes.

"Control, this is Launch Command. ESV Bluewing is ready for launch."

"Roger, Launch Command. Stand-by for 10 minute countdown."

Flight Control did its final systems check and after several minutes handed Bluewing off to be sent into space. "Launch Command, this is Control. You may proceed with 10 minute countdown."

"Roger that, control. ESV Bluewing, this is Launch Command. We are go for launch."

"Roger that LC. Bluewing confirms 'go' for ten minute count down."

"This is Launch Command. Begin 10 minute countdown on my mark. Three, two, one, mark."

It was the longest 10 minutes of Emma's life. It was also the shortest. Electric motors began to whine under the strain of the blast shield being raised. As the ESV's engines came to life Emma, felt both exhilarated and scared to death. She was totally unprepared for the rumble of the rocket engine when it was ignited at T minus 7 seconds. Suddenly, she felt the pressure increase to her NPD and it startled her. She thought she heard someone say "Tally ho!" just before the engines went full throttle and propelled Bluewing down the track like it was shot from a cannon.

The sound was deafening and she was nearing sensory overload. The craft had portholes that strafed both sides of the fuselage, but it was dark outside and she found it difficult to discern forward movement visually. Emma closed her eyes and crossed her arms over her chest at the last moment remembering what Commander Pickett had told her.

She felt considerable pressure push her against the seat as Bluewing rushed toward the ski-jump. About the time she was able to comprehend what was happening, the NPD tightened around her torso and legs, and the G force pressure changed abruptly from pushing her back, to pushing her down, then abruptly back again. A long moment passed, as she struggled to deal with the 'G' forces pressing upon her body.

The intercom crackled again. "Control, this is Bluewing. OMS is on line. The board is normal. Rolling right one-eight-zero degrees."

"Roger that, Bluewing, confirm all systems normal. Prepare for SRB sep."

A light appeared in Emma's porthole as the ESV performed its roll. It was planet Earth as she had only seen in pictures. The view was quite literally, breathtaking, although the 'G' force against her body was contributing greatly to that. In spite of the noise and vibration, she found herself actually beginning to enjoy the experience.

"Sixty seconds to SRB sep on my mark…three, two, one, mark!"

"Roger that!" she heard a voice half shout.

SRB sep, short for Solid Rocket Booster separation, was noticeable to the ESVs occupants, but it was not dramatic.

After what seemed a long moment she heard, "SRB sep in three, two, one." The rumbling immediately eased which was especially noticeable to the passengers.

Nearly seven minutes into the flight something began to happen that didn't feel right to Emma. There was a change in the sound of the ESV's engines. Then she remembered her training. ESV main engines are throttled back to keep from accelerating over 3Gs. If she remembered correctly, the ride would smooth out altogether and the engines would cut off completely. Ninety seconds later her memory was rewarded.

"Bluewing, this is Control. She's all yours, Commander. Have a good flight."

"Roger that Control. Great job, LC. See you on the flip."

Emma was suddenly aware of being weightless, even though she was secured to her seat.

"Ladies and gentlemen, this is Comm One. That lighter than air feeling you are now experiencing means we have reached escape velocity and in a few moments we will be in orbit. The pulsing sound you will occasionally hear comes from the ship's maneuvering thrusters. We will be making one complete revolution around the Earth to position ourselves into high orbit for approach to EP3. We should be docking with the platform in about 90 minutes. Because of good weather on our east coast, in approximately 55 minutes you should be able to get a glimpse of the Turbine Line through the starboard, or right side portholes. Talking is permitted. Please stay in your seats. If you would like a drink, water is available in the blue colored canister overhead."

One common aspect of being flown into space is that it makes you thirsty. Almost everyone simultaneously reached for their small water canister and drained it. The water was refreshingly cool.

Chapter Two

"Man's mind and spirit grow with the space
In which they are allowed to operate."
Krafft A. Ehricke, rocket pioneer

Phelps, a self proclaimed survivalist, studied the small group ambling along the creek below, trying to determine their intent and whether, or not they had discovered the location of his compound nestled just beyond the cliff's edge. A slight westerly breeze had been in the air all morning probably accounting for why he hadn't heard them approaching. They weren't being all that quiet. Were they just following the stream looking for food, or hoping to find other survivors like himself? Phelps really didn't care. He wished to remain undetected and wanted them gone.

The survivalist wondered if the AeroStream's silver reflection in the distance was the reason they had come. He would know by the actions they took in the next few minutes.

The small troop consisted of five men whose ages ranged from late teenage to early fifties. Judging from the distance, two either had rifles, or shotguns slung across their backs. They carried small packs, suggesting to Phelps they were marauders, moving from place to place looking for food and water. With any luck, they would continue to follow the ash choked creek on its southwest course and eventually pass from view.

He watched motionless from the heights. On a second thought, he made one quick look back at the camper to see if it was emitting any smoke. 'Damn!' he quietly exclaimed. Dot was cooking something. The smoke was hardly noticeable, but in this landscape it could be easily seen if anyone cared to look. Suddenly, he became aware of the aroma of food cooking, and in his heightened state it smelled incredibly good.

No one in the group had looked up and Phelps was thankful for that, until they began to leave the creek bed one by one and move in his direction. They weren't making any noise now. He knew he was in trouble when the men began making their ascent toward his position at the top of the ridge. They had to have seen the smoke and smelled the food, he thought. Two climbed to his right, while the remaining three took the easier approach to his left. He would have to act quickly, calculating they would reach the compound summit in less than twenty minutes. "I should have painted that damned camper sooner." he scolded himself.

~~~~

Orbiting Earth Platform #3 had incorporated into its superstructure three large slowly spinning cylindrical shapes. The rotating cylinder design, as opposed to a wheel shape, increased the square footage area of artificial gravity on the space platform. The cylinders housed living quarters which were set up similar to a hotel. Built into this hotel-like setting were training rooms, offices, a comprehensive science lab, and a staffed medical facility with an OR. The platform also had an observatory equipped with optical, radio, and gamma x-ray telescopes, satellite links to Earth for radio/TV/internet, and three ESV docking ports. The operational logistics for supply, maintenance, staffing and support for one outpost in space were quite an undertaking, let alone two additional OEPs, a lunar platform and a lunar colony, but GPATT had proven over and over, it was up to the task.

EP3's brilliant metallic composite superstructure was immense, and viewing it on approach against the monochromatic void of outer space was a moving experience for most. It may not have resembled a conventional hotel on the outside, but on the inside it was functionally identical in every sense, including the amenities, facilities and operational challenges. Part of its design incorporated the modular room, food handling, heat, A/C, water and waste systems used on cruise ships which are known for their economy of space and scale. This also meant nothing was wasted and everything was recycled.

With the exception of some battery backup, solar power was the primary source of energy for the orbiting platforms and lunar colony, both photovoltaic (solar VP) which converts sunlight into electricity via direct process silicon-based cells, and solar concentrating thermal, a process which involves heating water to produce steam to run generators. The solar thermal systems also provided process heat and steam for a variety of additional applications in the silent cold of space.

Several hours after takeoff, Emma's seat speakers once again came to life. "EP3, this is ESV Bluewing on approach for dock."

"Roger Commander, this is EP3... you are cleared for docking port number two."

"Acknowledged, EP3, docking port number two. ETA is eight minutes."

Emma expected a bit more comm chatter for the docking procedure than three sentences, but that was all there was. Docking was achieved through a laser guided computer so precise, when Bluewing docked with EP3 the locking mechanism wasn't felt by anyone on the ESV, or on EP3. Though confirmed by green lights over Bluewing's docking portal, the pilot had to be advised by the EP3 command center that docking was secure and transfer to the platform could commence.

"Ladies and gentlemen, this is Comm One. Welcome to EP3. We'll be letting you stretch your legs in just a few moments. Remember your utility bags. Move slowly and carefully. You shouldn't have to worry too much about floating off. Your Mag Lon boots should do the trick until you enter the hamster cage. That's what we call the cylinder shaped part of the platform. There you will experience the feeling of some gravity due to centripetal force. You should all have maps of the platform. There is also an information station inside the docking port. We will be debarking 'last on-first off." At that moment everyone's safety harness disengaged and retracted to preflight condition. The de-boarding process had begun.

It was a strange sensation to be walking in Mag Lon boots and no gravity, yet Emma mastered the effort quickly and was off to her living quarters. After she settled in, she made her way to the twenty-four hour dining facility for something to eat.

"So, how was my driving?" Emma heard a somewhat familiar voice from behind her. She turned to find Commander Pickett smiling at her for the second time that day.

"A bit bumpy at first, but you seemed to get the hang of it."

"You're pretty cool for someone who just had their very first spaceship ride. I was so wired after my first ride I needed some liquid therapy before I could relax."

She giggled. "To be honest, I was scared to death. When I got to my room I had to throw up."

The ESV pilot laughed. "You used the bag, I hope."

"Yes. But I don't know what to do with it." she admitted with some embarrassment.

"Read your handbook. I believe you'll find instructions in there. You're okay now, I hope?"

"Fine. Actually, I'm hungry"

"Mind if I join you?"

"Yeah. Sure." she responded.

They selected cheeseburgers with all the fixings, iced tea, and specially formulated nutritional supplements in the form of some rather tasty snack chips. In fact, various foodstuffs were enhanced with calcium and other minerals and vitamins to help counter some of the negative effects of living in a microgravity environment. It was easier than taking a pill every day, but if a pill was preferred, or a vitamin drink, those were available, too.

Emma was surprised to find how much normal food was offered. That was partially due to the fact the dining facility was located in the 'hamster cage' whose simulated gravity, along with the Mag Lon, helped to keep most of the food in place. Solid foods, such as hamburgers and fried chicken, were relatively easy to handle because they were pre-cooked and could be easily reheated. Liquids and food combinations that were part liquid still had to be confined in some sort of container that dispensed the contents easily, could withstand both freezing and heating, and took up almost no space as waste.

Drinks, however, were cleverly unique. Designers and engineers were asked to come up with a drinking system that incorporated the following components; public, personal, no waste, accommodated hot, or cold drinks, spill-proof, self cleaning, sanitary, portable, re-useable, minimal storage. Some of the technology utilized in this system had been in place for decades, in restaurants and stadiums, in the form of beer and soda dispensing. But the innovative part of the system didn't involve dispensing and storage. Liquids were already being kept in airtight bulk containers ensuring potability and minimal storage. They could be heated, refrigerated, and easily dispensed. The challenge lay in the public, personal, re-usable, sanitary, and portable elements.

Designers came up with the SmartCup system, a 12 oz. hot- cold container that was portable, and could be filled, emptied and cleaned in nearly every room on the platform with the help of some sophisticated plumbing. Whenever you wanted something to drink, you simply grabbed a SmartCup, placed it in a SmartCup port and pressed the touchpad for the drink you wanted. The system would empty any existing contents, clean and sanitize the interior, clean and dry the exterior, recycle the cleaning agent and any leftover beverage, fill it with the selected beverage, and complete the cycle in exactly 15 seconds. If just a refill was desired, sensors allowed the SmartCup to bypass the cycle and top off your beverage to its 12 oz. capacity, cleaning only the exterior of the cup, simply by pressing REFILL before the drink selection was made.

The SmartCup also had an ingenious mouthpiece that was leak-proof if dropped, or knocked over because it could only be activated by pressing your lips against it. The SmartCup drinking system effectively met all the design challenges put before it.

"Will you be going to the Moon?" he asked Emma.

"Day after tomorrow. I have some work to do here, first." she said, trying to figure out how to take a drink from the SmartCup.

Noticing her dilemma he said "See this?" pointing to the mouthpiece. "Just put your mouth over it."

Emma followed his instruction and was immediately rewarded. "You know, it would have taken me all day to figure that out."

Commander Adam Pickett was born in Norfolk, Virginia. At the age of four, his parents moved to Solomons Island, Maryland not far from the Cedar Point Naval Weapons Testing Station located at the mouth of the Patuxent River. He attended Patuxent High School and joined the track team where he excelled in cross country running. He also enrolled in the Naval Junior ROTC. He performed well academically and was recruited by the Naval Academy. After becoming a Naval aviator, Adam applied for ESV training with GPATT and was accepted immediately. At 30 years of age, he had been an ESV commander for about a year and a half. This was his seventh mission. Adam was 5' 9" tall, with a medium build. He had close cropped hair and grey eyes. He was confident, cute, and possessed a semi photographic memory, but he had to work at math.

"So, what's a nice girl like you…"

"Doing in outer space?" she interjected.

"Yeah, what are you doing up here?"

"Research."

"You're a student?" he asked, somewhat surprised.

"I'm a GPATT techie on special assignment."

Emma Cross was a geophysicist with a PhD from the University of Colorado in Boulder. She had a Bachelor of Science in Geophysics, a Masters in Hydrology Sciences, and a PHD in Applied Astrophysical and Planetary Sciences. She stood 5' 6" in her stocking feet, had shoulder length brown hair and pale green eyes. She was plain, but not unattractive, quiet, but witty and she appeared aloof most of the time.

"I'm impressed. Just what is it you are working on?"

"Well, I'm going to be working on the Moon." she answered with just a hint of sarcasm.

"Yeah, you did indicate that, sort of, didn't you. Let me rephrase." He glanced at his watch. "Damn! I gotta go. Could we pick this back up later, say tomorrow around 19:30 hours? That's 7:30 p.m. for you civilian types. I'll meet you right here."

He was off before she could respond, and now she was feeling some regret at her sarcastic response to his question, but that was all part of the flirt, wasn't it? Was she flirting? Emma had dated a few guys, though the relationships were usually short because she was devoted to work and school. That's what she told herself, anyway. Inwardly, she longed for a steady guy. In reality, there was rarely any chemistry with the men she had dated. But with Adam the chemistry seemed to be there and she found herself pleased with his attention. At dinner, she promised herself she would be more forthcoming.

As the day progressed Emma became more distracted and hardly heard a word at the EP3 orientation seminar. She hoped Adam wouldn't be turned off by the fact she was investigating the lunar core drilling incident, which had been officially closed for some time. The real reason she was there had to do with her published master's thesis, which didn't quite resonate with conventional thought regarding the Moon's geology and history.

Selenologists, those who study the Moon's geology, generally believed the planetoid to be a solid dead body with only the possibility of a very small, metallic core, if any. As far water existing, the only H2O would be in the form of small quantities of surface ice found in impact craters and imported by whatever formed the crater. But that hinged on which theory one ascribed to regarding lunar formation.

Ask how the Moon was formed and you might hear several hypotheses. For example, the *fission hypothesis* suggests the Earth lost a piece of its mass in an explosion, which is how the Pacific Ocean was formed. The Pacific Basin, however, is believed to be younger than the Moon so, it is somewhat ignored for that reason. And unlike Earth, the Moon is iron deficient.

Lunar capture contends the Moon was grabbed by Earth's gravity. Possible, though improbable because a close encounter with another moving body would in all likelihood, produced a collision sending out debris, some of which should have remained in orbit.

The *co-accretion hypothesis* maintains the Earth and the Moon were formed as a double system when our solar system expanded. This would seem to make sense, except it does not explain 'angular momentum', a reference to the dynamics of an object rotating about a particular reference point, the way the Moon goes around the Earth..

For the present, the popular theoretical explanation for the origin of the Moon is the *giant impact theory*. It assumes the Earth-Moon relationship was produced early in the formation of our solar system. The two bodies collided with a glancing blow, an impact that should have put enough material into orbit around Earth to have eventually accumulated to form the Moon. That being said, the theory doesn't explain why there is no other debris also in orbit around the Earth, nor why the Moon's volatile elements are inconsistent with Earth.

Emma's doctoral thesis theorized, irrespective of any particular formation theory, the Moon possessed an active molten core and sub-surface aquifers, which she partially based on a comparative analysis of both Earth and Moon geology. She developed the idea when she discovered that the question of the origin of water on Earth, and why it contains more water than the other planets in the solar system, really hadn't been clarified. She felt this was a hugely important aspect of any plausible lunar formation hypothesis, none of which any of the current theories address.

As with the Earth and Moon, there are also various popular theories as to how the world's oceans were formed. For example; the cooling of primordial Earth caused water vapor to be held in the atmosphere resulting in the retention of water, along with ice comets and water ice containing asteroids that brought water to pre-historic Earth. There is also photolysis, radiation that can break down chemical bonds on the Earth's surface, and biochemical synthesis. It is believed that some or all of these factors have contributed to the vast oceans we have today.

Emma had hypothesized, because it was generally accepted when the earth was in its planetesimal stage water was probably already present, the possibility of discovering water on the Moon was not much of a stretch. With respect to the Moon having a molten core, there was enough surface evidence to support magma activity in lunar history. The fact there were no current observable eruptions, or magma flows, and none had been discovered dating from the somewhat distant lunar past, was not suggestive of a non-molten core, at least not to her.

Emma's academic adviser at the time was so impressed with her work, he helped her to get it published in several scientific magazines and journals. That she was the daughter of a geology professor helped some, too. And when several members of the GPATT team were killed while drilling core samples on the Moon, Emma's thesis was thrust to the forefront, with the speed and suddenness of a phreatic volcanic eruption, in a clamor for information that would explain what had happened.

Chapter Three

*"From now on we'll live in a world
where man has walked on the Moon.
It's not a miracle, we just decided to go."*
Jim Lovell – Apollo Mission
Command Module Pilot

Dick Phelps was 6' 2" tall, 190 pounds and in good physical condition. He wore his hair close- cropped, which Dot cut regularly. And though it was just the two of them, he and Dot both maintained their usual grooming habits. Phelps always had a moustache, but occasionally wouldn't shave until the itch of his new growth drove him to it. He was an educated man and had served six years in the Army Reserve which afforded him good posture, self confidence, and served as a spring board for his interest in survival techniques.

Dorothy Phelps was a tall plain looking girl, with short straight black hair, but she had quite a figure. During the summer months around the house, she was usually seen in a two piece bathing suit. Inside the camper a two piece was all she ever wore. Dot was devoted to Dick and went along with just about anything he wanted to do, although she insisted on some discussion about most things before she would commit to them.

As Phelps hurried back to the AeroStream, he wondered about where the five men had come from. It never occurred to him that a little less than two years earlier, not long after he and Dot had settled into the camper, he had given away his position over the radio, bragging thoughtlessly to some chap on EP3 about how long he thought they could hold out. The town of

Waldron lay fifteen miles to the west of the compound. It was the closest town and where he had appropriated the majority of his supplies, including the AeroStream. Phelps thought, perhaps someone from Waldron had noticed what he had been buying and realized he was stockpiling. He had tried to be discreet, even secretive, but Waldron wasn't that large a town. Maybe this person who had also survived, up to now, figured it out and decided to come looking for him. But these men had approached from the east, which logic implied, they arrived at his location by way of Route 80 originating out of Danville.

The five were actually all from North Little Rock. They knew there wasn't much left in the east so, they followed the Holla Bend River to the Route 27 bridge at Dardanelle. Little Rock was buried in ash and the river, muddy as it was, provided the least demanding path for travel out of the city. Even they had some sense of caution, choosing to stay away from what they believed were the more populated areas. Together, they reasoned the smaller towns would present them with less trouble and a better advantage if trouble did present itself. From the Route 27 bridge, they moved southwest into Danville and picked up Route 80 on the southern end of town, which took them west toward the town of Waldron. It was no easy trek. Most of the lakes, rivers and streams were swollen and often unrecognizable. Roadways were recurrently obstructed with drifts of ash which made driving any distance nearly impossible, assuming a vehicle could be found that hadn't been choked dead by the ash. Remarkably, much of the ash had been washed away in places by months of rain. And although most living things were dead and gone, much of the inanimate remained. Satellites, unaffected by the cataclysm, continued to operate, and as batteries were available, GPS still worked. That's how the five were able to navigate from town to town. In the late morning sunshine (a more common occurrence as the ash dissipated) the AeroStream shown like a beacon that the five couldn't resist investigating.

~~~~

On December 15, 1972 the Apollo 17 lunar module landed on the Moon at 20° 11' 26"N   30° 46' 18" E on the southeastern rim of Mare Serenitatis, or Sea of Serenity. It differed dramatically from the Apollo 15 mission site located at the foot of the Apennine Mountain Range. The Apennines rise up more than 15,000 feet along the southeastern edge of Mare Imbrium, or Sea of Rains. As a comparison, these lunar mountains are higher above ground level than the east side of the Sierra Nevadas in California. The Apollo 17 site was chosen for its wide flat topography. GPATT selected the same site to establish the first lunar colony for similar reasons. The area was also an ideal place for habitat pod construction, not to mention the fact the needed logistical information was readily available, having been obtained from the previous Apollo missions.

It had taken four years for GPATT engineers to design, build and test several configurations considered for a lunar surface habitat. It took only six days for a trained 8 person team to construct a 30'x15'x10' arch shaped building on the lunar surface. The structures themselves had three basic components; a modular airlock entry/exit system, titanium Track Lock tubing, and two and a half inch thick structurally engineered fabric called

S2F which was a combination of bullet proof vest and self sealing spacesuit technologies.

The airlock module was an eight-sided box with airtight interlocking edges whose panels could be literally snapped together in about an hour. The fabric walls were secured over the track-lock tubing creating an airtight space that also protected against radiation. And if something were to penetrate the S2F shell, such as a small meteorite, or hand tool, sticky layers of resin filled fabric would temporarily seal the opening until a permanent repair could be made. Outside storage areas and tanks were also shielded with S2F.

Apollo Seventeen, as the colony was commonly referred, was more an outpost for scientific study than a lunar colony, yet that was changing because the site was constantly being expanded. When the drilling incident occurred there were 18 people living and working there. Three of those, who made up the core sample drill team, were working in the Mare Crisium plain, which from Earth, particularly during a full moon, can be seen as a smaller stand alone dark area closest to the Moon's outer edge. Depending on the angle, the plain could be described as the right eye of the 'face' of the 'Man in the Moon'. This particular plain is easily identified because the same side of the Moon always faces Earth.

At some point in Earth's past, gravitational effects slowed the Moon's rotation until it matched its own orbital period around the Earth. When that happened, the effect stabilized resulting in having the same side of the Moon permanently point toward Earth. Many of the moons circling other planets also behave in the same way. And though we observe the various phases of the Moon's light reflected surface, it is always the same side. Those familiar phases of the Moon have to do with its relative position to the Earth and Sun, not its own rotation.

The drilling team had been dispatched to the Mare Crisium plain on a twofold mission. Their primary aspect involved extreme depth core sampling. The second and minor aspect was to investigate an anomalous formation that had intrigued a small group of scientists. Photographs taken on previous space missions presented a series of pictures revealing what appeared to be transparent, dome-like shapes along the north Mare edge. Examination of frame LS3-51-21.6 in the series revealed an object that was brighter than any other natural feature. Through high resolution scanning this bright spot, to some, resembled a head similar to the famous Face on Mars photograph. Even though a semi-translucent haze exists between the camera and the object, some thought the anomaly possessed characteristics found in monuments.

Situated on a hillside, it had symmetry and what appeared to be a nose, mouth and eyes. Several observers excitedly believed they were genuine facial features not just a collection of random bright and dark spots in the image.

A second irregularity, fittingly referred to as the 'bird' was a cross shaped structure next to the face. These scientists insisted this structure did not resemble any lunar geology and believed it to be made of metal.

The 'control tower' is a third object to the right of the 'bird'. It protrudes through the main dome like an airport control tower, hence the name. One observer said it seemed uncharacteristic compared to familiar lunar geology.

One team member asserted, "There is no reason to suspect photographic defects, or imaging flaws. The shapes cannot be explained by any natural process. Their proximity to each other suggests that they are artificial. I must therefore conclude all of them were constructed." To the casual observer, however, all three just looked like rocks in the distance.

Core samples being their main objective, the drilling team proceeded due west, but slightly south of the anomalies. There were six GPS satellites orbiting the Moon providing a real-time position of the Rover on the lunar surface. This helped them to navigate the flat, but irregular landscape between Apollo Seventeen and the far edge of the Mare Crisium Plain. The team planned to take a core sample along the eastern edge of the rim, after which, they would investigate the supposed monument like shapes to the north. The Moon was in its first quarter phase so there would be plenty of illumination to make their initial observations and take ground level photographs. Using a specially designed digital camera, they made one noted observation on route and reported - light distortion at that distance made the features unremarkable.

"Here, take a look at this, twelve o'clock, just above the base and slightly left." Roman handed his drill specialist the digital view camera. It was an ingenious auto-focus image-stabilizing instrument which was placed right up against the helmet visor. It had only two buttons. One controlled the zoom and the other engaged the camera shutter. It had one drawback over conventional binoculars. The image was a digital interpretation on a six inch screen, and at considerable distances, most images were adversely subject to light distortion.

"Definitely something there." Mike said as he continued scanning. "But I can't tell what it is. Too bright." He handed the viewer to Skip. "At this distance it's hard to tell what it is, but it is bright, I'll give you that. Maybe that means something."

Skip put the viewer up to his visor then handed it to Roman, but said nothing.

"What do you think?" Roman asked.

Skip responded by vocally imitating the familiar high pitched musical tones of a famous 1960's sci-fi television series.

"Well, there you have it." Mike said with triumphant sarcasm. "A truly professional opinion."

Skip responded defensively. "Hey, I see puppy dogs in clouds. That doesn't mean they're actually there."

Roman and Mike simultaneously turned and glared at Skip with feigned exasperation.

"Okay." Skip relented. "Hate to disappoint, but I don't think it's a cabin hideaway for Martians. Looks to me like a natural formation, not dissimilar to formations found in Badlands National Park, South Dakota. But we are way too far away for a meaningful assessment. Based on the photographs we looked at, my guess is they are shield volcanoes made of silica-rich lava that erupted from localized vents. That would at least explain their shapes and bright appearance." Glaring back at Mike and Roman he sarcastically added, "And that's my professional opinion."

Roman made a note of each one's personal observation after which they continued on in the Rover to the drill site. He kept a watchful eye on the anomalies as they rode along, but when they eventually passed from view they passed from memory as well and he began to mentally prepare for the dig. This whole notion of artificial structures on the Moon was exciting to some, particularly those scientists back on Earth, but to his crew whose mission was to investigate those anomalies fist hand, it was disquieting.

Mike gave the command to stop the Rover. Checking his GPS coordinates he remarked, "This is close enough for GPATT work!"

Satisfied with Mike's coordinates, Roman announced, "Gentlemen, start your engines."

They went to work immediately without saying another word, setting up the drill rig and photovoltaic cells that would help power the apparatus. Once the site was ready, they would end their shift and retreat to Apollo Seventeen in the Rover. The next morning they would return to the drill site with a supply of pipe.

In reality, morning was a relative thing on the Moon because of the long periods of sunlight and darkness. The time zone used on the Moon was Central (US and Canada) in conjunction with the time zone in which Ronald Reagan Jump Port was located. Once they finished obtaining core samples from this area, they would then move to investigate the so called anomalous structures on the northern rim of the plain, but Roman knew that wouldn't happen until the end of the week. The next day they returned to the bore point and began their steady penetration into the lunar mantle.

Apollo astronauts had used seismometers during their visits to the Moon and discovered it wasn't as geologically inactive as science had assumed. Small moonquakes were detected occurring well below the surface. At the time, they were believed to be caused by the gravitational pull of Earth. It had also been determined that tiny fractures appeared at the surface from which gas escapes. In 1999 data from Lunar spacecraft suggested the Moon's core was small and probably no more than four percent of its mass, significantly smaller than Earth whose core is approximately 30 percent of its total mass. But as often happens, scientific opinion modified (because of this new data) from the Moon's core being small and inactive to probably small and slightly active. The discovery of escaping gas suggested the core was still hot, but not necessarily molten. And though the gas couldn't be seen by the naked eye, it might account for the hazy effect in the image that produced the anomalies in frame LS3-51-21.6, which was one reason why they were there.

GPATT's current model of the interior of the Moon was developed from data obtained using the seismometers left behind from the Apollo missions. Its mass appeared to be absent any voids giving rise to the popularly held belief that the Moon was composed of solid rock. And because the Moon does not have a dipolar magnetic field like the Earth, there is no geo-dynamo at its core and, therefore, not molten.

Small disturbances to the Moon's rotation, however, had suggested to some the core, though small, might still be molten. Another explanation considered was the Moon is not spherical. It's shaped like an egg with one of the small ends pointing toward Earth, so the Moon's center of mass is not at its geometric center. It was theorized to be about 1.2 miles off-center. Armed with this information GPATT held it was quite safe to probe deeply into the planetoid.

The core drilling team, however, would not get to investigate the anomalies identified in frame LS3-51-21.6 . They had drilled several thousand feet by day four and were approaching the depth limit of their probe when the drill stopped turning. Skip had been standing at the controls on the side of the rig keeping an eye on the hole.

He raised his arms indicating he hadn't done anything unusual, and didn't know what was wrong. Roman and Mike started moving toward Skip to assist with inspecting the equipment when the ground began to rumble. That was all the warning they received. Pipe was suddenly ejected from the hole in a geyser of steam, followed by pieces of jagged rock and more steam that exploded outwardly. Mike was hit by a piece of sharply twisted pipe which struck him with such force, it launched his body the entire length of a football field away from the bore hole. His visor had completely shattered making him the first casualty. Large stone chips with sharp edges tore through Skip's spacesuit and fractured his helmet visor. He wasn't seriously injured, but his suit depressurized instantly. The geyser toppled the drill rig, which fell on Roman pinning him to the ground. He hadn't realized flying stone chips created parallel tears in the leg of his suit that the self sealing fabric couldn't handle. His oxygen had leaked out and was depleted well before the rescue party arrived in response to his EPIRB (emergency position indicating radio beacon) signal.

The ground quaked continuously in that region and steam gushed steadily from the bore hole for two months, then stopped abruptly. Because the Moon has no atmosphere the water vapor dissipated into space. Inexplicably, for those two months, a cloud trail could be seen from Earth whenever the Moon was illuminated by the sun. The event left many questions in its wake, but it answered one question with certainty; there was water in quantity on the Moon.

Chapter Four

*"Our generation has inherited an incredibly beautiful world
from our parents and they from their parents.
It is in our hands whether our children and their children
inherit the same world."*
Sir Richard Charles Nicholas Branson

Humans have various personal strengths and weaknesses, depending on one's point of view, which can propel them to greatness, or keep them in the shadows. Most people, if their personal situations remain relatively stable, rarely get tried beyond their comfort zones. As a result, their personal strengths and weaknesses are rarely observed. But whether they have to do with a relationship, a job, school, or on the playground these either help improve personal situations, or worsen them. And yet, there is a characteristic embedded within the human race which is neither strength, nor weakness that has kept humanity from extinction for over 6,000 years and allowed us to survive the cataclysmic events of our history on this planet.

This characteristic is random and doesn't surface in everyone, but it presents itself in enough people in times of great calamity to keep our species from dying out. The five men approaching the bluff over Dutch Creek possessed this characteristic. It had brought them together and kept them alive when most of humanity had perished. It allowed their bodies to resists disease, breathe polluted air, drink foul water and eat spoiled food without deadly consequences. It also provided them with the wherewithal to endure long periods of hunger, thirst and adversity when most men and women could not.

Basic instinct was inherent of this characteristic, and a man forced into unprepared survival, oftentimes proceeds imprudently on that natural impulse. And though it had served them well, the unique characteristic they possessed would soon be tested against someone who had also survived the ash, not so much by instinct, but through strength of intelligence, which had gifted him the foresight to prepare for the encounter that awaited them all.

Hoping it would never come, Phelps had planned for this day. He was intrinsically pragmatic. If he could survive, others could too, and it would just be a matter of time before limited resources triggered a migratory hunt for food. From the outset, the Phelps' compound structures were positioned for strategic advantage with weapons, knives, water and ammo placed in each one of them. They were aligned in a crude semi-circle facing the edge of the cliff and the fire road, and each one had a small window on all four sides. Phelps' mental picture of such a confrontation, however, began on the fire road approach to the compound, not from the cliff face. No matter. He would be ready. Phelps always figured if he was ever discovered, it would more than likely be by a small group no larger than six people, and they would be desperate. Unlike the five men approaching, he would not have to make hasty decisions, or rash judgments due to a weakened condition stemming from an empty belly, or a parched throat. He would, however, react quickly and with deadly force against any threat, and Phelps felt threatened by the men ascending the cliff. Their advancing tactics confirmed this in his mind.

~~~~

Commander Adam Pickett was right on schedule. It was 7:30 precisely when he strolled up to Emma's table.

"19:30." she said cheerily, as he sat down.

"Very good, you remembered." he grinned, pleased she was there.

Emma smiled shyly and looked down at the SmartCup she was holding.

"What are you drinking?" Adam asked.

"Nothing, yet."

"Well, if you want something stronger than tea, we'll have to go to the bar."

"There's a bar up here?"

"Yep, you can eat there too. Alcohol has to be paid for and dispensed by a bartender, even up here. Come on, I'm buying. It's not far."

Along the way, Emma couldn't help thinking about how strange it seemed to have a bar on a space station. 'And why not?' she asked herself. If mankind was going to be serious about space travel, a bar had to be in the picture somewhere. After several minutes of light conversation, they arrived at the Tail of the Comet, ordered their drinks and sat down intent on getting to know each other.

"You can see your drink with these." Emma said, examining the transparent SmartCup in her hand.

"Yeah, you only find them here in the bar, and only if the drink contains alcohol. Comes with a built in counter, too, just in case the bartender thinks you've had one too many."

"It counts your drinks? Pretty ingenious."

"So, where were we?"

"Well, you were giving me lessons on how to use one of these" she said holding up the SmartCup, "and how to tell military time from civilian time, then you left."

"That's right, I was. And you were going to tell me what you are doing up here."

"No I wasn't."

"Right. It was more like you were trying to avoid telling me what you are doing up here."

"There ya go."

"What? Is it a secret, or something?"

"No. I just didn't want to go into it for the purpose of idle chit chat."

That comment did not sit well with Adam. This was the third time he had tried to talk Emma, and she continued to be coy. He liked her, but his intuition was telling him he was getting nowhere, and his efforts were growing tiresome so, he looked for an opening to end the conversation politely thinking this was all just a waste of time. After what was felt to be an appropriate amount of time, he found the opening he was looking for.

"So, when are you scheduled to skip over to the Moon?"

"I'm leaving tomorrow morning."

"That would be 09:30." he said flatly.

"That's right. How did you …oh, you're piloting the ESV aren't you?"

"Yes, I am, and I really have a lot to do in preparation for the flight." Adam gulped down the rest of his drink and looked Emma in the eye. "Guess I'll see you in the morning." he said with feigned cheerfulness. And for the second time in as many days Adam Pickett had departed before she could respond, leaving her alone in the bar.

The encounter had not gone the way Emma had expected. The interval had been way too short. Adam sounded genuine enough with his exit, but Emma was confused. Her mind started racing to explain what had just happened. She went to bed trying to dismiss the negative feelings she had, but she couldn't sleep.

Emma tossed and turned for several hours trying to make herself feel better, to no avail. It wouldn't be until the next morning, when Adam halfheartedly waved to her at breakfast, as he walked out of the dining area, that she completely understood. She had been playing with Adam, not realizing she had taken it too far. Lesson learned. The next time, hoping there would be a next time, she would be more forthcoming.

The flight from OEP3 to OLP1 in stationary position above the Apollo Seventeen lunar site was far less stressful than the jump from Earth. The ride was quiet and smooth and the ship's forward motion was imperceptible.

Before taking up residence on the Moon, Emma would see Adam only twice. On a pass through early in the flight he smiled and said "Hello" to her. She was happy to see him and wanted very much to have a do-over of their previous encounter. But as pleasant as he seemed with his "Hello", he offered no opportunity for conversation. She longed for one more chance to speak with him.

During the long flight to OLP1 Emma spent the time reviewing her research and recalling events that led to her current assignment. When the drilling team was killed by the eruption on the edge of the Mare Crisium plain, the Moon had already begun its waxing phase. This helped to mask the newly created lunar vapor trail giving GPATT extra time to do damage control.

They handled it as an industrial accident. The headlines read *Lunar Drilling Kills Three as Gas Pocket Explodes*. When the lunar vapor trail became visible it was treated with excitement rather than alarm, although some officials at GPATT were privately concerned.

A full year after the lunar accident the global warming argument hit a new high. For years the notion of global warming had been hotly debated particularly in the United States. Air pollution was at the forefront of the argument. In particular, man made CO_2 emissions were blamed as the culprit for the increase in these atmospheric gasses. It was argued, heat from the sun's rays trapped by these gases created what is known as the "greenhouse effect". Climatological models said increasing concentrations of greenhouse gases led to runaway heating of Earth's atmosphere. What some scientists predicted as a result of this heating, or 'greenhouse effect' was a significant rise in Earth's sea levels due to melting polar ice, thereby destroying coastal cities and towns. The picture painted by this model was simple and very easy to understand, lending it credibility in the public eye.

In reality, carbon dioxide is produced in far larger quantities by many natural means including volcanic out-gassing, carbon dioxide from animals, bacteria, decaying vegetation and Earth's oceans. These far outweigh man's production of CO_2. The human carbon dioxide emissions footprint is small by comparison. And with all that CO_2 production going on, clouds and water vapor still account for 90 percent of the total composition of Earth's atmosphere. Add the remaining constituent gases and CO_2 still only equals approximately .038 percent of the atmosphere. And in spite of its popular bad reputation, carbon dioxide is a very important and beneficial element to all life on planet Earth.

Through hard science Emma knew the atmosphere was a bit more dynamic and complex than what was presented by the simple greenhouse effect model. It is a very active environment. A real greenhouse is a physical barrier that prevents convection. Earth's atmosphere is not a greenhouse, nor does it act like a blanket around the Earth. It actually promotes convection. A real greenhouse works by modulating convection, while the so-called 'greenhouse effect' works by modulating radiation so, the impression of actual greenhouse-like activity in the Earth's atmosphere is technically incorrect.

Greenhouse gases do not actually trap Earth's heat, but they can slow the transfer of energy from Earth to space. And though it may be delayed, heat is eventually released due to atmospheric and cosmic drivers of climate change, such as volcanoes, clouds, thermals, and hurricanes. One fact not presented in the global warming argument is that the sun is not diminishing as many of the uninitiated believe. Our sun, albeit very slowly, is actually growing in size and intensity as it expends fuel, and as such, it will eventually extinguish all life on Earth. Fortunately for mankind, that time is still a long way off.

Emma's research strongly indicated solar activity more precisely matched the plot of Earth's temperature change over the last 150 years, and it corroborated the post-WWII temperature dip, when global CO_2 levels were rising. Solar activity would at least support observations made by U.S. spacecraft that parts of the Martian polar ice caps have been receding.

Still, events had occurred to suggest Earth was warming, such as the thinning of the Ross Ice Shelf, boundary recession of artic polar ice, diminished number of glaciers, a slight increase of average Earth temperatures over the past 150 years, and a slight, but almost imperceptible rise in sea level. Until recently, all of these in Emma's mind could just as easily be attributed to cyclical changes.

As a geologist, Emma knew that in the contiguous United States, a few feet below the surface of the ground, the year round temperature consistently hovered at a cool fifty-five degrees Fahrenheit. Twelve months after the lunar accident, that temperature had risen to fifty-seven degrees providing the global warming devotees some of their most potent rhetoric. In the two years following, the temperature continued to rise and was now sixty-five degrees, yet atmospheric temps and carbon dioxide emissions had remained relatively constant. She suspected the current global warming indicators were not being produced by anything that was taking place in Earth's atmosphere. So if carbon dioxide and the 'greenhouse effect' were not responsible for this new spike in the globe's temperature, what was? Emma was going to the Moon in an effort to find out.

Other phenomena also occurred following the 'lunar accident' that found their way into her research. For example, in Yellowstone National Park 'Old Faithful' geyser was behaving strangely. The temperature of the geyser's water had always been relatively constant. Between the mid 1980s and mid '90s measuring probes were lowered down into Old Faithful to a depth of 72 feet. Water temperature at that depth was 244 degrees Fahrenheit, the same temperature that was recorded in 1942. On a recent reading the temperature at 72 feet had risen to 287 degrees Fahrenheit.

The geyser's eruptions also normally lasted anywhere from one and a half to five minutes and usually shot 3,700 to 8,400 gallons of boiling water to an average height of 145 feet at intervals approximately 90 minutes apart.

Current measurements showed eruptions were shooting 10,200 gallons of water 216 feet high lasting a full 7 minutes at nearly regular intervals of 74 minutes. Old Faithful was getting hotter, and discharging more water, higher, longer and in shorter intervals.

Trees in the park had also started dying, though this was thought not too unusual considering a large part of Yellowstone is situated directly over a huge magma chamber. But this incident was unique because the trees and plant life were dying in unusual patterns and unlikely places throughout the park. Tree dead zones also began to appear in nearby states for unexplained reasons.

The seventeen year locusts had also arrived, billions of them. *Magicicada septendecim,* or periodic cicada is a resident of the eastern United States known for mass emergences every seventeen years in the north, and every thirteen years in the south. Some scientists believe these mass emergences are related to the insect's survival. The cicada is not really a locust and it is harmless to humans and animals, but it does damage trees and shrubbery when it lays its eggs under the plant's bark. Periodic cicadas in the United States are grouped in a numbering scheme known as broods. Numbers one through seventeen identify broods that emerge every seventeen years. Numbers eighteen through thirty identify broods that emerge every thirteen years. But not all broods emerge at the same time. Different broods depending on their location emerge in different years. As an example, Brood

III, the Iowan Brood emerged in 1997. Brood XIX the Great Southern Brood emerged in 1994. Brood XXIII, the Lower Mississippi River Valley Brood is a thirteen-year brood which emerged in 2002.

Emma was not so much intrigued by the sheer numbers of the insects, as much as she was the areas they were emerging in. Of the thirty, or so broods within the numbering scheme, twenty-seven had suddenly emerged at the same time and off cycle. Reports of off cycle emergences had also come from Australia, Thailand, Japan and Korea.

Glacier disappearance was also on the rise. Glaciers are made of crystallized snow which is pulled by gravity to lower elevations where the now compacted snow either breaks off and melts, or forms ice sheets that eventually break apart as icebergs. In Greenland three of the Earth's largest, the Helheim, Jakobshavns and Kangerdlugssuaq glaciers had retreated almost to their sources. Iceland's lower elevation glaciers had completely disappeared and the island's snow covering was vanishing. Yet the higher altitude glaciers in Tibet, Nepal and the Himalayas showed no such drastic changes.

In conjunction, ice shelf calving was dramatically increasing. When the end of an ice shelf breaks off in pieces, it is called calving. An ice shelf is a floating sheet of ice attached to the coastline extending quite some distance over water. They usually have level, or gently undulating surfaces. They are relatively thick, rising two meters, or more. Ice shelves grow by snow accumulation and by the seaward flow of land glaciers.

Two years after the lunar accident, the calving process of numerous ice shelves accelerated in size and speed. The Ward Hunt Ice Shelf, located on the north coast of Ellesmere Island in Canada's Nunavut territory, broke into ten separate pieces, all of which Emma noted, were floating independently and melting into the sea. The Ayles ice shelf also broke away from Ellesmere Island. But even more significant to Emma was new evidence indicating the Greenland ice sheet had begun to melt. Scientists had predicted, if this ice sheet melted completely, it could raise the Earth's oceans by 23 feet.

Although Emma was a geophysicist, part of her research effort for this project was to review any natural abnormalities occurring around the globe that were reported. One such aberration involved changes in salt water tides. To most people, tides are nothing more than the rising and falling heights of the sea caused by the gravitational forces of the Moon. All one had to do was spend a single day at the beach and watch the water's edge progressively move closer to land then surreptitiously retreat. Tidal changes are even more noticeable along docks where the depth of the water can be seen relative to a stationary object such as a pier, or bulkhead. Emma knew, however, that forces behind tides were slightly more complicated than just the Moon's pull on Earth's oceans. A tide produced at a given location is not only the result of the changing positions of the Moon, but also the Sun, the effects of the rotation of the Earth, shape of the sea floor, and the wind.

Normal high and low tides had recently become amplified in certain areas. But this was not unusual considering the changing and complex nature of tides. The anomaly that caught Emma's attention was associated with a tidal bore in India. A tidal bore is a phenomenon in which the leading edge of an incoming tide forms a wave that travels inland up a river, or bay against the current.

Bores occur in relatively few locations around the world so, when a report about one made the news it usually involved some dramatic consequence.

The Hugli River in northeastern India is part of the Ganges river system 155 miles north of the Bay of Bengal. Along its banks resides the heavily industrialized population of Bengal, an important shipping route. It is also well known for the onrush of its spring tidal bore which threatens shipping and can damage coastal property. The Hugli tidal bore is usually a whopping six feet in height and travels up river at the quick average speed of thirteen miles an hour.

The most recent bore was measured at double the average speed and height, surging past the Farakka Barrage, a man made barrier which helps to diminished the severity of the bore's charge. And though the path of death and destruction left in its wake made headlines worldwide, the newsworthy aspect of the event for Emma was the bore's height, speed and unexpected time of arrival. It was two months ahead of schedule.

An earlier event that made global news nearly two years after the accident was the eruption at Ascension Island. It was the first eruption since the island's discovery over 500 years ago. Ascension is mostly wasteland located south of the equator along the western edge of the Mid-Atlantic Ridge, an underwater mountain range in the middle of the Atlantic and Arctic Oceans that begins just 3oo miles south of the North Pole and runs all the way down to Bouvet Island just above Antarctica. Ascension was primarily a small military installation and telecommunications relay station shared by Great Britain and the United States. It was discovered on Ascension Day, 1501, by the Portuguese navigator Joao da Nova. The island is actually the summit of a stratovolcano that rises over 9000 feet above the sea floor and almost 2500 feet above sea level. The eruption was actually a slow moving magma flow that destroyed Wideawake Airfield, the golf course and the Georgetown Obsidian Hotel. It did not take long for the island to be deemed unsafe and quickly evacuated. Of interest to Emma was that magma continued to ooze from vents on the eastern side of the tiny island. Similar events had also occurred at the Marshal Islands in the western Pacific, where slow moving magma flows were belched to the surface with all the ceremony of catsup being poured from a bottle, but completely destroying several of the uninhabited atolls.

The most recent oddity on her list of anomalies came from a news brief she happened to catch on the 11o'clock news, not long after the Ascension Island eruption, and just two days before her flight. The TV screen showed a woman holding a huge Alaskan red king crab.

"Paralithodes camtschaticus" the reporter said expertly, "is the most coveted commercially sold king crab in the world and the most expensive per pound. It is a very large animal with a leg span reaching six feet. This particular species is caught in the Bering Sea and is difficult to catch, but it is one of the most preferred crabs for eating and is claimed to be tastier than lobster. The red king crab is a claret stained color while it is alive. Its gets its popular name from the color it turns when cooked. The short four day seasonal catch of Alaskan red king crabs from the Bering Sea is usually around 16 million pounds. This year only three million pounds were harvested. King crab fisheries have been declining in recent decades, but nothing of this magnitude. The explanation for this year's poor catch is under investigation, but it is being contended by some that over fishing is the primary contributing factor."

The real truth was that no one really knew why the catch of giant crabs was dwindling. Over fishing was only one theory. Global warming was another. Emma had her own ideas about it, along with all of the other phenomena in her research, but she couldn't and wouldn't propose anything until she had facts to support her explanation, whatever that would be.

Chapter Five

*"For the Lord your God is bringing you into a good land,
a land whose stones are iron,
and out of whose hills you can dig copper."*
Deuteronomy 8: 6-8

Richard and Dorothy Phelps were only two of several thousand Americans who, recognizing the signs of impending doom, acted to prepare for the worst. Some dug underground shelters, others stored supplies in their homes and garages, and many, like the Phelps, literally headed for the hills. Richard and Dot had no family. That made it a trifle easier to keep their scheme a secret. They told no one, and they were very careful to hide their activities from everyone. Forty-five year old Richard Phelps had determined early on if global conditions proceeded the way he anticipated, the only way anyone could survive would be to isolate themselves in a secret location and stock it. His fear was not the act of survival, for he was confident in his abilities to do that. What concerned him most was being discovered by others, which would require protecting his cache and defending it against human predators.

He had scouted an old tertiary fire road that hadn't seen any traffic for decades. The site he selected was so far off the beaten track, that it would have been difficult to locate even from the air. It was remote, to say the least. For over a year Richard and Dot had been developing and stocking their little compound. They had six twelve foot by twelve foot sheds filled neatly with water, food, survival gear, clothes, medical supplies, and just about any necessity you could think of, including an M4 Carbine, several shotguns, a 9mm pistol, a .357 magnum revolver and 1,000 rounds of ammo for each. They also had six 700 lb propane tanks and fifty smaller tanks of the size used with gas grills. Phelps even drilled a well that was hand pump operated. And everything was covered with camouflage netting.

To acclimate themselves and determine what items they would need to survive alone for several years, they practiced their survival techniques by turning off their electricity and water. They held mock scenarios for handling injuries, illness and exposure to the elements, especially the cold. They camped out regularly to get used to being alone and to find ways to fight the boredom and loneliness they expected to experience. They practiced for severe conditions, but in reality they would be relatively comfortable in their camper. They had numerous electronic devices that could be powered by generator which included a flat screen TV and a DVD player. They were judicious about the use of fuel and food, and they calculated that the 677 DVDs, 321 CDs and the 550 books and magazines in their collection would keep them entertained for a long time.

They researched what type of long range radio equipment would be required to communicate with other survivors, including the military, or some remnant thereof, whom they were confident would be there when the dust settled. They were well prepared. Dick Phelps also made sure Dot could handle the weapons as well as he, though Dot never thought for a minute she would ever be facing the confrontation her husband believed was coming up the cliff .

~~~~

The signs were apparent to visionaries years before Emma Cross was even born; predictions, calculations, presumptions, expectations, and warnings that the demand for copper would outpace supply and accelerate. Auguries would eventually reach the public consciousness in the form of news stories;

LONDON - The price of Copper on the LME rose on worries South American supply might fall on account of an ongoing strike, while price movements were exaggerated in heavy trading in China. Accordingly, copper prices have more than doubled in the past two years. Workers in the copper industry, in the meantime, naturally want a larger piece of the rising profits pie, which has led to dozens of labor disputes in the last 12 months alone.

LIMA - An ongoing strike at Abancay Southern in Peru is hindering output and estimates point to a possible 60 percent loss of annual production. Workers for the world's largest copper producer started their strike indefinitely yesterday for better wages. It is all happening at a time when the copper market is having trouble meeting demand. It is estimated production will fall short of demand by 300,000 tons in the coming year.

NEW YORK - US data released earlier showed The Institute for Supply Management (ISM) non-manufacturing business index fell more than expected negatively impacting today's upward trend. Meanwhile equities markets, closely linked to metals prices, were higher today in spite of copper inventory being low. Poor equity markets mean investors take their money out of metals to cover losses, and flee towards safer bets. A major contributor to demand outpacing supply are the booming economies of China, Indonesia, India, and East Africa which need massive amounts of copper to support their burgeoning infrastructures.

TOKYO – SATU Global Technologies, the electronics giant has acquired Arequipa Geologies of Peru, the seventh largest producer of copper ore in the world in an undisclosed offer for the purpose of adding to its fast growing copper wire business. SATU's chairman was quoted as saying "Without copper, we simply can't build out on modern society. Tubing, plumbing for houses, offices, wiring in cars and motors, just to name a few, are made with copper. You can't even light a light bulb without copper."

LOS ANGELES – Environmental groups have been applying pressure on the California legislature and members of congress to restrict the mining of metals due to the extreme and disruptive impact current techniques have on the surface of the landscape. The California legislature is currently reviewing a bill that is gaining a lot of momentum which would eliminate certain types of strip mining altogether in the state.

WASH. DC – A bill recently passed by the House imposing sanctions on imports from countries whose mining techniques are not in accordance with current federal guidelines for the US is expected to sail through the Senate with little to no opposition. The President hailed the action saying "...we must continue to be a global leader when it comes to the world environment."

For nearly 6,000 years, copper has played a significant part in the history of mankind. The oldest civilizations of Earth; Iraq, China, Egypt, Greece and Sumeria all contain evidence of early copper use. During the Roman Empire copper was mined on Cyprus, which is the origin of the metal's name. It was called Cyprium, "metal of Cyprus". The bright orange colored metal is a chemical element in the periodic table having the symbol Cu. It is an essential trace nutrient to plants and animals and it is found in the bloodstream of humans. In certain amounts copper is poisonous. For that very reason, it is incorporated into marine paint because it retards marine growth, particularly on boat hulls. Like gold, silver and aluminum, copper is a ductile metal, which refers to how much a material can be deformed before it breaks.

Copper is an excellent electrical conductor, heat conductor, building material, and component of various alloys. Its uses and applications are numerous and include plumbing, electric motors, wiring, circuit boards, relays, bus-bars, solder, switches, structural engineering, roofing, rain gutters, paint pigment, coins, jewelry, cookware, medical imaging, germicidal, biomedical, ceramics, musical instruments, electrical grounding and telecommunications.

It is also a metal that does not react with water, although the oxygen in the air will react slowly with it to form a protective layer of copper oxide on its surface giving it a green patina, as in the Statue of Liberty. The Turbine Line towers were purposely made from a copper alloy because of the metal's non reactive property with water.

The most common source of copper on Earth is the mineral chalcopyrite, an ore that accounted for half of all copper production. There are other secondary ores containing copper as well, but in nowhere near the density. A number of countries had sizable reserves of the metal, which was extracted through large open pit mines, but due to increased demand, supply was dwindling. It had been estimated decades earlier that at the current usage rate, the Earth would run out of copper in less than half a century.

And so, GPATT was formed by the United States, the UK, Russia, Japan and numerous contractors worldwide for the purpose of mining copper on Mars for use on Earth. The endeavor would involve traveling, living and working in space, on the Moon and on Mars. It would also involve mining and shipping material from an environment extremely hostile to humans. The world's demand for renewable energy was driving its appetite for copper, and man would travel all the way to Planet Mars to satisfy that hunger.

In the world's search for low cost, environmentally friendly, renewable energy, new technologies had developed such as, wave-water action piston-powered generators and solar convection towers for driving turbine generators. These new technologies required thousands of miles of copper wiring for power and transmission lines. Demand for copper had become so voracious that the time had finally come when the strain on Earth's resources, the negative impact of mining techniques on the environment, and advances in technology had mankind eyeing the planets as new locales to exploit. Mars was prime real estate.

Extracting copper from ore is accomplished one of two ways; through pyro-metallurgical (fire), or hydro-metallurgical (water) techniques, neither of which is difficult on Earth. These extraction techniques, however, presented GPATT with special challenges in the Mars environment. Mining the ore was not too difficult. Techniques were relatively the same on Earth. But transporting just ore back to Earth for processing would be way too inefficient. Extraction of the metal from the ore while it was still on Mars was the challenge. On the plus side, copper ore concentrations were much higher on Mars, making the closed processing fire and water extraction systems that GPATT engineers designed, more productive and cost efficient.

Mars is sometimes called the red planet. Named for the Roman god of war, it is the fourth celestial body from the sun, Earth's neighbor and a standout in the night sky. The reddish appearance is not from an over abundance of copper on the surface, but rather from hematite (rust). The copper is actually below the surface.

Mars is categorized as a terrestrial planet meaning it is very much like Earth. It has an atmosphere, thin and poisonous, comprised of 96 percent CO_2, 2 percent oxygen and smaller amounts of other un-breathable gasses. It has a similar rotational period and seasonal cycle to that of Earth. Its surface features have valleys, deserts and ice caps like those of Earth. It is home to the highest known mountain in the solar system, Olympus Mons, and the largest known canyon, Valles Marineris. Possessing these common elements with Earth was beneficial for planning missions to the red planet because operations could first be practiced in Earth's safe environment.

Of particular interest to GPATT, other than copper, was that there is water on Mars. In 2007 the government space agency had announced that if Mars' southern polar ice cap melted, it would cover the entire planet with water to a depth approximately thirty-six feet. Even larger amounts of water are thought to exist beneath Mars' mantle. The ability of a world to develop and sustain life favors planets which have liquid water on their surface. However, even with water and an atmosphere, habitable life as we know it is not possible on the red planet because Mars' orbit lies half an Astronomical Unit beyond the habitable zone of the Sun.

GPATT's interest in the water on Mars wasn't for sustaining life, though, it was for wresting copper from the ore using the hydro-metallurgical extraction method. The availability of water was extremely important to their mission because transporting water to Mars for ore processing was simply out of the question.

~~~~

Emma had been napping when she was awakened by the muffled sound of maneuvering thrusters which fired in several short bursts. A few moments later she heard the now familiar docking chatter and voice of Commander Adam Pickett over the intercom.

"LP One, this is ESV Bluewing on approach."

"Roger Commander. You are cleared for docking port one."

"Docking port one, acknowledged, ETA is ten minutes."

Emma could now see LP1 from her window. She noted immediately, it was the same design as EP3, but with only one cylinder, or hamster cage, as the structures were referred to. The Moon was in its waxing gibbous phase and LP1 and Apollo Seventeen were both still illuminated by the Sun, which meant her investigation of the bore site would not be hampered, or delayed. Hopefully the site would be relatively undisturbed.

As Emma was proceeding through the terminal area of LP1, she caught sight of Adam walking ahead of her. Catching up to him, she gently grabbed him by the arm.

When he turned and saw who it was he flatly responded, "Hey."

"I owe you an apology." she confessed searching his face for some recognition.

"For what?" he said blankly.

"I don't know, being a smartass?"

Adam folded his arms, but said nothing. He was beginning to enjoy her attempt at eating humble pie.

"I'm here to investigate the explosion that happened at Mare Crisium. I don't know, I just thought..." her voice trailed off.

"Thought what?" he half demanded forcing the conversation to continue.

"I don't know, maybe that you might not be interested in talking to me, once you found out why I was here."

"Are you kidding?"

"No, why?"

"Well, because you looked all...unapproachable at the jump port, and then that I'm smarter than you attitude on EP3. I figured you wanted me to get lost because I'm just a rocket jockey."

"Well, I sort of figured that you were like that with all women. But I don't think that now."

"Oh, and what's changed in a day and a half?"

"Me. I didn't give you much of a chance. I'd really like another try, to be friends. At least let me buy you a drink to make up for my, uh, prejudging you."

"All right, I'd like that."

"Okay, um, how about 19:30 hours tomorrow? I'll meet you at the - Blue Moon Saloon is it?"

"That's what they call it. Okay, 7:30. See you then."

Emma checked into her quarters on LP1, logged into GPATT.net, confirmed her appointment with the mission coordinator for the next morning and retired for the evening. She was feeling better having set things right with Adam. She owed him that, whether, or not anything developed between them.

The next day she arrived at the OLP1 Office of Mission Logistics, promptly at 10 a.m. and was met by Major Derek Woo. Mission Operations Officer Woo was a dark haired, clean shaven, medium built military man dressed in GAPTT fatigues just like everyone else on the platform. The only noticeable difference, other than his military haircut, was the rank insignia on his collar and unit patch on his shoulder. Emma found him to be friendly and talkative, but guarded.

They shook hands, "Major Woo?"

"Yes. Miss Cross, I presume?"

"Pleased to meet you. Thank you for meeting with me."

"Not at all. I have been asked to cooperate in any way I can. Please, sit down. I have been told that you are here to investigate the Mare Crisium incident."

"Yes. Actually, I have several assignments, but that is the main one."

"I thought that had already been done. The report submitted by the investigating team said they hit a gas pocket. Have you seen the report? I can get a copy for you."

Emma thought she sensed some defensive posturing. "Oh, no thank you. I have a copy. I'm not really here to redo their work. They did a great job for what they did. I'm a geologist and I've been asked to take a look at what happened from a geologic perspective."

Woo nodded, but said nothing.

"Matter of fact, I'm not really here to find out what the drilling team did, or didn't do. I read the report and as far as I'm concerned, they didn't do anything wrong. I'm here simply to try and determine what happened below the surface. You see, GPATT didn't expect to run into any gas pockets, let alone one that would explode. Frankly, based on our data, it shouldn't have happened."

Woo seemed to relax a bit. "I'm at your disposal." he said pleasantly. "Would you like something to drink?"

"Coffee, creamer and sugar would be great."

Woo filled two SmartCups and gave one to Emma. As a way to place the Major even more at ease, she decided to ask him about the Mars mission, and the mining vessel launched weeks earlier.

"Major, I'm curious about a couple of things. Why was Cyprium Prospector built in orbit around the Moon, and why all the mining equipment lying around if mining is not allowed on the Moon?"

"Well, for one thing, Cyprium Prospector is a Trojan class vessel. It is enormous, and way too big to have been launched from Earth. They thought of it as a kind of Trojan horse, hence the classification. Everything that was needed to supply a complete mining operation for an extended stay on Mars was packed into the Prospector, and on the return trip it will, hopefully, be full of processed ore. Imagine sixteen Titanic sized passenger ships stacked two ships wide, two ships high and four ships in length and you'll get an idea of its size. It's basically a cargo hauler in the sea of space. Secondly, the engineers and designers calculated that maximum efficiency with all kinds of things would be obtained if it was constructed out here.

For example, there are no construction delays due to weather in space, and the size and weight of construction materials are far easier to physically move around in a weightless environment. Less fuel is used because the ship does not have to escape Earth's gravity, but something that large would never be able to anyhow. The trip to Mars is also shorter based on perigee and apogee of the Moon, Earth and Mars orbital paths. As far as mining equipment, and I am assuming you are referring to the equipment at Apollo Seventeen, it's there for training purposes only. You are correct, mining is not allowed on the Moon at present, but it is an excellent place to train mining techniques for operating in a hostile environment. And Mars is a hostile environment. Now, how may I be of assistance?"

"Well, for starters I'll need quarters."

"That has already been arranged. You will keep the quarters you are in now on LP1, and you will also have quarters down at the colony."

"Thank you. How do I get around in case I need transportation?"

"While you are on the Moon, a Lunar Rover and two cadres will be at your disposal. They will take you where you want to go. You will be limited of course and excursions must be scheduled through this office, along with a mission plan which is similar to a flight plan. Your cadres can handle that for you. Naturally, you will have complete access to the accident site. As far as going back and forth from the Moon to LP1, there is a shuttle, but you will be limited by its schedule, which is once a week. On occasion it may run twice a week and you'll know about it. Oh, and while you are on the surface, you will have the same computer systems and communications access you have on LP1, although I must caution you, solar flares are more disruptive out here."

"Excellent. I understand that there is seismographic equipment in place."

"Correct. I can provide you with a grid that shows sensor placement. There are computers both here and down at the colony that receive real-time data from the sensors and you can access all the data history from either location."

"What condition is the site in?"

"Believe it or not, it hasn't been touched. There are a lot of boot prints and tracks out there, but my people only did what was necessary for their investigation, and to get the bodies back, oh yes, and the drilling rig. No one has been out there since."

"Now, should I contact you, or someone at the colony when I need something?"

Before Major Woo could respond an enunciator sounded. "Right on cue." he said smiling as Lieutenant Jefferson walked into the office. "Miss Cross, this is Lieutenant Emmitt Carver Jefferson. He has been assigned to be your liaison while you are here."

Jefferson was a tall close cropped wedge of muscle, young and eager to please. Emma wondered how long he had been in space, considering his physique and what she had learned about losing muscle mass while living in space.

"Pleased to meet you, mam."

"If you need anything Miss Cross, directions, information, resources, or if you have a problem with anything, he's your man. The lieutenant is attached to LP1 and he will remain on the platform, but his services include your needs on the Moon. He takes the shuttle down and back every time it runs so, you'll get to meet with him at least once a week, and it's another way to keep in touch."

"You can reach me anytime by touching your comm badge." Jefferson offered.

"I don't have a comm badge."

"We'll get you one. This is a comm badge." he said pointing to a black square of plastic on his uniform breast pocket. "It's kinda like a cell phone. Touch it, say the name of the person you want to reach and it sends a signal through your earphone to the receiving badge. The person on the other end touches their comm badge and it opens up an encrypted line of voice communication between the two. When the conversation is over you touch the badge again and it breaks the connection. They stay activated all the time and the batteries last for two years. Get me anytime, day or night. Now, if you don't answer a regular call, a message is left on the Net in your 'inbox'. And by the way, you'll have to keep this with you 24/7 while you are here."

"You said a regular call. Is there some other kind?"

"Yes. The badge beeps once indicating a regular call, priority one, or what we call a P-1. For example, to contact me you would touch your comm badge and say Lieutenant Jefferson, P-one. My badge will beep once every five seconds for twenty-five seconds, then it will stop and an alert will be sent to my inbox telling me you attempted to call, noting the time and the date. You may choose not to answer a P-1 for various reasons. If the call is urgent you will get two beeps, same duration. That's a priority two, P-2. You may choose not to answer those as well, but two beeps means someone really wants to get hold of you. Three beeps require a mandatory response. If you don't respond to a P-3 call a search team goes looking for you. The badge is also a GPS locator. You can run..." he said pausing. Emma and Major Woo smiled acknowledging the well used but unfinished phrase. He then added "Prioity-3 is usually reserved for emergencies."

"Well then, I guess all I need to know at this point is when the next shuttle leaves."

"I believe the next one leaves in about 46 hours. The schedule is always on the message board counting the number of hours until departure and arrival."

Major Woo handed Emma a paper chart of the seismometer sensor grid. "Is there anything else I can do for you, Miss Cross?"

"No thank you Major, you have been very helpful."

"Then I'll leave you with Lieutenant Jefferson."

The Lieutenant escorted Emma to get her comm badge. When he confirmed it was working properly, and she knew how to use it, he departed leaving her with a reminder not to separate herself from it, it truly would be her lifeline. He also requested she make her calls to him Priority-2. He never received P-2 calls anyhow, and that way he would know it was she who was calling.

~~~~

Unlike landings and takeoffs from Earth, the shuttle down to the lunar colony was a relatively short, but direct shot from LP1. Emma had plenty of time to prepare for her departure to Apollo Seventeen. She spent some of that afternoon going over data and new information. The rest of the time was spent getting ready for her 7:30 p.m. rendezvous with Commander Adam Pickett.

To Emma's surprise, the Blue Moon Saloon was a rather cozy place with its wood accents and colored lighting. You could almost forget you were on a space station. Emma was sitting at the bar sipping on her first drink when Adam arrived.

"You're early." he said pleasantly.

"Only by a few minutes. What would you like?"

"I'll have a Guinness." Adam said to the bartender.

"You can get that up here?"

"Yep, the bar stocks about twenty different brews and Guinness is one of them. Trouble is, when they run out of something it takes a while to get it restocked. They usually wait for at least half of the tanks to run dry before they change out the empties. It's either, feast or famine."

The bartender returned with a transparent SmartCup filled with Adam's drink. He could see that it was still foaming inside the way a Guinness does when it's poured into a glass.

"What are you having?" Adam asked.

"White zinfandel."

"I like that, too."

Emma raised her drink and said, "Cheers."

"Slainte." he responded as they tapped their cups together.

Emma looked down at her drink and smiled in a way that suggested a slight embarrassment. "So, you want to know what I'm doing up here, eh?"

"Well, yes, I am interested. Seemed to me like a good place to start up a conversation at the time."

"It was. I'm sorry. I don't know what my problem was. Let's blame it on post traumatic stress syndrome from being launched into space at a thousand miles an hour."

"I can buy that. Heck of a ride though, wasn't it?"

"That's an understatement."

"Are you criticizing my driving?" he said teasingly.

"No, no. I wouldn't do that." She responded emphatically. They both laughed.

"So, what are you going to do now that you are up here?"

"Wow. I never really thought about what that might mean. It's not every day you wake up and just fly up to the Moon, you know?" Emma's senses were suddenly heightened with that realization.

"Actually, I do know." Adam said without much excitement.

"Yeah, I guess you do. But wow! Me! I'm going to be on the Moon, tomorrow! That's incredible!"

"Don't get out much, do ya?" Adam said with his chin leaning on his hand like this was all so ho-hum.

"Not to outer space, no, but here I am."

"And why did you say you were here, again?" he said sarcastically.

"Right. You want the long version, or the short?"

"Oh, the long one, absolutely."

"Sure you have the time?"

"Oh yeah. I've got nothing scheduled for the rest of the evening. I'm all yours."

"Okay. I'm a geophysicist."

"That much I know."

"Right. Well, when I was in graduate school I did my thesis on the probability of water existing on the Moon."

"We know it's there now."

"Yes, but back then no one thought there was, not in any significant amount. Anyway, it got published with the help of my advisor, and my Dad."

"Your Dad?"

"Yeah, he's a professor of geology, sort of well known. He's done stuff for the space agency. That helped me get it published in a few scientific journals. That's a big deal to some, you know."

"I would imagine that it might be a big deal to have your paper published, especially if you were only a grad student. How did you come up with your idea?"

"Well, I read something in college somewhere that suggested no one really knew why water existed on some planets and not others. Think about how galaxies and solar systems are formed, or are thought to be formed, particularly during the planetesimal phase. Matter is spinning and expanding outward, material is mixing and colliding with other material. I began to wonder why all of the planets in our solar system were so different if they descended from the same primordial accretion disc. I mean, I understand some of the reasons for the differences involve time, distance, temperature and collision with other objects. But at the time, I figured it all came from the same basic stuff. That's how I looked at it, at least. Other celestial bodies and planets have water. So I figured there was a pretty high probability that water existed on the Moon, below the surface of course and in significant quantities. I must have defended my thesis pretty well because here I am. I mean, that's why I'm here, because the accident at Mare Crisium proved there was water below the surface, and I'm the only one who's really done any significant work on the subject, I guess. Actually, when you think about it, it was a long shot."

"Wait a minute, I thought GPATT had already explained what happened - there was a gas pocket."

"Well, yeah, that vapor trail had a lot of water in it. Steam is water in a gas state."

"I know that. I guess I just didn't think of it quite that way."

"What did you think they meant by a gas pocket?"

"Natural gas, not breathable air, or steam from water. That's a pretty significant discovery. Wonder why they played it down?"

"I don't know. Maybe they didn't want it to be a big deal because it would divert attention from the Mars mission. Anyway, I'm here to see about what's under the surface, because they don't want something like that to happen again, and I'm also here to do some research on global warming."

"Uh, oh. You're not one of those green earth fanatics are you?"

"You have a problem with environmentalism?"

"Not at all, just extremists."

"Good. I'm not an extremist, I value human life above all other life, but I am for protecting the planet and preserving its natural resources. So, what do you do out here when you are not flying ESVs?"

"Training for the next Mars mission."

"You're going to Mars?"

"I'd like to."

"I don't understand."

"Not everyone who trains for spaceflight gets to go into space. At any given time there is always a group of people who are 'mission ready'. But first you have to make it into the 'ready pool'. Once there, you have to get selected for a mission, and selection depends on a number of factors like age, weight, mission type and duration, specialty, and training completed. Training is constantly being revised and updated. I want to be assigned to a Mars mission so, its' training, training, training regardless of any curse."

"Did you just say, curse? What curse?"

"No one has told you about the Mars curse?"

"No. Is it something I should know about?"

"Everyone connected with the Mars mission knows about the Mars curse! But then, you're not really here about the mission. Sorry, everybody up here is connected to the mission in some form or other. Naturally, I assumed you knew."

"Nope. So tell me."

"All right. Nearly 50 percent of all launch attempts to Mars have failed for one reason or another. It's joked about there is actually some force trying to prevent us from exploring Mars. They call it the 'Mars Curse.' I don't even know how it got started. Hardly anyone ever mentions it."

"Except you."

"Right. I guess the reason no one speaks of it any more is because most of those failures occurred early in the program."

"You might have something there."

Adam and Emma spent the rest of their evening together chatting and getting to know each other in the normal way people do, through a series of strategically executed short forays designed to discern information about each other's personality, character, dating status, all sorts of things. By the end of the evening, their reconnaissance had determined they both wanted to do more reconnaissance.

Chapter Six

"We shall move out there, not because we want to,
but because we have to."
Edward Gilfillan – Migration to the Stars

The five men took longer than the twenty minutes Dick Phelps thought it would take to climb up to the compound. It was closer to forty-five minutes before the first one appeared atop the cliff. The man took a quick survey of the compound, then looked directly below him for a long moment observing the two that accompanied him. He then shifted his gaze to his right, ostensibly watching the progress of the rest of his party who were intent on remaining purposely out of sight.

Nearing the top of the cliff, one of the men shouted up at the man standing above them. "Hey, Barry what did ya find?"

"Shut up, you asshole!" he whispered loudly in response and quickly crouched to minimize his silhouette. He didn't see Phelps, or anyone for that matter, but he was astute enough to observe the smoke had stopped emanating from the camper and he could no longer smell the pungent pleasing odor of food being cooked. There were no signs of life, and that worried him. Phelps watched as the other two clumsily appeared and crouched low, obviously waiting for Barry to give them a command. They were tired and out of breath from the exertion so, they rested quietly for a few moments.

"Looks like no one is home." the third man opined, breaking the silence.

"They're here, all right." responded Barry quietly.

"Where are they? Did you see somebody?"

"No. But I know they're here. Spread out, and be quiet about it."

At Barry's command the three men slowly approached the small compound. They had formulated no plan if they encountered anyone so, they were unprepared when challenged by Phelps.

~~~~

Within the cold inky vastness of the solar system an object was moving with predetermined precision set upon a course of direct intercept with the fourth planet. That distant rust colored orb called Mars was unaware of the object's approach, unaware of its intentions to harvest some of the bounty the red planet holds. In exchange for this larceny, the object would leave permanent scars upon the landscape, intent on returning again and again on an errand to satisfy its master's voracious appetite for energy.

From Earth a voyage to Mars could take as little as 130 days, significantly less than the nearly two years estimated in 2001. This reduction in time is dependent upon two things; the red planet's closest approach to Earth, which occurs every 1.6 years, and new advances in ion propulsion. For use inside the microgravity of space an electrostatic propulsion system was specifically chosen to give flight to Cyprium Prospector. Electrostatic, or ion propulsion uses xenon gas for propellant. Xenon is highly stable and virtually non reactive with other elements. The gas flows into the engine where it receives an electrical charge converting atoms to ions. This allows them to be pushed around by electrical voltage. A pair of grids electrified to 1300 volts accelerates the ions to very high speed and expels them from the engine creating thrust.

The disadvantage of ion engines is they have very low initial thrust so, they cannot be used to escape Earth's gravity, but they have an important advantage in space.

Xenon ions travel at almost 22 miles per second, or 77,000 mph. This is about 10 times faster than the exhaust from conventional rocket engines. Ion engines also use only a very small amount of xenon at a time. Though the initial thrust is very low it slowly builds up, eventually attaining speeds far beyond the reach of conventional propellants. An ion engine also uses 10 times less propellant than its chemical counterparts, and unlike chemical engines, which have fixed burn times, ion engines can be operated for significantly long periods. Another big plus for the ion engine is the electricity for this remarkable system can be provided by solar arrays.

If everything went according to plan, Cyprium Prospector could complete a round trip in approximately one year, a desired maximum GPATT had determined was optimal for the human body to live in space. GPATT engineers had precisely calculated mining operations of two months in duration would require ten months total travel time in space. That window of opportunity had to coincide with the half of Mars' orbital path around the sun which was closest to Earth. This first mining mission, however, would require an extra month be added to the journey to account for establishing a habitable, working, operations and processing facility on the surface of Mars.

Three Trojan class vessels would be needed to make the mining venture worthwhile. Six were planned. Cyprium Prospector was the prototype and it would serve as the model for future voyages. As with everything, building Cyprium Prospector was not without controversy, the primary one being whether it was better to build one large vehicle that carried everything, or send multiple smaller craft to Mars ahead of the human payload. The issue was debated vigorously and provided loads of material for pundits and talking heads. The single payload approach won out, at least until a colony could be established on Mars. Not until then was it felt smaller unmanned vessels could be inserted into the mix, when risk and control would be greatly improved at the destination end.

Cyprium Prospector's senior officer, Commander Aviv Tamari, was reviewing the Mission Travel and Performance Schedule Log, or 'weather report' as it came to be called by the bridge personnel, as he had every day since the great ship had been launched. It noted the time, date, distance to Mars, ETA to Mars, distance from Earth, various engine and systems performance indicators, solar brightness, external temperature, internal temperature, humidity, oxygen levels, air quality, solar activity observed, anomalies picked up by radar, telescope observations, and a hundred other items that required monitoring regularly. With the exception of some travel data, the weather report was virtually the same most every day, and that made him happy. As the Commander, he also received and reviewed fitness reports and training schedules.

Commander Tamari was a lean dark-haired "forty something", as he was known to say, when asked about his age. Aviv was actually thirty-eight. He stood five feet eleven and one half inches in his GPATT issued boots. He was a likable sort, unmarried, though he shared a condo with Afsana (Sana) Halperin, a girl he had known from school in Eilat, Israel's southernmost city. Eilat is also a resort and port on the Gulf of Aqaba in the Red Sea that straddles the geographic line separating the continents of Africa and Asia.

For most of the time they had known each other, Aviv and Sana had been friends, sometimes more than friends, but not really boyfriend girlfriend. They liked each other and were attracted to each other. They went on dates, and even liked the way each other kissed, but they just couldn't seem to get the fire of a romance burning. Oh, the combustibles were there, it just took a long time before they finally ignited, years in fact. Their careers had taken them away from each other, only to reunite them again in their thirties at GPATT. What they seemed to have trouble igniting in those early years found no difficulty now. They were very much in love. Sana wanted to get married, as did Aviv, but only after this once in a lifetime mission had ended, just in case something happened.

Aviv was thinking of her as he perused the 'weather report'. He enjoyed the fact Sana would also be reviewing the same data each day. She was an electrical engineer assigned to a team that monitored from Earth, more accurately, from EP3, various systems on board Cyprium Prospector . The team rotated shifts one month on EP3, one month on Earth. And due to her particular job assignment, she was also responsible for all radio communications between Cyprium Prospector and Earth. This allowed her the unique privilege of directly contacting Aviv whenever she wanted. Despite the lag time between responses, it was two way communication with her significant other, just not the kind of conversation either one of them longed for.

This particular morning Aviv was melancholy and he allowed himself a daydream about her that abruptly ended with a start, just the sort you get when someone unexpectedly walks up from behind and calls your name.

"Commander?" It was Ensign Manda Richardson. She was from the forward observatory, also called the crow's nest. One of the duties of the forward observatory was to monitor activity in space, particularly in the path of Cyprium Prospector.

Aviv jumped in his seat.

"Ben zona!" (son of a bitch) he exclaimed, earning looks from the bridge crew.

"Sorry, Sir. I didn't mean to startle you."

After a long moment, and several deep breaths trying to regain his composure, he responded, "That's all right ensign, wasn't your fault. What is it?"

"Sir, we've been monitoring some meteor activity for several days."

"I'm aware of it."

"Mister Powell asked me to tell you that we may need to slow the ship to avoid the activity. It will delay our ETA by about 24 hours. He wanted to give you a heads up for this afternoon's briefing."

"Very well, thank you, ensign."

Having been literally snapped back into reality, Aviv once again directed his attention to the training performance reports. The residents of Cyprium Prospector were not only experts with their particular specialty, they also had to be proficient at surviving and working in a hostile environment. That meant training. For starters, the entire crew was EMT certified, even though there was a medical staff on board. Everyone had to know how to construct and repair the self sealing fabric S2F habitation structures and make them environment stable for human life. They had to know space suit operation and safety, life support systems equipment, electrical power systems, HVAC, plumbing, waste handling, and fire suppression techniques. GPATT wanted to ensure that in an emergency anyone could respond. Their very lives might depend on it.

The crew were quite familiar with the layout of the complex to be built on Mars because they had practiced erecting it several times on Earth, and on the Moon. While aboard Cyprium Prospector, they continuously studied every aspect of what was involved for living and working on Mars, and they practiced their techniques over and over, Aviv included. He was due at fire suppression training in five minutes. A tone sounded on his comm badge indicating he had a message. It was from Sana, but it would have to wait until later. Short of an emergency, even the mission commander was required to follow the training schedule.

~~~~

Emma got SAS her first day on the Moon. She was green and feeling queasy. Mechlazine and ginger ale brought her some relief, but it took a full day for her stomach to calm down. She decided she preferred LP1 to the lunar surface. At least on LP1 the feeling of gravity seemed better, or so she thought. Adam contacted her to say good-bye. He was returning to Earth and would not be back for two weeks.

"I hear that if you suck on a raw onion, it will cure your SAS." he offered.

"Thanks. See you when you get back, if I'm still alive." She felt terrible. Was he kidding? The thought of sucking on an onion only made her more nauseated. But she wasn't so sick to know she would miss him.

For the next six days Emma familiarized herself with her new surroundings and the people who were stationed there. Lieutenant Jefferson was well acquainted with the fifty current lunar residents and he had made sure Emma received a proper introduction to them all, especially the two person detail assigned to her, Danny Cooper and Dave Hubbard. Everyone was friendly and they so enjoyed seeing a new face. She felt like a celebrity for the first few days and then it was business as usual.

As promised, Jefferson went to see her the following Monday on the shuttle, which was its usual schedule. He advised her the next shuttle was planned for the coming Friday in case she wanted to spend the weekend on LP1. She accepted cheerfully knowing Adam would be back by then.

Upon concluding her first two days at the lunar colony, Emma settled into a daily routine. She was up at six am without an alarm clock, had her coffee and breakfast, and was in what passed for an office by seven. She checked her data twice each morning and twice each afternoon. After the evening meal, she would analyze the data, make notes, read, or watch TV and retire around eleven p.m. Occasionally, she would check out the dayroom to see what was going on, but for the most part, she had her nose in her work compiling and studying the data produced, including data from instruments located on LP1.

Dave and Danny kept busy recalibrating various equipment and rechecking the onboard systems of their vehicles. Aside from that, they considered Emma an easy detail on the edge of boring. They preferred to be out wandering the landscape in the Rover, which required wearing a spacesuit. Emma hated spacesuits. She considered them bulky, restrictive and imposing. They were all of those things, yet sooner, or later her job would require she don one in order to visit the bore site.

By the time the shuttle arrived the following Friday at the Apollo Seventeen colony, most of the information Emma had collected dealt with solar brightness and lunar seismic activity. The data suggested solar brightness had increased somewhat, probably due to the fact a new solar cycle had begun. Seismic sensors on the lunar surface registered seemingly constant activity at very low levels.

She allowed herself no conclusions, as she had yet to compare either data set with any significant historical data. That would have to wait. Adam's ship had docked and she was anxious to see him.

Emma arrived at shuttle departure a full half hour before it was scheduled to return to LP1. She had packed light, as most of her personal things were still in her quarters on the lunar platform. She was more excited than she would have believed herself to be only two weeks prior. She and Adam had exchanged several messages since their last encounter, and on her call with him last evening, she detected that he was anxious to see her. It was unusual, but the only duty Adam had to pull was a four hour relief shift in the Command Center's screen room from 12:00 to 16:00 hours Friday afternoon. After that, he was free until his return sortie to Earth on Sunday. She planned to meet him in the Blue Moon Saloon at half past four, or 16:30 hours as Adam would say.

The Command Center was one of the more visually interesting places on LP1. Upon entering, the first noticeable characteristic was the low light level. It was akin to being in a theater during a show, or a movie. Most of the light emanated from displays, control consoles and small

LEDs in the floor. The screen room's most notable feature, aside from the low light, was that it was filled with video displays. Some were monochrome, though most were color. Four figures manned consoles glowing with multicolored lights which helped them monitor the complex array. There were displays for RADARs, telescope feeds, internal security cameras, docking port and exterior observation cameras, along with several cameras at the Apollo Seventeen colony. There was even one for a camera erected at the bore site.

For his four hour shift, Adam served as the Watch Officer in the screen room, not an ironic title, because that is what the duty consisted of; watching. Usually, it was a long four hours of boredom, especially if there was no activity, because you were not allowed to do anything but monitor the displays. There were to be no distractions while on duty in the Command Center. The four technicians were slightly busier than the Watch Officer because they had other minor duties to perform in conjunction with monitoring the screens.

In the middle of twenty-five UTC clocks hanging on the left hand wall of the screen room, the extra one for (BST) British Summer Time, there was one digital clock for time zone UTC 6-S. Time zones are defined as the twenty-four regions on the Earth, about 15° of longitude apart, circumnavigating the globe that have the same time everywhere within them. Many follow their geographic meridian, although, political and geographical requisites can result in irregular-shaped zones. Most adjacent time zones are exactly one hour apart, and by convention, they used to compute their local time based on Greenwich Mean Time (GMT), which refers to mean solar time at the Royal Observatory Greenwich, London.

Due to variations in the Earth's rotation and tilt, GMT did not proceed at a constant rate. In order to correct this, Coordinated Universal Time (UTC) was introduced. Atomic clocks used to be adjusted annually. Now, leap seconds are inserted to keep the UTC within 0.9 seconds of GMT, which has been replaced by the acronym UT1.

UTC 6-S was used for GPATT standard time because that was the time zone in which the RJP was located. The digital display read 14:15 hours when Adam returned from his middle of shift break. He checked in with the four technicians, then arbitrarily decided to study a bank of six flat panel displays monitoring live lunar views provided by cameras on the exterior of LP1.

One particular screen provided a spectacular view from camera EC-10 aimed along a portion of LP1's bright superstructure with a curved illuminated portion of the Moon in the immediate background against the blackness of space. He quickly recognized the Grimaldi Crater which is located in the equatorial region of Southwestern Oceanus Procellarum.

It was a rare occurrence to observe anything moving on these screens without GPATT having initiated the activity, and as nothing had been scheduled during Adam's watch, no activity was expected.

"What's that?!" Adam suddenly shouted, pointing at one of the monochrome displays.

The four technicians looked up immediately and focused on the screen. One of them quickly checked his console and said "Whatever it is we're recording it!"

"It's not on RADAR." said another tech, frantically working his console.

The five of them watched as a perfectly round two dimensional spinning white circular shape with a crisp edge moved with steady precision across the screen and out of view.

"What the heck was that?!" Adam asked. No one responded because they didn't really have an answer. "Where's that camera?"

"It's EC-10, Commander, top center of the hamster cage."

"Can we track that thing?"

One of the techs rushed to another console and the view on the screen began to shift left. After a moment it stopped.

"What happened?!"

"That's as far as it goes, Commander."

"Is it on any other monitor?"

They all quickly scanned every screen in the room, but without result.

"Who else could have seen it?!"

"Well there's the observatory, but I..."

"Call up there, man!" Adam excitedly commanded.

In hurried low tones the technician began conversing with somebody over the comm. "I've got someone in the observatory, Sir. No one up there saw anything, or sees anything and they have a pretty good view from up there."

"Commander?" another tech called out. "We're not picking up anything on any of our instruments. Maybe it was just a ghost image."

"In relation to this platform what is its heading?"

"Toward Earth, Sir."

"Is there a camera pointing that way?"

"EC-4, right there." said the tech pointing to one of the monitors connected to that particular external camera. They watched for a long moment, eyes glued to the screen, which had its lower left corner filled with a trailing piece of superstructure with Earth in the distance. The white spinning circle seen on the other monitor did not make an appearance.

"Play that back!" Adam commanded. The image appeared against the black of space and began spinning its way across the screen.

"Stop!" Adam shouted. "Did that come from the lunar surface, or from behind the Moon?" None of them could tell. It was strictly two dimensional. Its depth could not be perceived in the video. And as sharp and in focus as its outer edge seemed to be, they couldn't discern any other characteristics to explain what it was, except it was spinning in an apparent counter-clockwise direction.

"Does that look like a ghost to you?" he asked sharply.

"If it was solid, we should have picked it up on RADAR, or on another camera." responded the technician who still had an open comm with the observatory.

"Commander, we see shit all the time on these screens that we can't explain." one of the other technicians added.

"Like that?"

"Well, not exactly. Sometimes spots, or what looks to us like flashes and shooting stars."

"Let me tell you boys something. A few years ago I got to see some classified video taken by the space shuttle Endeavor. It was part of a series of early space shuttle videos that had inadvertently recorded, shall we say, objects moving through space. That thing you see there has been recorded before. That's no ghost."

"What is it then, Commander?"

"Let's just say that it hasn't been identified. What's the protocol for this sort of thing?"

"We would ordinarily treat this as a visual anomaly and note it in the log. We...we have no evidence to the contrary."

"Not this one, boys. I want this treated as a UFO sighting. Get this to whomever, right away."

"Aye. aye Sir."

~~~~

The shuttle carrying Emma back to LP1 docked at approximately 13:30. She wouldn't meet with Adam until 4:30 p.m., another three hours so, she spent the rest of the afternoon working. She hadn't married up the historical data with her current readings on solar brightness, although, she felt confident the summary wouldn't tell her anything new. The sun had begun a new cycle some two years earlier, predictably bringing with it a new interval of increased solar illumination and radiation only slightly higher than historical levels, which could account for some slight increase of global warmth on Earth. It would also help corroborate the government's earlier explanation for the receding polar ice caps on Mars. She wouldn't rule out some correlation with the unusual phenomena taking place on the Earth, but she wasn't ready to rule it *in*, either. Neither had she the opportunity to combine the historical lunar seismic data with the post accident time frame and current readings. She was looking forward to doing that, but for the remainder of the day Emma had decided to review the third item of study on her mission agenda; anomalies in series photograph LS3-51-21.6.

Unfortunately, there were no subsequent current photographs to compare with frame LS3-51-21.6. The latest information available was from the observation notes of the now deceased drilling team members, and those were inconclusive.

Incredulously, someone, or no one had remembered to commission a high altitude surface imaging satellite in orbit around the Moon. It had been discussed and agreed upon in planning meetings such a satellite was an obvious required piece of equipment, but for reasons unknown it was never added to anyone's action item list. Apparently, everyone thought someone else was taking care of it. Unfortunately, the building and launching of Cyprium Prospector had eclipsed the lowly imaging satellite, along with the bore site drilling incident. Consequently, Emma would have to make a physical inspection the site of the anomalies, a trip she did not relish.

As exciting as it had been, having her theory highlighted immediately after the Mare Crisium incident, the work Emma was doing now seemed rather unimportant and anticlimactic, even if she was on the Moon. In fact, she was beginning to dread the rather uneventful, unexciting analysis she would in all likelihood have to present to GPATT, unless the anomalies otherwise proved to be constructs, which she doubted.

Emma was seated in the Blue Moon Saloon sitting at her familiar spot when Adam arrived promptly at 16:30 hours. A casual observer would recognize immediately they were quite attracted to each other. Their smiles, body language and eye contact spoke volumes if anyone cared to pay attention.

"Hi." Adam said first, as he searched her face for a response to seeing him for the first time in nearly two weeks.

"Hi." she answered softly, conspicuously pleased to see him.

"I missed you."

"I'm glad. I missed you a little bit, too."

"Just a little bit?"

"Yeah." she said crinkling her nose and shrugging her shoulders, meaning 'I really missed you a lot'.

"Is that for me?" he asked, pointing to a second SmartCup that appeared to be filled with his preferred beverage.

"Yep, Guinness."

"Ooo, good." Adam picked up the drink, tapped her SmartCup with his and said "Slainte!" (pronounced - se lan cha)

"What's that mean?"'

"It's Irish for 'good health'. It's like saying, 'cheers'."

"Are you Irish?"

"No. A buddy of mine is. I learned the expression from him and apparently, that's all the Gaelic he knows, too!"

They both laughed and sipped on their drinks.

"So, how is your investigation going up here?"

"Slow. I got SAS my first day down on the surface, as you may recall. The rest of my time has been spent gathering data, taking readings. I haven't even been able to compare the relatively current data with historical data, but I'm almost there. Today, I spent the afternoon looking at surface anomalies in some old photograph a couple of scientists think are constructs, but I seriously doubt it, and I don't have any new photos to compare them with because there is no imaging satellite orbiting the Moon to take any new pictures. Seems someone forgot all about that, which means I'll have to ride out there, and I'm not looking forward to it."

"I can tell."

"Oh, I'm sorry. I haven't had the opportunity to have a whole lot of conversation with anybody up here. What have you been up too?"

"The usual, just driving my bus, but this afternoon..." Adam paused, looked about to see if anyone was in earshot, lowered his voice and continued, "...while I was on watch in the Command Center we had an incident."

"An incident? Pray, tell. What excitement of other events do you have? I'll bet it beats all the excitement I've had since I've been here, present company excluded of course."

"I've got a better idea. Why don't I just show you?"

"Ooo, intrigue."

"Let's take a walk." he said grabbing her by the hand.

"To where?"

"The Command Center."

"Isn't that off limits?"

"Not to me. The watch officer on duty now is a friend of mine. He'll let you in if you're with me. We can tell him I'm taking you on a tour. Better yet, didn't you tell me you have a level two clearance?"

"Yes, so?"

"With that level you can go in by yourself, provided you have a need."

"And what need would that be?"

"Well, you are investigating the bore site accident so, you need to be aware of any anomaly that might contribute to an explanation of what happened there. I'll tell him, that, uh, we're there to look at an anomaly."

"What anomaly?"

"That's what I want to show you."

Buxton 'Stoney' Hunt looked up from his desk behind the command console when he heard the Command Center door actuator sound. "General Pickett, Sir." he stated cheerfully in his best southern accent when he saw Adam peer from behind the door.

"My compliments, General Hunt, may I present Miss Emma Cross?"

"A Southern belle, delighted." responded Stoney.

"Please to meet you, General." Emma said extending her hand and eying his uniform for a star signifying his rank, at which Stoney began to laugh.

"My apologies." Stoney said, still smiling broadly. "Inside joke. I'm not really a general. You see, Adam is distantly related to Major General George Pickett, Army of Northern Virginia, and I am distantly related to Brigadier General Henry J. Hunt, Army of the Potomac."

"The Civil War?"

"That is correct, mam." affirmed Stoney.

"Pickett I've heard of, Hunt I have not, sorry." Emma said apologetically.

"An unsung hero to be sure, but don't feel too bad, most people haven't. He was the Union artillery commander at the Battle of Gettysburg."

Adam chimed in. "I didn't know that either, but he let me know as soon as he found out my name was Pickett."

"So, didn't you get enough of this place this afternoon, or are you giving guided tours now?" said Stoney.

"Actually, this is kind of work related. Emma is investigating the drilling accident. She's level two, by the way." he added pointing to her I.D. badge. "Part of her work involves researching unusual anomalous activity. I want to show her the video from this afternoon."

Stoney looked skeptically at them both.

"She is level two, and besides, I out rank you." Adam said smugly.

"Not in here you don't."

"Point taken." Adam answered with feigned humility. Technically, Stoney was a half level below Adam in rank, but the 'Officer of the Watch', regardless of individual rank, was the highest ranking person in the Command Center, second only to the CC Commander.

Stoney played the clip on one of the console monitors. Playback over a live feed was against GPATT protocol. All three watched, as the spinning white disc glided across the screen.

"What is that?" Emma whispered, looking up at Adam, then at Stoney.

"A ghost, it's nothing." Stoney responded with finality.

"Yeah, it's nothing." echoed Adam looking hard at Stoney. "Come on." he said to Emma. "Thanks, General. Mum's the word."

"It was nice to meet you, General." Emma said as she was pulled away by Adam.

"Same here. See you around campus."

Adam didn't speak a word and didn't let go of Emma's hand until after they were seated back at the Blue Moon. Emma broke the silence.

"That was your excitement? What exactly were we looking at? What did he mean, 'ghost'?"

Adam leaned in close. "Several years ago I had the opportunity to see a series of videos taken from several space shuttle missions. The videos were recordings of things like space walks, or the cargo boom in operation, things that were happening outside the shuttle. Those videos recorded unidentified images in the background moving through space. The image on the clip that you just saw was taken today. It was also recorded by the space shuttle Endeavor's cameras."

"Endeavor? That was a long time ago." Emma said not making the immediate connection.

Adam looked directly into Emma's eyes waiting for the association. "Yes." was all he said.

"That's different technology. What do you think it is?" she asked wondering how he would respond.

"I don't know what the heck it is." he gasped sitting back in his chair. "I know what it looks like, but it didn't show up on RADAR, or any other external camera, and apparently no one else on the platform saw it. We only have an unidentified.....'thing'... moving across the screen, and with such mechanical precision!" he whispered excitedly. "We have two known videos of an identical image, taken years apart with different video technology, which to me rules out mechanical, or photographic aberration."

"So you think this thing is a UFO?"

"I think it looks like a UFO on the screen, but the rest of it doesn't seem to track."

"What are you going to do?"

"Ahh, nothing." he said with exasperation, as he looked down at his drink. "I sent the video through channels. Some one will look into it. Maybe I just overreacted. It was a lot more exciting this afternoon."

"Well, it is an interesting video, in light of what I was working on today."

"Oh? I thought your work was in geology, not extraterrestrials, or ghosts."

"You might just be surprised."

"Yeah, how's that?"

Emma stood. "Why don't you order some supper. I like just about everything. When I come back, I'll have something to show you." she said cheerfully. "Be right back." she added, and was off.

Adam was hungry so, he ordered lasagna and Greek salad for both of them. Their food was ready by the time Emma returned. She handed him a large grey envelope.

"What's this?"

"Open it."

Adam pulled out a 16 by 20 inch black and white photograph that appeared to be lunar landscape.

"That is a photo of the northern edge of Mare Crisium taken on one of the Apollo missions. I don't remember which one, and that looks like lasagna and salad." she added eyeing the food.

"Greek salad." he answered

"Good choice. I love Greek salad."

"Why do you have this photo? Oh, right, Mare Crisium, the bore site is there. But you said the northern edge. The bore site is on the western edge."

"That's right. But this doesn't have anything to do with the drilling incident. This has to do with one of my other assignments."

"Which is what?"

"I'm supposed to examine several possible constructs, right there." she said pointing to the bright spots in the frame.

"Constructs?"

"Yeah, a couple of scientists think the Martians might have a summer home there." Emma responded nonchalantly.

Adam looked at Emma with half a smile trying to decide if she was being serious, or if he was being pranked. She immediately understood the look on his face.

"Seriously." she said breaking the silence. "Oh, I don't personally believe that, but I have been asked to inspect three distinct shapes out there that more paranoid minds think might provide solid evidence of off-worlders."

"Shapes? What does that mean? What kind of shapes? You mean buildings?"

"Not exactly. More like monuments."

"Monuments? Monuments of what?"

"I don't know. One is supposed to look like a bird, another one looks like a face and the third one looks like an airport control tower. If you asked me, it takes a pretty good imagination to see all that in this photo. But somebody somewhere has played around with the image and believes they see these things. They either know some one high up, or they presented a very compelling case because I have to go out there and take a look."

"Why you?"

"Let's just say, the other side of the Martian condo claim is these shapes are geologic formations, and I am a geologist. It lends credibility, if you know what I mean. Of course, if I get out there and it is extraterrestrial, that flying saucer film of yours will get lots of play."

"I don't even want to think about that. Chasing UFOs is one thing. Catching up with them is an entirely different matter." Adam took a long pull on his drink.

"Let's not get too excited, until after I have a look. Besides, from what I can tell, the shapes only resemble those things. I mean come on, didn't you ever imagine faces, or animal shapes in wallpaper, or carpet patterns, or clouds?"

"Of course, but I didn't imagine that video."

"That one I can't explain either, but I'll bet you breakfast it's something really stupid and we'll have a good laugh over it when we find out what it is."

Adam smiled. He knew Emma was probably right, though he wouldn't completely give up on the possibility of extraterrestrials flying around out there somewhere. The two spent the rest of their short weekend together sharing meals and talking, an activity of which they never seemed to tire. They watched a movie and completed three intervals exercising, an all important activity for space living. Emma would be going home in two weeks and Adam wouldn't be venturing into space for another month. The next time they saw each other would be back on Earth.

Adam's spinning disc never reappeared. No one else had ever seen it either, except for that one space shuttle mission video, which unfortunately was filled with all kinds of unusual phenomenon that was explained away as image aberrations, reflections and dust. He was never questioned about the report he filed, nor was it ever even acknowledged. As far as he knew, the sighting was being treated as image noise, unimportant and therefore not investigated.

Three months after the sighting, however, a report with video filed by one Captain Adam Pickett found its way to an obscure office somewhere in the bowels of the Pentagon.

"They're getting careless." said the man with the black tie.

"How's that?" asked a second younger man sitting at one of three desks in the room.

"This is the fourth sighting."

"I thought it was the second?"

"Well. I suppose it's time you knew. You've been here long enough."

"Knew what?" said the younger man, as he turned in his chair toward the man with the black tie.

"Roswell was the first..."

"I had a feeling." the second man interrupted.

"... John Glenn was the second, Shuttle Endeavor was the third, and now we have Captain Adam Pickett."

"Is he a risk?"

"I don't think so. He hasn't been blabbing."

"What should we do?"

"They need to be made aware so, it doesn't happen again. And remember..."

"I know, this conversation never happened. What about his report?"

"Encrypt it and file it with the others. As far as you know, it doesn't exist."

Chapter Seven

*"Who has confidence in himself
will gain the confidence of others."*
Rabbi Lieb Lazarow

Dot sat quietly inside the camper door nearly invisible behind the black mesh screen, her two weapons at the ready. The AeroStream was situated at the apex of the semi-circle formed by the compound structures, giving it the best view of the drive into the compound and the edge of the cliff. Before long the three men crept into her line of sight. She could also see Dick kneeling behind the makeshift blind taking aim at them. She wondered where the other two were, remembering Dick had said there were five. She took no action, preferring to wait for a cue from her husband. The quiet was intense and she longed to hear Dick's voice in conversation breaking the silence. Roo Roo was on her lap growling low. Dot attempted to keep her quiet, so as not to give away her presence in the camper. For the time being, she was only an observer, not a participant, but that was about to change.

Barry concentrated on the AeroStream for a moment. He could see now it was partially painted tan, an obvious attempt at camouflage. A ladder was still leaning against its side, with paint and roller on the ground, as though someone had recently put them down. He was now certain, whoever lived here had detected their presence well before they made it to the top. His eyes swept the compound looking for signs of movement. Seeing nothing, he changed his gaze to the desolate landscape of bare tree trunks. He saw nothing nor heard anything that might indicate the whereabouts of whoever lived there. He switched his gaze back to the camper and began to move toward it.

~~~~

Charles Wallace Powell (Charlie) was the chief navigator for Cyprium Prospector. He had a small staff who assisted him with monitoring, calculating and observing everything that had to do with directing the giant space barge safely to Mars. On his recommendation the huge craft was slowed to avoid a meteorite cloud moving through the Solar System on a path that intersected Cyprium Prospector's projected course. Charlie and his group had been monitoring the cloud for two weeks. They were prepared for its passing and felt comfortable with the calculations they had made and their decision to slow the craft, as opposed to altering course to avoid a collision.

To most of the crew, the passing meteor cluster was an exciting happenstance, compared to the often dull existence they experienced day to day on Cyprium Prospector. It evoked the same wonder and curiosity that other cosmic events do, such as a comet, or lunar eclipse, viewed from Earth. And even though the meteorites would be a bit muted against the darkness of space, everyone wanted a look. Their journey would be delayed nearly twenty-four hours, for a not too sparse collection of rocks that would only be visible for an hour and twenty-two minutes as they crossed the path ahead of the great ship.

Surprisingly, the shower of space debris did not whoosh by in a flash, as some had thought. There were no smoke, or vapor trails, nor were the meteorites in the mass tumbling wildly. They did not appear to be traveling at any great speed, as one might expect in space, only slightly less than 200 mph.

Contents of the cloud varied in diameter, from marble to baseball size, as well as in shape, from round to sharp and amoeboid. Most were charcoal in color and nearly all of them sparkled as though they contained precious metals and gems. But this passing swarm was not comprised of the usual chondrites which are similar in composition to normal terrestrial rocks found on Earth. These were iron meteorites, very dense nonporous specimens that were much heavier than most comparably-sized rocks. And at 200 mph, a grouping of iron meteorites, even in such dispersed concentration, could wreak havoc on the Cyprium Prospector. This grouping, though, moved harmlessly well ahead of the Trojan Class giant and would never be seen again.

"Are you sure?" the chief navigator demanded.

"Aye, Sir. We've been continuously monitoring the cloud, and it has moved beyond our flight path and is no longer a threat. The time computations were off by ninety seconds, but that is an acceptable margin of error."

"Tell that to the guy who's two minutes ahead of us." Charlie responded with sarcasm, and then touching his comm badge he said loudly, "Navigation to Bridge!"

"This is the Bridge, go ahead." responded Aviv's now familiar voice.

"Resume speed at your pleasure, Commander. We are clear of the meteorite cloud."

"Thank you, Mister Powell, well done."

"Miss Urbanic," Aviv called out to the helm officer, "resume speed."

"Aye aye, Sir. Bringing engines back to full."

~~~~

Emma was only somewhat intrigued by Adam's UFO video. Admittedly, there had been some pretty compelling evidence gathered over time regarding the existence of UFOs, but UFOs were like Bigfoot; there were numerous videos, eyewitness accounts and sightings, however, there never seemed to be any really hard evidence that shouted "Here's the proof!"

Besides, so much science fiction had become reality over the years most people probably wouldn't get all that excited to learn a Bigfoot, or UFO had plopped right down in their own backyard.

Emma couldn't explain Adam's mysterious moving disc, but she was fairly confident the monumental structures in frame LS3-51-21.6 were nothing more than natural geologic formations, interesting only to lunar geologists. She was also convinced she really didn't have to visit the bore site, either, because she was able to collect all the data she required from the several K5 Strong Motion Inertial Seismometers which had been placed at the various lunar landing sites and at the bore site. She had used much older equipment during her college and grad school days, adequate at the time, though not as technologically advanced.

Capable of detecting seismic waves generated by quakes, explosions and other seismic sources, the K5s had been continually measuring and recording motion within the lunar surface. Their operating principle was fairly simple. A mass, like a ball, is contained within a system framework, like a box. The ball is usually attached to the system by a spring that holds it in a fixed position. Any motion of the ground moves the box while the ball tends not to move. By measuring and recording the motion between the box and the ball, the motion of the ground can be determined. Of course, these units were all electronic now, enabling them to be tied into a computer. Emma could analyze the data without ever having to step foot on the Moon. Unfortunately for her, the job assignment required an onsite inspection, as well as a visit to the site of the three anomalies.

Though Emma had immersed herself into her work, in the end she could add little to what was already known. She had a voluminous catalogue of seismic activity, though it was not much more than a record showing frequency, timing and size of ground motion that had occurred. Unlike Earth, seismic mapping of the Moon was only partially complete. This meant scientists were not totally certain about the Moon's inner makeup. It was believed no water, gas pockets, or molten core existed based on the current data. This was the reason why the bore site accident was unforeseen. Ironically, incomplete mapping was the one reason it should have been foreseen. Regardless, the data did not help Emma explain the accident, it only recorded it had happened. The data did show an increase in moonquakes and what appeared to be volcanic activity immediately following the accident. As such, a moonwalk was unavoidable.

Danny Cooper and Dave Hubbard had submitted the mission plan request to Major Woo's office and prepared the rover for Emma's trip to the bore site. They estimated it would take from twelve to sixteen hours to navigate the rover to the site, travel to the anomalies and return to the Apollo Seventeen compound. A real plus for the trip was that this rover was an updated version of the first open style lunar rovers; it was enclosed and looked more like an RV and that meant Emma would have to don a spacesuit only while outside the rover.

Dave was the designated mission commander, and would not be required to leave the confines of the rover. That meant Danny was assigned to accompany Emma on her exploration of the site. He would also share driving duties. To save time, Emma and Danny suited up just ahead of their arrival. They spent twenty-six minutes on the lunar surface examining the site and collecting samples of rock that had been spewed from the now inactive fumarole.

The samples would confirm the existence of subterranean water and show evidence of intense heat. Emma also discovered several large fissures a short distance east of the site. And though she could discern nothing else, it was puzzling to Emma that so much water vapor had seemed to escape from such a few comparably sized openings in the Moon's crust.

The ride across the Mare Crisium plain to the anomaly site was almost boringly uneventful until a little blinking yellow light appeared inside the rover on the overhead console.

"Well, that's not good." Dave said reaching up to tap the blinking amber rectangle.

"What's not good? What's not good?" Emma inquired, somewhat concerned.

"Sorry, Miss Cross. We won't be going to the anomaly site." Dave touched his comm badge which was being fed through the Rover's powerful transmitter. "Apollo Seventeen Base, this is Lunar Rover Two. Over"

"Go ahead, Rover Two."

"We've got a flag yellow on our secondary scrubber. Aborting mission and returning to base. Over."

Emma was listening intently wanting to understand the comment "That's not good." just uttered by Dave.

"Do you need assistance? Over."

"Negative, Base. We can make it back. We are Oscar Kilo. Rover Two, out."

"What's the matter? Why are we going back? Who is Oscar Kilo?" Emma asked without trying to sound scared.

Danny turned toward Emma and explained what was happening. "That warning light means there may be something wrong with the Rover's secondary air scrubber. We breathe through the primary scrubber. The secondary scrubber is our backup. There may be something wrong, and then again maybe not, but we don't operate unless both systems are working properly so, when one goes off line, the mission gets scrubbed until we get it fixed. Nothing to worry about. We always have our spacesuits if the primary should go, too. Oh, and Oscar Kilo is GPATT jargon for 'okay'."

Emma's assignment had come to an abrupt end, which was Oscar Kilo with her. GPATT wasn't going to schedule a special trip just to go back and look at anomalies. They only reason it was considered in the first place was because the accident site was close enough to make a side trip. She would complete her report to GPATT and happily meet with Adam the next day to discuss her opinion and theory on what she had found.

~~~~

"Wasn't sure I'd get to see you this trip." Adam said as he sat down next to Emma at their usual table in the Blue Moon Saloon.

"I wasn't either. My field trip got cut short so, I was able to catch the shuttle, but I had to run for it. I thought I was going to be stuck down there for one more week."

"What happened?"

"The secondary 'air thingy' had a flag yellow..."

"So they scrubbed the mission." Adam interjected. "That's pretty much SOP, and lucky for me."

"Yeah?" she said, obviously pleased at the comment.

"Yeah." Adam breathed as he leaned closer to Emma.

She responded by leaning even closer and they softly kissed their first kiss. She hadn't been kissed like that in quite some time, and it fulfilled her hope and expectation of what a first kiss should be. Suddenly aware of her surroundings, she sat up straight, slightly embarrassed she had kissed Adam that way in public.

"What's the matter?" he asked.

"Nothing."

"I'm sorry, maybe I shouldn't have done that."

"It was nice." she responded softly, and he immediately understood her reaction.

"Yes, it was." he countered, and then politely changed the subject. "So, you said you thought you would be going back to Earth day after tomorrow. Does that still hold?"

"It does, and if I'm not mistaken, you are listed as the pilot."

"Bus driver."

"You shouldn't be so cavalier. I know more than a few people who would trade jobs with you in a New York minute."

"Oh, it's just my way of keeping things in perspective."

"Just be careful. That kind of comment falling on the wrong ears could get you reassigned."

"Okay, Mom."

"Sorry. I shouldn't have said that."

"That's okay, you're probably right, anyway."

"It's just that... I think your job is pretty amazing. Not just anybody can do what you do."

"All right, enough about me. What happens with you next, now that you have finished up here."

"Well, I have to present my findings to the people who hired me, and I'm afraid I don't have anything new to tell them. I don't think they are going to be happy about it."

"Did it ever occur to you, that what you have to tell them might be exactly what they want to hear?"

"To tell you the truth, I don't really know what they expect me to tell them. Maybe that's a good thing."

"Then just tell them what you know, tell them what you found, support it with your data. I wouldn't worry about whether they like it, or not."

"That's exactly what I plan to do."

"Good. So, what did you find out?"

"Well, I was able to confirm pretty much what is already known. The Moon has subsurface ice and an inner hot spot that were brought into contact with each other through the drilling operation. That wasn't previously thought possible, but ejecta samples taken from the site strongly indicate water and heat interaction."

"How do you know that?"

"Because the rock samples show characteristics and striation patterns typically found under those conditions, and much of the material is exactly like what is often spewed from an erupting volcano on Earth, only in smaller amounts. That usually means there is a liquid core. Somehow a molten chamber, or some subterranean vein had been breached and came into contact with ice, which melted resulting in huge amounts of steam being released into space. Based on what was known, no one could have predicted the event. What confounds me is the location of the molten material and the amount of steam that was vented."

"What do you mean?"

"Well, we generally think of the planets in terms of spinning spheres. Spinning establishes gravitational forces which would keep a molten core at the center of the sphere, like it does with the Earth. Planet-wide cooling would tend to keep the core even more confined to the center of the sphere, even if the spinning slows down, like it has with the Moon. It was believed by many, because the moon is cool, comparatively speaking, and had virtually stopped spinning, because its spin is only as fast as its orbital revolution around the Earth, it had no molten core. The evidence is now clear there is molten material, but, and here is the interesting part, it's not at the center. It's off-center, based on the depth the drill team achieved and the limited seismic mapping done to date, but more study is needed to say that conclusively. They're going to think I'm nuts if I say that."

"Which part?" Adam asked intrigued with her enthusiasm on what he considered was a dry subject.

"The off-center part."

"Wait, wait, wait. How could it be off center? You just said..."

"I know what I said. According to known data, there shouldn't be a molten core at all, but molten material came out of that bore hole, and from the data I collected, it didn't come from the center of the Moon. Aside from the fact that the Moon's center of mass is slightly off center, it defies what we know about lunar geology, volcanic activity and planetary development, although, it just might lend credibility to the 'giant impact theory'. That could explain why the magma chamber is not at the center and why it wasn't detected before."

"That's a pretty significant discovery."

"And then when I present my data showing increased solar brightness and lunar temps, coupled with things like the Martian polar ice caps receding, all of which points to global warming being related to solar activity, the global warming folks at GPATT will go ballistic."

"Is that your scientific explanation for what is happening on Earth?"

"No."

"No?"

"I'm not sure."

"You are going to tell them you're not sure?"

"I can't tell them any more than what I think the data could suggest."

"What the heck does that mean?"

"It means more study is needed to be conclusive. I just took a look around. There's only so much one person can do. It is the Moon, after all. If they want to know definitively, that will require more equipment, more manpower and more time. It all depends on how much more they want to know."

"You're kidding me."

"Absolutely not. Why would I kid about it?"

"You've just made the discovery of the decade, maybe even the century, and you're worried about whether, or not GPATT is going to like it? Unbelievable! You're going to be famous!"

~~~~

Foggy Bottom Station was a long escalator ride up to street level from where Washington DC's light-rail subway deposited Emma. The Metro, as it is called, had a rather sizable rectangular hole in the ground at 23rd and I Streets, Northwest, which was quite convenient to George Washington University. GPATT corporate offices were located adjacent to several school buildings making the stop convenient for commuters.

Through mutual endeavors, GPATT was able to utilize some of the school's resources, in this instance, a small auditorium in Ross Hall which is part of the School of Medicine and Health Sciences. It was there Emma would conclude her assignment.

The auditorium, though undersized, was not filled with people. A small group of sixteen sat mostly in the center of the first several rows of seats to watch and hear Emma's presentation. She thought the atmosphere cozy and not intimidating. Perhaps it was intended, because her reception did not have much warmth.

The presentation delivery was made with practiced professionalism and with seemingly expert knowledge. Emma had a talent for making dry data interesting. At the end of her remarks, she recalled Adam's words to her about becoming famous. There was no clapping. There were no accolades, or congratulations. There were a few questions. The first two were from a serious dark-haired man who did not identify himself.

"Miss Cross..."

"It's Doctor Cross, you pompous ass." Emma thought to herself. Actually, she preferred not to use her title except for when she was in a professional environment, because in her mind there was no respect from academics unless you had degrees.

"...the best scientific minds have suggested the Moon, in all likelihood, does not have a molten core with the caveat, that if it did, it would be very small. I find it intriguing you are suggesting there is molten material under the lunar surface at a depth that falls short of where the Moon's solid core has scientifically been determined to be. Has anyone reviewed your data for confirmation?"

"No. Not yet. I haven't been asked to..."

The man interrupted. "Your conclusion as to the cause of that unfortunate incident would seem to bolster the well known 'giant impact theory', which you make singular reference to. Have you any other proof, aside from a few rock samples, which supports your rather fantastic conclusion?"

"No. Certainly, my findings are not completely conclusive, but I think the evidence is exciting and highly suggestive, and I would recommend additional study to be more definitive."

"Miss Cross?" another voice called out. Emma just cringed. It belonged to a middle aged woman who also failed to identify herself. Inwardly Emma seethed. These people are rude.

"Yes?" she responded as pleasantly as she could.

"Have you done any work in the area of global warming?"

"I did two papers on global warming in graduate school."

"Anything outside the classroom?"

"No. Just this."

"Are you really suggesting that global warming is solely the result of increased solar brightness, and not air pollution? How else would you explain all the things that are happening?"

"I believe my data strongly suggests an increase in temperatures within the solar system. I think that should be taken into account in the global warming debate. I am not suggesting it is a conclusive explanation for global warming, or any of the phenomena alleged to be related to global warming."

"Do you think it is related?"

"I believe it is a contributing factor."

"Are you entertaining any theories, Doctor Cross?" The question came from Dr. Kenneth Wagner, GPATT Director and head of Lunar Affairs, and the person who had recruited her for the assignment. He was a kind man whom Emma liked. He was soft-spoken and possessed a warm pleasant tone of voice.

Emma did not speak immediately, choosing to phrase her response carefully. She wanted Dr. Wagner's question, "Are you entertaining any theories, Doctor Cross?" (emphasis on 'Doctor Cross') to sink in with her audience. She made them wait just long enough.

"Not at this time." she said quietly.

Dr. Wagner walked over to the podium. "Thank you, Doctor Cross. Ladies and gentlemen, that concludes our presentation." The attendees rose quietly and left the auditorium. "Do you have a few minutes?" he solicitously asked Emma.

"Yes."

They adjourned to a small office reserved for visitors, opposite the lecture hall's main entrance, and sat down.

"That was different." Emma offered, to start up the conversation. She was feeling a little inadequate at the moment.

"Actually, that was pretty normal for this group."

"Judging from what I just experienced, I don't think I'll be invited back. Who were they, anyway?"

"Intellectuals mostly, engineers, scientists like yourself, a few corporate types, a bean counter or two, decision makers all, to be sure. But I am the Director. You did a nice job Emma." he said reassuringly.

"Thanks, but I'm not sure they thought so."

"I know a few people who will be disappointed you didn't get to check out those anomalous formations, but the rest of your work is impressive. You did a thorough job."

"Thanks."

"You haven't told us everything, though, have you?" he asked in a tone that said 'You can trust me, tell me what you're really thinking.'

Emma flushed slightly.

"I can tell the wheels are turning in your head." he prodded gently."Look, a good scientist doesn't always say everything that might be on her mind so, off the record, what do you think is going on down here and on the Moon?"

"Then you also know a good scientist doesn't make rash unsubstantiated comments about what they think." she politely rebuked him.

"Touché. But you have made observations. I'm interested. I'm interested in your ideas about what you see. I'm not going to hold you to them, and if it makes you feel better, this conversation is just between us."

Emma was silent, confirming Dr. Wagner's intuition she was holding back. He continued with his gentle assault.

"I'm going to have someone review your data." She didn't like the sound of that. "A second opinion if you will. I'm sure the same conclusions will be drawn." he said reassuringly. "And it will give your study credibility. You do realize your magma chamber hypothesis is a big discovery, once it is confirmed." The comment stroked her bruised ego.

"Dr. Wagner, I really appreciate your giving me this assignment. I owe you for that."

"Then talk to me." he pleaded softly

"Have my work reviewed. If it is accepted as a valid body of work, I'll talk to you about my ideas. In the mean time, I will continue with my research."

Chapter Eight

"And there shall be signs in the Sun, and in the Moon,
and in the Stars;
and upon the Earth distress of nations, with perplexity;
the sea and the waves roaring;
men's hearts failing them for fear, and for looking after those
things which are coming on earth:
for the powers of heaven shall be shaken"
Gospel of Luke 21: 25-26

Three months to the day since Emma's presentation to GPATT (she hadn't heard a word from Dr. Wagner) Cyprium Prospector was on station in geosynchronous orbit above the planned habitat and ore processing site on Mars in the Planum Australe region. It would stay on station for 12 weeks, which was the estimated length of time it would take to set up the Mars facility and fill Cyprium Prospector's cargo hold with processed ore.

Planum Australe is the name of the southern polar plain on Mars. It is partially covered by ice in places which are over a mile thick. The southern ice cap was chosen over its much larger counterpart because there is a huge cyclonic storm traveling in the northern polar region. Martian storms are usually composed of dust, but this one is made up of water ice clouds similar to storm systems on Earth. Four times the size of the state of Texas, this super hurricane generates wind speeds of up to 900 mph, effectively ruling out any current consideration for mining operations in much of that hemisphere.

The selected habitat and processing site was located on a relatively smooth area of Martian landscape situated between, and chosen for, its proximity to the outer ice formations of the southern cap and Chasma Australe, monolithic erosional structures that have resulted in the removal of greater than half a mile thick stacks of layered deposits of exposed copper ore. But that is a clinical description of the landscape, and grossly inadequate.

Chasma Australe is a stunning arrangement of sheer, straight, sharp-edged vertical escarpments colored a deep reddish-orange, which merge with brown-black shadows that rival, and in some cases, surpass the colossal splendor of the Grand Canyon on Earth. Unlike the Grand Canyon, Chasma Australe is a single sided escarpment, not a river valley, whose rock formations are set against a butterscotch colored sky, except for the pink and red of sunrise and sunset, which render color contrasts unmatched on Earth.

The crew were ready. Cyprium Prospector had been awash in activity for five days in preparation for departure to the Martian surface. As soon as geosynchronous orbit had been achieved, material and equipment began descending to the planet below. The fact that Mars' gravity is 62 percent less than Earth's was a significant factor in planning mining missions to the red planet. It meant enough fuel could be carried on board to supply the ore carriers. Cyprium Prospector had what were called manned ore transports (MOT) or 'mots'. MOTs were small space tugs used to haul partially processed ore and equipment between Mars and Cyprium Prospector. They required a crew of two and could carry six people while attached to a partially processed ore container (PPOC), or a piece of heavy equipment. Twenty-four hour operations had commenced and would continue non-stop for the next three months. Naturally, fuel was critical, but less gravity and a thinner atmosphere meant less fuel would be required.

Although the voyage had been a wondrous achievement thus far, it was about to move into its second and most critical phase; living and mining on a hostile alien planet. The site became known as Mars BC, after the largest copper mine on Earth, the Bingham Canyon Copper mine. Subtitled, the Richest Hole on Earth, the Bingham Canyon Mine is located twenty miles southwest of Salt Lake City, Utah. Not only the largest copper mine in the world, it is the largest of all man-made excavations, the largest hole dug in the Earth, and it just may be the greatest single metal deposit ever discovered. Though still in operation, Bingham Canyon had ceased being a source of notable mineral specimens, which are only present now in very low grades and distributed throughout the granite-like rock as tiny grains. But that didn't matter to the mining crew because it was still the grand-daddy of all mines, and they were confident Mars BC would one day be just as big, and perhaps even bigger.

~~~~

Emma's research had been a small item in the news for some weeks. Global warming proponents decried that portion of her work citing Emma's own words that more study was needed. Conservative media touted it as being clear evidence the 'greenhouse effect' theory was nothing more than *hot air*. Her data relating to the bore site incident was extremely interesting to the planetary science folks, to which they responded by adding more new theories of their own regarding the origins of life and the universe. Irrespective of her work's appeal, or lack thereof, it brought her no job offers, or requests for speaking engagements, save from a few of the local high schools in south Texas. It was, however, accepted as a valid study, and as such, Emma would have to open up somewhat to Dr. Wagner about her ideas.

She continued with her study of the unusual phenomenon occurring around the globe, which were only a curiosity to most, but alarming to her. There were even documentaries on television about a number of these phenomenon, much of which were said to be linked to global warming - a result of the 'greenhouse effect' caused by man's burning of fossil fuels. Some of the evidence was compelling to be sure, but Emma was far from ready to throw in the towel on the global warming controversy. She took her own counsel and proceeded to do more research.

The idea of global warming, sometimes incorrectly called climate change, had been around for a long time. Nearly everyone in the industrialized world was familiar with the concept and believed they had a fair perception of its effect. Extremists argued flatulence and excrement from animals high on the food chain were partially to blame. Public understanding generally held that global warming was caused by air pollution, which was primarily the result of burning fossil fuel for energy and transportation. The pollution stayed in the atmosphere, occasionally falling as acid rain, building up overtime to such an extent it was endangering plant, animal and aquatic life. It was also causing Earth's ice to melt which raised sea levels, and therefore would lead to the destruction of real estate along coastlines. And now, the signs of impending doom were spreading. It seemed the predictions about the consequences of global warming were coming to pass.

Emma and others noted with interest the increase in the rise and fall of sea tides, the deterioration of ice shelves in some parts of the world, an increase in global humidity levels, a burst in global plant growth, changes in aquatic life behavior, such as, the off season migration of seabirds, the disappearance of the northwest salmon fishery, an explosion in land crab populations and the increased presence of whales and other marine mammals in the North Atlantic. Even insect species were undergoing change, notably an increase in flies and mosquitoes. In numerous areas of the globe conditions resembled some of the biblical plagues of Egypt. All were attributed to man's carbon footprint. What wasn't completely agreed upon as a result of this climate change was the significant increase in the temperature of Earth's crust and increase in volcanic activity.

The media had been doing its part in reporting all the unusual activity, failing not to point out global warming's part in the play. However, there were two aspects of climate change the global warming drum beaters and the media rarely touched upon. The first was that CO_2 levels had peaked several years earlier and had actually begun to drop. Cleaner and highly efficient fuel burning technology had been developed, along with small increases in the use of nuclear power for heat and energy production. Together they contributed to the reduction of CO_2 emissions in those areas by nearly 60 percent. Windmills, telecommuting, hydrogen fuel powered autos, small HYCOM powered cars (a combination of solar-gas-electric engines) had reduced oil consumption for transportation by 40 percent in the United States alone. That had the added benefit of reducing the United States dependence on foreign oil by 67 percent and the number was climbing.

The second aspect often ignored was the worldwide economic recession associated with the effects that were predicted. To be fair, a hit on the global economy received a mention now and then, but nothing like the attention that was given to the impact on the environment. Perhaps the media felt that aspect was expressly implied. In any event, few seemed to be listening as the sea began to reclaim the land. For months the waves and tides of the Atlantic Ocean had been threatening the barrier and coastal islands all along the eastern seaboard of the United States. Now these areas had become swamped. It wasn't until then the media really ramped up. From Chatham Massachusetts to Key West Florida the Atlantic Ocean had begun to redraw the coastline. Bermuda and other low lying Caribbean islands started to become swamped, or completely submerged. South America, Japan, the South Pacific Islands, Indonesia, the British Isles, and Latin America were next to experience the effects of rising tides and sea levels.

It seemed to happen overnight. People went to bed in the evening only to wake the next morning to discover once familiar ground was now knee deep in water. But it only seemed that way. Depending on the elevation of the landscape, coastal flooding reached inland anywhere from a few feet to over 50 miles along some rivers, which backed up and flooded towns and communities along their banks. Coastal roads were inaccessible, as were homes, businesses, marinas and seaports. Local economies fell like so many dominoes. The tourist industry in the Americas was nearly eliminated, coastal infrastructure collapsed and jobs ceased to exist. Phone communications and power went down. Oil, gasoline, food and water were rationed.

Only emergency travel was allowed. Martial law was in effect in many countries around the globe. The damage was inestimable. Millions were on the move inland and to higher elevations. The chaos that ensued was like nothing the world had ever seen. High-ground had become the new wealth secured in many instances by bloodshed and force.

Humans are adaptive, however, and most of the refugees, high-tiders as they were known, were able to escape the slow, but steady onslaught of water. The world had been holding its collective breath, strained to the breaking point, but remarkably humanity did not break. It did not weaken, or become more primitive, rather it got stronger in the face of adversity, and globally, humankind reached out to their neighbors. But the worst was yet to come.

In the months following Emma's return from space, a quite disagreement had begun to develop in the scientific community over the alleged climate change effects which were occurring and threatening civilization. The disagreement emanated from the science of geology. Increases in Earth's mantle temperatures and volcanic activity puzzled scientists. They had begun to question the origins of some of the phenomenon allegedly caused by the 'greenhouse effect'. Dr. Wagner had been closely following the debate. He was concerned over the enlarging body of news reports covering the many strange things happening globally, particularly those dealing with volcanic activity. Somewhere between the first real perceptible encroachment of the water, and the chaos that ensued, Dr. Wagner contacted Emma. She wasn't aware of it at the time, but that meeting would conclude with another ESV ride into space.

Emma could only guess what the GPATT director wanted to discuss. All he could tell her was that he needed to see her as soon as possible on an urgent matter that couldn't be voiced over the phone. Based on that tiny bit of bait, Emma travelled to Washington, DC and GPATT corporate headquarters. This time she met with the Director, not in some college lecture hall anti-room, but in Dr. Wagner's private office inside GPATT corporate.

GPATT headquarters was an impressive domain, richly decorated, roomy and full of well heeled types. The intent was to impart the feeling of power, importance and success, all of which were not lost on Emma. Dr. Wagner, who was very much a people person, received Emma in the luxurious waiting area and escorted her back to his nicely appointed office.

"This is gorgeous!" she exclaimed. It was near decadent in its mahogany and gold leaf, and of course, copper accents. There were beautiful detailed representations of technology all over Dr. Wagner's office utilizing copper; a sculpture made of copper cable, 2D and 3D art on the walls, scale replicas of a wind turbine, solar wind tower, an ESV, OEP3 and Cyprium Prospector.

"Would you like something to drink? Just name it." he offered cheerfully.

"No, thank you." replied Emma engrossed with the model of OEP3. "So, what's with all the cloak and dagger?"

"That's one of the things I like about you, Emma, direct and to the point."

"One of the things I like about you, Dr. Wagner, is that you are always straightforward with me."

"I apologize for the mystery Emma, but some things just can't be discussed over the phone. The mystery ends right now, but before I begin, I want to know if you are ready to tell me anything."

"Like what?" she responded quizzically.

"The last time you were here I asked you to tell me what you weren't saying in your report. I was curious, in light of recent events, whether you were ready to share anything now. Besides, your work was validated, at which point you agreed to share your thoughts with me."

"You didn't have me come all the way to Washington just to ask me that?" she said avoiding the question, though she felt more compelled to share her thoughts with him now than before.

"Actually, I have some ideas of my own. I just wanted to test them first. You must have a pretty long list by now." he said peering at a report in his hand. She knew immediately he was referring to her compilation of worldwide phenomenon.

"Yes."

Dr. Wagner looked at her over the top of his reading glasses with a look that indicated he was waiting for the next part of her one word response.

"And I can tell you that I am not in complete agreement with popular assessment." she added.

"Which is?"

"That not all of the events are related to global warming."

"Anything specific?"

"Some of the ice melt, increased temperature of the Earth's crust, volcanic activity."

"Thank you."

"For what?"

"Confirming some of my own suspicions. When you refused to voice your misgivings to me, I was incented to perform a little research of my own. I wanted to know what it was you weren't telling me."

"I didn't know what to tell you. All I knew at the time was that something didn't seem right. I didn't know what."

"How about now?"

"Honestly? I think something other than global warming is triggering the phenomenon we are seeing. It feels geologic in nature, but I don't know what it is, and I can't just come out and say that. I have nothing to back it up."

"Well, if it's any consolation, I think something else is going on too, and we are not alone. That's why I asked you to come to Washington. I want you to find out what it is."

"Me? You already have a gaggle of geologists at your disposal. What could I tell you that they can't already?"

"You're right, down here there's probably not much that you could add. However, there is no one with your perspective working on the problem in outer space."

Emma paused for a moment. "I never really thought about studying Earth geology from space before. I mean, I know aerial and satellite pictures can add perspective."

"Think of it as being a bit more objective, you know, not being so close to the action."

"What exactly do you want me to do up there?"

"I want you to solve the problem. And do it quickly, I'm not feeling very optimistic about what I see." he said raising the report in his hand.

"What is that?" she asked acknowledging the report.

"Your list."

~~~~

The relationship between Adam and Emma had developed at a somewhat slower than usual pace, primarily because of Adam's job. Had it not been for the fact Emma lived in relative proximity to the jump port, Adam's primary duty station, their brief encounters in outer space would more than likely have ended there. They didn't have the luxury of a typical free evening, or a weekend free work schedule, although they managed to see each other frequently enough. Absence did make their hearts grow fonder to the point where their relationship did become serious.

Emma was able to manage one free weekend before ascending to her lookouts on the OEPs which nicely coincided with Adam's schedule. The two decided to spend it together on South Padre Island, Texas, which had for the moment, been enigmatically spared from the rising seas. Tidal forces was the explanation provided as to why the Texas coastline had been unaffected. Their first evening was spent dining at the Wahoo Grille, known for its great seafood and breathtaking harbor sunset views.

"So tell me, how do you rate all these exotic assignments?" Adam teased.

"Just lucky, I guess. Actually, I was surprised Dr. Wagner called. After the reception my presentation got at GPATT, I wasn't sure I'd ever hear from him again."

"Well, your presentation was obviously better than you thought."

"I guess. At least this time I won't have to go stomping around on the Moon in a spacesuit. I'll be on the OEPs the whole time."

"And how much time will that be?"

"I really don't know. I'll be doing my own thing at my own pace, but that doesn't mean I can drag my feet. Dr. Wagner is hoping I come up with some answers quickly."

"Answers to what?"

"All the unusual things that are going on."

"You mean the global warming stuff?"

"It's not all due to that."

"Care to tickle me with some of your theories?"

"I'm not sure what's going on. I just don't believe every strange happening is the result of global warming."

"I think the evidence is rather compelling." Adam countered. "How else would you explain a world-wide burst in plant growth, more clouds and the devastating rise in sea level?"

"Fair question, but how would you explain why huge areas of vegetation are now dying, along with large animal populations in tropical and subtropical climates? And what's with all the volcanic activity?"

"Well, there's been some, but not the Mount Saint Helen's kind."

"We haven't seen that kind of activity, I'll grant you that. But there's plenty of activity. Why do you think all the trees are dying in Yellowstone?" she asked

"I, uh..." Adam stammered.

"Because a large portion of the park sits right over a huge magma chamber, and something is causing that chamber to get hotter." Emma said answering her own question.

"And going into space will provide you with answers?"

"Dr. Wagner thinks it might."

Sipping their drinks as the conversation paused, they sat quietly for a long moment, enjoying the view from their table in the restaurant and being in one another's company. Emma broke the silence.

"Adam? What's happening?" she asked in a subdued tone he immediately recognized. The scientist had let down her guard and was allowing herself to be vulnerable in front of him. In this moment she was afraid. Conditions globally had continued to worsen and all anyone could do was blame it on global warming. No other explanations, or sensible solutions had presented themselves. Emma wanted Adam to tell her everything would be all right and the planet would set itself right again. But he couldn't tell her that, and though he wanted to comfort her he had no words to offer.

"Hopefully, you will be able to tell us." he said softly.

Apart from that brief moment, when Emma allowed herself to wax melancholy, the evening was perfect. The conversation was pleasant, the weather was delightful and the food was delicious. For Emma, it was as good as it gets, romantically, and she longed to be with Adam completely.

~~~~

EP3 served as the hub for EP1, EP2 and LP1 orbiting the Moon. EP1 was suspended just over the edge of Antarctica with views that changed continuously from southern South America, southern Africa, Australia and New Guinea. EP2 was usually centered over Afghanistan but also floated over Eurasia drifting back and forth across the continent from Great Britain to Japan. EP3 was perched in geosynchronous position over Canada and encompassed North America and Greenland. Primarily observation stations, EPs 1& 2 were actually downsized versions of EP3, and whose hamster cages were also smaller.

As Emma had already spent time on EP3, albeit in a different role, she decided to begin her new assignment on EP1. There was no driving logic to her plan, she just needed a starting point. Depending upon what she observed there, would decide which platform to visit next.

Emma had seen the popular TV documentaries on global warming, climate change and pollution, along with their environmental impact on plants, animals and the Earth. She was familiar with the science and the scientists behind the studies on changing Earth temperatures, receding ice, increases in desert areas and loss of fertile growing land. She had personally studied satellite thermal imagery graphically portraying those changes which could not be denied. Emma was as familiar with the evidence documenting change to the planet as anyone. And yet, she, Dr. Wagner, and a small group of others felt something else was occurring partially masked by the attention being paid to global phenomenon. Emma would consider all the evidence again, but this time with a perspective that included her personal scrutiny from perches in high orbit above the Earth.

The views from the EPs were breathtaking, though they were often obscured by clouds. RADAR and satellite imagery was actually better than the raw view available from a space station, because those could see through clouds, but even technology didn't notice everything. Even with the help of technology Emma really didn't know what she was looking for. This was Dr. Wagner's idea and his intuition was uncanny sometimes. So, here she was gazing down at planet Earth, observing the way an eagle high up on some rocky crag might look for movement, indicating prey.

Emma spent several days on EP1 overlooking the southern hemisphere, gazing, thinking, staring at the land masses and their outlines against the sea. Several times each day she would study satellite imagery, then return to her perch peering down at Earth through the lenses of telescopes. Nothing clicked. She moved on to EP2 continuing with the same precise routine. At her request, EP2 tracked its way eastward across Europe where it took up station over Sakhalin Island, Russia's largest island separated from coast by the Strait of Tartary. There Emma tarried to observe one of the most active volcanic stretches on the surface of the Earth.

"The gods must be awake." Emma joked to herself staring out the window of her observation post. She was looking at an unmistakable string of islands off the coast of Korea which comprised the nation of Japan. Steam, or smoke was curiously emanating from numerous locations along the island chain.

"Never would have seen that from down there." she added, somewhat bewildered. "That's certainly one for my list. Guess it's time to report in."

"That's why I'm calling." Emma spoke into her Comm badge. "The Japanese Meteorological Agency, a/k/a the JMA, claims there are over 100 active volcanoes where the Pacific plate butts against the North American and Philippine Sea plates. They lie along part of a line known as the ring of fire. This makes Japan a very active area, geologically speaking. The caveat here is the JMA defines active volcano as having erupted within the most recent 10,000 years. In actuality, they only monitor about two dozen places that have fumarolic activity. Some hardly even qualify as volcanoes in the way most people think about them, although from up here it looks like more than two dozen. The Kamchatka peninsula is also very active, but oddly nothing is coming from its highest peak, Klyuchevskaya. "

"So, my scheme is bearing fruit!" answered the director enthusiastically.

"I don't know what it means, but you were right in asserting I might not have picked up on any of this for quite a while, if I hadn't taken the assignment. Can I get a world-wide infrared satellite image of the Earth no more than 48 hours old? "

"I'll see what I can do. Thanks for the update, Emma. Keep me informed. Good-bye."

Emma was excited about her discovery. She hadn't really expected to observe anything significant, although, now she was encouraged she just might find evidence to help explain things. This discovery certainly coincided with the rise in volcanic activity being reported. Interestingly, no one had been able to definitively explain the increase in frequency of volcanic activity. She was hopeful global infrared imaging would provide some clues. Emma decided until something else caught her eye she would focus her attention on the world's high profile volcanoes particularly along the ring of fire. Maybe that would provide her with some elucidation.

The *ring of fire* is an area of regular geologic activity that nearly encircles the entire Pacific basin. In an almost horse-shoe shape, it stretches from New Zealand, New Guinea and Indonesia, through Japan, into the Aleutian Islands arc, then down the western edge of the Americas terminating with Mount Erebus in Antarctica, the southernmost active volcano on Earth.

An example of just how active the ring of fire is lies beneath the western United States in a region called the Cascade Volcanic Arc. It contains 20 major volcanoes and over 4,000 separate volcanic vents, stratovolcanoes, shield volcanoes, lava domes, cinder cones and a few isolated examples of rarer volcanic forms such as tuyas, a distinctive, flat-topped, steep-sided volcano that is formed when lava erupts through a thick glacier, or ice sheet.

All this activity is a direct result of tectonics, the movement and collision of Earth's crust plates being subducted beneath one another. Ninety percent of the world's earthquakes and eighty percent of the world's largest earthquakes occur along the ring of fire. The ring by itself has over 450 major volcanoes and is home to over seventy-five percent of the world's active and dormant volcanoes. Emma would have plenty to look at.

The morning after her call to Dr. Wagner, Emma once again took up her perch in EP2 over Sakhalin Island. The day before, she reported the Kamchatka peninsula was very active, although, there was a conspicuous lack of activity from its highest peak. This morning, she had something quite different to report. Klyuchevskaya was sporting a Karman Vortex Street.

Named after the fluid dynamics engineer, Theodore von Karman, a Karman Vortex Street (KVS) is a repeating pattern, or string of swirling whirlpool like vortices seen in fluids and gases. They are best observed directly over top of the vortices themselves. Emma had a bird's eye view. This KVS contained eight, easily identifiable swirls, or holes in the cloud trail emanating from mount Klyuchevskaya.

"Great guga muga, there's a KVS!" she exclaimed excitedly.

After fifteen minutes of studying Klyuchevskaya's KVS, it occurred to her excited brain to consider the possibility there just might be other volcanoes behaving the same way. Diverting her gaze southward she noticed another large vapor trail. This one emanated from the center of Japan's main island.

"Fuji-san!" she gasped melodramatically.

Mount Fuji is Japan's highest mountain at 12,338 feet. Up until this moment, this usually snow covered slightly active volcano was classified as 'low risk' for eruption. But there was definitely vapor coming from its peak, and vapor uncharacteristically observed rising from mountain peaks is often the harbinger of an earthquake, or an eruption.

"Time to call *Tremor Man*." Emma said to herself.

Eric Kimbrough was one of Emma's college associates and a good friend. He was given the moniker 'tremor man' because earthquakes were his passion in school. Eric worked for the USGS Earthquake Center in their Denver Colorado office on the Earthquake Hazards Program, a continuous near-real-time monitoring of tremors and quakes across the United States called ANSS (Advanced National Seismic System), and across the world called GSN (Global Seismographic Network).

"Eric Kimbrough." said the distracted voice on the other end of the line.

"Tremor Man!"

"Rockie Top, is that you?"

"Yeah, it's me. How've you been?"

"Great! Just great! Little busy at the moment."

"I had a feeling."

"Oh, man. You wouldn't believe what's going on."

"Actually, I would."

"The *ring* has really been rockin'. The plates have been banging the crap out of each other. You ought to see the Cascade Arc readings. Sensors have been going off all over the place." Eric said excitedly.

"How about Klyuchevskaya and Fuji?"

"Yeah, the big 'K' and Fuji started just six hours ago."

"You should see the KVS coming from big K." Emma said smugly.

"KVS?! Really?"

"I'm looking right at it."

"You've gotta send me the pictures."

"I will, as soon as I download them from my camera."

"Camera? Where the heck are you?"

"EP2." she said as plainly as she might have said 'In my car'.

"EP2? What's EP2?" Eric asked somewhat confused. Emma didn't respond hoping he would figure it out. She wasn't disappointed.

"You mean the space station? Are you shitting me?"

"Pretty cool, huh?"

"Man. You get around. What is this, your third time in outer space?"

"Second."

"More global warming stuff for GPATT, huh?"

"Sort of. Listen, I need a favor."

"Name it."

"Can you get me a chart of Richter Magnitudes 2.5 and higher with their occurrence frequency for the last three months, and can you differentiate those associated with volcanic activity?"

"Yeah, sure. Might take a day or two."

"That will be fine. It will take me that long to get over to EP3."

"What's going on? You know something?"

"Honestly, T-man, I don't know anything. I'm just trying to figure it out like a lot of people. You got anything?" she asked, trying to throw him off.

"No. There are a couple of theories being quietly floated, but I can tell you, global warming ain't one of them. And anything you hear about changes in ocean salinity contributing to earthquakes is crap. Something else is going on, but we don't know what. Crust temps are up, cracks are widening and new ones are appearing and..., hey, you didn't hear that from me."

"No worries."

"Rockie?"

"Yes?"

"If you find out something...you know what I'm saying?" Eric said in a serious tone.

"Yes."

"You will let me know, right?" There was concern in his voice.

"I promise, Eric."

"Okay." he breathed somewhat reassured. "You call me if you need anything else."

"Thanks T-man. You're the best."

Three days later Emma was on EP3 studying charts and graphs she received from Eric. It was great information, but it was disappointingly unrevealing, or so it seemed to Emma.

Chapter Nine

"Atheism is a crutch for those
who cannot bear the reality of God."
Tom Stoppard- Playwright

The Lockheed built Hercules C-130-J was on a sortie out of Gardermoen Air Station fifty klicks north of Oslo in southern Norway, home to the 135th Air Wing and the 335th Squadron of the Royal Norwegian Air Force. This four engine turbo-prop heavy transport had a crew of three; a pilot, co-pilot and loadmaster. It had cleared the barrier islands west of Bergen and was on a direct approach toward Scotland's Shetland Islands. From there it would alter course slightly northward toward the Danish controlled Faeroe Islands. Passing the Faeroes, the large grey aircraft would change course one final time on a heading due north to the Norwegian overseas outpost of Jan Mayen Island. Ordinarily, C-130s would fly in from Bodø Main Air Station in northern Norway only two hours east of the outpost by air, but this one was on a training mission from one of the most advanced Hercules C-130 installations in all of Europe.

Only thirty-four miles long, Jan Mayen is a small volcanic island in the North Atlantic 300 miles east of Scoresbysund, Greenland, 600 miles west of North Cape, Norway and approximately 600 miles north of Iceland. It has no exploitable natural resources, no ports or harbors, limited offshore anchorage and no economic activity, except to provide services for employees of Norway's military radio and meteorological stations. Main access to the island is gained via one 5,200 foot long gravel paved airstrip, which is easily negotiated by a Hercules C-130.

The island's human population work for the Norwegian Defense Force, or the Norwegian Meteorological Institute, all of whom live in the settlement of Olonkinbyen. The outpost's primary purpose is to support a military radio transmitter. Jan Mayen's most prominent feature is Beerenberg Volcano, the world's northernmost active volcano. Covered partially by a glacier, Beerenberg is a towering stratovolcano whose near perfect symmetrical cone reaches skyward 9100 feet above sea level.

The co-pilot, scrutinizing his in-flight checklist, called the airstrip for a weather update. He already knew the weather. A large area of high pressure was dominating the North Atlantic, the ceiling was unlimited and the sky was clear as crystal. But this was the military, and weather checks were part of normal flight procedures. The co-pilot keyed his microphone.

"Jan Mayen Field - Jan Mayen Field, this is NDF transport Golf Alpha Sierra - Flight 3, requesting weather check. Over." There was no response. The pilot, who could also hear the conversation through his headset, turned toward the co-pilot.

"Give them a second. It's an outpost, after all. They don't get much flight traffic."

The huge craft continued on smoothly, its four engines droning with such synchronized precision the noise produced made it sound like they were one. After a few minutes the co-pilot keyed his microphone a second time. "Jan Mayen Field - Jan Mayen Field, this is NDF transport Golf Alpha Sierra - Flight 3 requesting weather check. Over." The co-pilot looked over at the pilot for confirmation of the radio's silence.

"What time is it?" asked the pilot.

"13:30." responded the co-pilot as he glanced at his chronometer.

"Lunchtime should be over. What frequency do they monitor?"

"148.020 kHz AM." the co-pilot responded after a quick glance at the setting.

"Get a radio check from Bodø."

The co-pilot complied. "Bodø Tower, Bodø Tower, this is NDF Golf Alpha Sierra - Flight 3, requesting radio check. Over."

The heavy transport's radio received an immediate response. "Golf Alpha Sierra - Flight 3, this is Air Station Bodø, reading you Lima Charlie. Over."

"Roger that, Bodø, thanks. Flight 3 out."

The co-pilot marked his check list; negative contact – JMF, 13:30hrs. The notation was the same at 14:00 hours. Approaching the island at 14:30, they discovered why the outpost had been silent.

~~~~

The Giske Point was a spooler, or more technically described, an 11,000 ton, 655 foot long, 112 foot wide, self-propelled, dynamically-positioned, single reel pipe-laying ship. Its hull was specially constructed to buttress a support structure for rotating a vertical reel for spooling rigid-walled underwater gas pipeline. The ship could accommodate laying a single line of pipe underwater to a maximum depth of 3,000 feet. The reel capacity could handle seven and a half miles of 12 inch diameter pipe to eighteen miles of 6 inch diameter pipe, at a lay rate of up to a half mile of pipe per hour. It looked like a floating carnival ride.

The ship had just wound a spool of 6" pipe from the spooling facility located on Norway's Vigra Island and was headed toward the Shetland Islands by way of the shipping lanes 30 nautical miles out. The crew was preparing to make its course change to the south when the lookout beckoned to the first mate to come out onto the starboard observation deck, five stories above sea level.

"What do you make of this? The horizon looks like it's moving."

"What do you mean, moving?" The mate took the image stabilizing binoculars from the lookout and held them up to his eyes. After a long moment, he turned and opened the bridge door and called in.

"RADAR? Do you have anything dead ahead?"

The radar operator waited for a refresh sweep of the antennae and responded, "No vessels. Screen is clear."

"Do you have anything, anything at all?" the mate demanded.

"There's a line across the screen." responded the operator. "Could be a small short in the array. I'll have it checked."

"What's the range of the line?" asked the mate.

"Eighteen miles."

"Tell me if it moves toward us."

After a long moment the radar operator tucked his chin, blinked and with curious surprise in his voice said, "Range, seventeen miles."

The mate looked through the glasses again. He called to the Captain.

The captain turned casually toward the mate. "What is it?"

The mate beckoned the Captain to come out on the platform, handed him the glasses and pointed. "Unless I'm wrong, we've got a wave coming right at us, and it's the biggest thing I've ever seen."

After a long look through his glasses the captain returned to the bridge barking orders."Hard a-port!"

"We'll never turn her in time." the mate challenged.

"Rudders amid ship!" the Captain countered. "Maintain your heading, full speed ahead, sound general quarters and activate the emergency beacon."

"Range!" hollered the mate.

"Fifteen miles." answered the radar operator. "What is it skipper?"

"Tsunami." the captain responded flatly. He looked at the mate. "Time." he demanded, wanting to know how long it would be before the wave struck the ship.

"Six to nine minutes." responded the mate.

The crew reacted to the general quarters alarm by donning their life vests and closing every hatch and companionway door they could get to within the few minutes they had before the inescapable occurred. Now, all they could do was watch, as the fast approaching wall of water bore down upon them.

The tsunami slammed into the bow of the Giske causing the vessel to become quickly overwhelmed by water. The ship heaved as a roaring wave rolled over the deck until the stern momentarily disappeared from view. The Giske Point was completely submerged. It shuddered hard slamming everyone on board to the deck. What followed was a momentary feeling of weightlessness then gravity took control. They felt the bow rise as though the ship was going to flip over. The bridge crew knew what was happening because they could see it. Those below decks could only try to hold on. A loud creaking was heard as the hull was stressed by the weight and pressure of the water that had suddenly come upon it. Forward motion stopped as the big ship was held in the wave's grasp then it lurched forward and returned to its familiar normal forward motion and the tsunami was gone. The bridge crew were dumbfounded. Not one window broke nor hatch gave way.

"All stop." stammered the Captain.

The first mate climbed to his feet and disengaged the azipod propulsion engines. Unlike internal combustion engines which required an external air source, azipods are electric and were still running. For two whole minutes no one spoke a word. Incredulously, no one was killed, or seriously hurt, although, the cook sustained a mild concussion, after being struck by a large aluminum stewpot when the ship heaved. The rest of the crew came topside and began to look around checking for wreckage. There was only minor damage to the spool support structure, but it had been rendered completely inoperative.

The RADAR operator broke the silence. "Did that really just happen?" He then gasped and soberly added, "Oh my God, we need to warn the mainland."

"It's too late." the Captain responded somberly. "It's too late."

~~~~

Eric Kimbrough called Emma from the Earthquake Center in Denver. It wasn't a pleasure call and he wasn't following up to see if Emma had received the charts.

"Eric! Hey, thanks man. The charts are just what I was looking for." she lied

"Rockie, I've been getting major motion from Jan Mayen for the past twenty-two minutes. You've got to look out your window up there and tell me what's going on."

"Holy shit! Are you kidding me?"

"No man. We're pretty sure it's Jan Mayen, and it's major."

"Okay, let me call you back. It will take me a couple of minutes to get up there."

"All right, but you'd better call me back!"

You can't run very well run on a space station, even in sections with artificial gravity. And though Emma hurried, it took fifteen long minutes to get dressed, climb to the observatory, train the optics on Jan Mayen Island and call Eric back.

"It's Beerenberg." Emma told him definitively.

"I knew it! Which way did it blow?" he demanded.

"Southwest, over the island." Emma said shocked at what she was witnessing. "T-man, you still there?"

"That means they're gone." Eric said quietly.

Beerenberg volcano had exploded in a violent lateral discharge, similar in manner to the Mount Saint Helens eruption of 1980, creating an avalanche that ravaged the west side of the island. The blast produced a 20 mile long fan of destruction Emma couldn't clearly see because ash and smoke were obliterating most of the island from view. The settlement, airstrip, radio and meteorological stations all were in the direct path of the onslaught. The main difference between the two eruptions was that there was little warning of the impending eruption for Beerenberg. No one escaped its fury.

"I should have seen this one coming." Eric said, remorsefully.

"How? How could you have possibly seen this coming?" she demanded, angry at his self inflicted guilt. "That island is on the world's smallest micro-plate, and is inconsequential, except for a stupid radio tower. With all the crazy things going on all over the world... pick a spot, make a prediction, and you'll probably be right! There wasn't any time, and you know it. You wouldn't have given that island a snowball's chance of blowing in this century, and neither would any one else, and if you think you are that good, you'd better tell me when and where the next one is going to blow."

"What do you mean, next one?"

"I mean the next one!" she shouted. "Did you even look at the charts you sent me?"

"No, not really, why?"

"We need to team up. How would you like to come up here?"

"Are you kidding me? I'd love it! But I can't just stop work and come up there. And how in the hell would I get up there anyway? I don't work for GPATT."

"I can fix it so USGS will loan you to GPATT. You'll continue to get paid through USGS, but the money will come from GPATT, and you'll get paid 24 hours a day as long as you are up here."

"I'm there. What do I need to do?"

"Pack a bag and I'll set it up. Someone from GPATT will contact you. They'll take car of everything. You're right, you can't just stop what you're doing and fly into outer space. You'll need a physical, an NPD and some training. I'll meet you at the jump port when you are ready, hopefully, no longer than three, or four weeks."

"You're coming back down?"

"In about a week. In the mean time take a look at your charts! See you in a few weeks."

There were no tsunami sensors in the North Atlantic, at least not beyond the Faroes, and so, there was no warning. The excitement generated by the explosion of Beerenberg was such, that those monitoring the event, including Tremor-man, hadn't stopped long enough to consider Jan Mayen was on the edge of the Atlantic Ridge, and the potential for what that meant. The massive undersea quake which had generated the eruption spawned a deadly mega-tsunami, the type scientists eagerly liked to theorize about with computer generated images on cable TV because of their size and destructive force. This one was rushing toward the porous coastline of Norway with its thousands of islands and innumerable water capillaries, some of which easily reached inland thirty miles or more.

By the time the wave reached the tiny Faroe Island group, it had already begun to inundate Norway's northern shores with an eight story high wave crest that would angle its way down that country's irregular coast like the blade of snow plow clearing a road. The wave would crash into Scotland and eventually overcome the famous earthen dykes of the Netherlands. The death and destruction left in its wake would be almost incalculable.

Emma stayed on EP3 for another six days, expectantly watching the Earth below. There were no new volcanic events within the six days following Beerenberg, although the ring of fire continued to pour forth smoke and steam. As she hadn't heard from Eric, or received any updates from the USGS, Emma correctly assumed Eric was busy training with GPATT. She wanted to stay on

EP3 a bit longer, but she hadn't seen Adam in a while, who had just returned from his latest mission. She picked him up at RJP and drove back to his apartment condo.

"So, what's been going on?" Adam asked as they got in the car.

"You know about the tsunami?" she asked.

"Of course. Who doesn't? It was big."

"That's an understatement. It was the largest tsunami in recorded history, a sixty-two foot wall of water by the time it reached the mainland. News sources said it went down the coast like a giant snow plow. Water reached inland 25 miles in some places. It devastated Norway's coast and it even reached the Netherlands. The dikes there were no match for it, but some experts claimed they did help some. They have been showing video on the news non- stop. The death toll is estimated to be in the millions. Can't even get relief efforts going because the water isn't receding fast enough."

Adam turned on the television as soon as they entered the apartment. The FOX news channel had been the first to pick up the story and the first to have videos of the tsunami's aftermath. They watched in disbelief as scene after scene showed death and devastation. It was evocative of the before and after pictures of the 2004 Indonesian tsunami in that, so much of civilization had just disappeared.

Bodies of people and dead animals floated about in the thousands. Debris was everywhere. Even parts of Scotland and Ireland lay in the tsunami's path. Eleven countries in all suffered direct wave impact. For those living in the strike zone who survived, the world had suddenly become unfamiliar, alien and inhospitable. Many would be alone and on their own for weeks without food, shelter, clothing, or medical supplies. The death toll would continue to mount due to a lack of food and fresh water, untreated injuries, and disease.

"Can you imagine what could have happened if a nuclear power plant had been destroyed?" Adam was thinking out loud not really expecting an answer.

"God help us." Emma intoned.

"God help us? Why didn't God stop this?" Adam responded quietly.

"That isn't how God works." Emma said still somewhat mesmerized by the devastation playing out on the TV.

"I wonder sometimes, if there really is a God when this kind of stuff happens."

"Of course, there is." Emma turned away from the television, her full attention now on Adam.

"Be nice if you could prove it."

"Prove God exists?" she asked surprisingly.

"That's the trouble. No one can. I saw a television show once where this scientist was discussing time. He noted humans were the only species on the planet aware of their own death, that their time on Earth is limited. He said mankind invented God out of a need to believe in a timeless existence after death, neither of which could be proven scientifically."

"So, because he says God can't be proven scientifically, He doesn't exist?"

"It was a pretty compelling argument."

"For an atheist."

"Well, you really can't prove He exists." challenged Adam who was no longer watching the television.

"Okay, you prove He doesn't exist."

"I believe the discussion is about proving He does exist so, the burden is on you."

"What about faith?"

"What about it? Having faith in something doesn't prove anything."

"Oh, really?" she quipped. "And I suppose faith has no place in science?"

"Well it wouldn't be science then, would it? It would be faith."

"Let me ask you a question. What is scientific method?"

"Uh, wow. I'm going to have to go back to my high schooldays for that one. It's a process by which a hypothesis is proven by an experiment that can be measured, observed and repeated."

"So, you're saying that, assuming God cannot be proven scientifically, he does not exist."

"It would make it easier."

"Phooey. When you die, when you're dead and gone two hundred years from now, how will the scientific method prove you existed?"

"There will be records that I existed, my birth certificate, stuff like that."

"Exactly. There will be a history of you, just like God, just like Christ."

"Well, I never thought about it that way."

"So, you are an atheist?"

"No! I believe in God."

"Prove it, and please, feel free to use the scientific method."

Adam paused for a moment to think about what he would say next. Had Emma trapped him with his own conflicting statements, or had he done it to himself?

"What's the matter, cat got your tongue?"

He allowed an embarrassing chuckle to escape. "I see what you mean."

"No you don't. Most people will say they believe in God, if you ask them. But to say that doesn't carry any stigma, or embarrassment because it requires no membership, no proof, no commitment, no knowledge, or history, and no defense. Rarely is anyone questioned when they say "I believe in God". It's actually harder to say that there is no god, because the odds are if you do, you will more than likely be questioned about it, prompting at the very least some minimal defense of your position. You say, "I believe in God", as do most, yet there is no science involved in making that statement, only faith. Does that make you a hypocrite, or a liar?"

"Okay, I see your point."

"Do you believe in Buddha?"

"There are people that do."

"Yes, but can they prove he was real?"

"Didn't you just get finished saying that you couldn't prove something like that?"

"No, I only said that scientific method can't necessarily prove everything. There are other methods available, for example, history. Would you say that most people accept their school history books as reliable and true? I mean, the people writing and publishing those books aren't trying to tell lies. They are trying to be as accurate as possible, right?"

"I feel like I'm being set up." Adam said cautiously.

"If it makes you feel any better, I accept the history in those books. I've got no reason to believe I'm being lied to. I believe they are reliable." Emma said genuinely.

"Okay. Me too."

"Those history books contain information that passes the test of bibliographical authority. Take Jesus and the New Testament. Did you know the New Testament has more bibliographical authority than the Greek Classics, or any piece of literature from antiquity?"

"What the heck does that mean?"

"Well, bibliographical authority refers to how manuscripts are transmitted through time. For example, how old are they, are they copies, how close to actual events were they transcribed. It's a test manuscripts have to pass for reliability. Now, scholars accept the existing manuscripts for the Greek Classics as being reliable. If you compare The New Testament texts with the Greek Classics using the test for bibliographical authority, the reliability of the Classics doesn't even come close to the New Testament manuscripts. That means the manuscripts used to document the life, death and resurrection of Jesus are highly reliable. Not only that, they are credible in content, because much of it was written by eyewitnesses, the second test of history. You can't say that about Buddha."

"That's interesting." he admitted honestly.

"The point is, you don't arbitrarily dismiss something as invalid, because you can't prove it scientifically. Just because God doesn't behave the way you think He should, is not a criteria for His existence, or of his love for humanity."

"Point taken. " he conceded. "I just wish all this wasn't happening."

"Neither do I. "

"You're a pretty smart person. Anyone ever tell you that?"

"My Dad." she said humbly.

The two of them sat fixated to the TV until it pained them to watch any longer. And as terribly shocking and widespread as this event was, Emma couldn't stop thinking about what was happening along the *ring of fire*.

Over the next two weeks Adam and Emma both worked relatively normal schedules, and as such, they were able to spend most of their free time together. But at the end of the interval, Adam resumed his spaceflight duties, and Emma met Eric at the jump port, both bound for EP3. From there they would shuttle over to EP2 in orbit over the Pacific to observe the *ring of fire*.

~~~~

As excited as he was to be on his way into outer space, Eric was not as prepared as he thought. At first, leaving Earth's gravitational forces was a 'rush', as he put it. However, before they docked with EP2, Eric developed a nasty case of SAS. It took him nearly three days before he could move about steadily, or eat anything solid.

"Well, look who's with the living!" Emma cheerfully exclaimed as Eric unsteadily entered the observatory for the first time. "Are you okay?"

"The past couple of days have been rough, but I think I'm finally ready for duty. Got my utility bag with me, though, just in case."

"That's a relief. Well, come here and take a look. It's a million dollar view."

"Wow." was all he could say for a very long moment. "I mean, I've seen pictures..."

"They just don't do it justice, do they?" Emma finished his sentence.

"No, mam." he said absorbed with the view.

"You keep looking. I'm going to get a cup of coffee and take a pee. Want anything?"

"Hot tea, milk and sugar." he responded somewhat robotically, as he was completely engaged with the scene below.

Emma had been gone a full ten minutes though it only seemed a moment to Eric.

"Hot tea, milk and sugar." she said handing the SmartCup to Eric.

They spent the next hour going over the equipment in the observatory, and another half hour reviewing the landscape below.

"What do you make of it?" Emma asked, gazing at the big blue ball beneath them.

"It's one heck of view. I still can't believe I'm here."

"No, I mean, what do you make of that?" she said pointing to the various vapor emitting volcanic peaks.

"Amazing, but I don't know what to make of it. There's never been anything like this in recorded history. I wonder how this will marry up to the phenomena you've been cataloging?"

"That's an interesting question. I'm curious to see how the level of activity correlates with geographic location, too. But since the ring is always active, I'm not sure the increase in activity means anything, by itself."

"Hopefully, the data will provide some clues. I will say this, being up here gives my work an entirely new perspective."

"Good. That's a good start. We need some new perspective, if we're going to figure this thing out. Okay, ready to get to work?"

"I sure am. What exactly do you want me to do, and just what are we looking for?"

"We're looking for an explanation." she said seriously. "I want you to do what you normally do; observe, gather data, correlate that data, tell me what you see happening, paint me a picture. Why is the ice melting? Why is the sea rising? Why the increase in quakes and eruptions? Why is the top half of the ring steaming? What's causing the crust temps to increase? Look over my research. I have a list of events occurring around the globe that are happening out of synch. Everyone seems to think global warming is the reason."

"It's as good as any explanation." Eric suddenly paused and looked at Emma. "That's not it, is it? Something else is going on. I knew it! What is it you're not telling me? What's going on?"

"Well, that's the challenge. We don't rightly know, but some at high levels are quietly skeptical Earth's problems are due to the *greenhouse effect* so, we are exploring other possibilities, whatever they might be. Global warming is certainly the easy way to explain what is happening, but I don't just want to explain these things away. I want to know what it all means, and why. I think something else is taking place, and so do a few others at GPATT."

"What could it be? Let me in on your theory."

"I don't have one. I'm just not convinced global warming is doing all this. Something is happening to the Earth that trapped gas and heat just don't fully explain. Do the phenomena have some other common denominator? Why has Mother Earth just suddenly gone on the fritz? I want you to help me put the puzzle together. And if we can't start by saying what's causing these events, let's start by identifying what isn't."

"Okay, I got it. I'll review your stuff first, then I'll redo your original request, only with a few tweaks of my own, and we'll see what we come up with. Okay!" he said clapping his hands together, "Where's my work station?"

Eric and Emma remained in space for nearly a month visiting all three Orbiting Earth Platforms. At the end of that time, they returned to Earth. Emma submitted a preliminary written report to Dr. Wagner with the promise of a personal presentation once Eric had completed his analysis. It had taken three weeks, but he had compiled a remarkable database. Utilizing USGS software he was able to develop some interesting 3D computer imaging of all geologic activity recorded in the past five years with their associated Richter levels, down to a 1/100th order of magnitude, if desired, along with any known anomalous events.

Eric was obviously pleased with his handiwork as he showed Emma the images and explained how the program worked.

"Is this cool, or what?" Eric said excitedly as they watched the striking graphics changing on the screen before them.

"Eric, this is impressive!"

"Yeah, man. I've been playing with it for hours. It does all kinds of shit!"

"What order of magnitude are we looking at?"

"This is just point five."

"Can you put this thing in motion for a given time frame?"

"I can dial this baby any way you want, but I have to warn you, too much data requested over too wide a time range causes it to run kind of slow."

"Have you discovered anything?"

"Not really. I've been too busy playing with it, and the neat thing is, it self updates. I got the program wired into our global sensors. Your anomalies, any new ones that is, would have to be manually added of course."

"All righty then, let's see what we've got."

A week later in Dr. Wagner's office Emma verbalized their findings as Eric ran his program.

"Impressive." Dr. Wagner said at the end. What's the cause?"

"Unfortunately, that hasn't presented itself yet." Emma said almost apologetically.

"But we know one heck of a lot more than we did." Wagner said confidently. "Tell me, Dr. Cross, does this bolster the ideas you say you don't have about what you think is happening?" he asked with humorous sarcasm.

Emma answered carefully and thoughtfully, measuring every word of her response. "It suggests to me, the data which has been collected and analyzed for a given time frame, and subsequent to a specific event, may be systemic."

"I'll take that as a yes. So, what now?" he asked.

"Well, I think we should study this imaging program some more. There are a thousand different ways to look at this, and we haven't begun to scratch the surface. We really need some time to tweak the data."

"How much time do you think you'll need?"

"I wish I knew. Could be days, weeks. I don't have an answer. I feel like we have arrived at that place on the map where X marks the spot, but nothing is there. You know it's the right place, it's just not the right time. And maybe that's it."

"What do you mean?" quizzed Eric.

"Something doesn't feel like it is synced up, like the time is off, before we can discover whatever it is. Beyond that, my forward direction has stopped so, it's time to start digging."

"Then dig. Get back to me when you have something."

For the next six months Emma did just that. She ran Eric's program to the point where she was doing it in her sleep. Once a week she would send Dr. Wagner an email. It read simply, 'Dear Dr. W, nothing to report, but progress is being made. The place continues to feel right but not the time.' signed, 'E'. In the seventh month, however, time had finally sync'd up.

Chapter Ten

"We learn geology
the morning after the earthquake."
Ralph Waldo Emerson

Cyprium Prospector still some months away from Earth, was on the return leg of its maiden voyage, and though the cargo holds were filled regrettably at eighty percent capacity, the mission had been an undeniable success. Training, training and more training had been credited to that success. But for a few very minor mishaps, the safety record of the mining operation was perfect. Construction complete times were within hours of actual estimates, and mining production had occurred within calculated timeframes. The only area of uncertainty involved the water processing. It took two weeks longer than anticipated to get working, which resulted in the twenty percent deficit to the cargo load. By the time Cyprium Prospector had reached eighty percent of its hauling capacity the mission had reached the end of its maximum departure range, forcing the great ship to leave Mars orbit. There just hadn't been enough time left to complete a full load.

One of Commander Aviv Tamari's worries was whether, or not Cyprium Prospector would be impacted by meteorites on its way to Mars. It was problematic when it came to detection and avoidance of such space traffic, particularly for the smaller sized objects. And yet, the mission had been happily void of any meteorite collisions. Now that they were on their way home from this unprecedented historical mission, Cyprium Prospector's commander and crew felt a bit more at ease regarding the possibility of such an event because they had deployed detection buoys in synchronous orbit around the sun between Earth and Mars at fixed intervals along their flight path. Although Cyprium Prospector would not follow the exact same course on the return trip, the buoys offered a degree of detection previously unavailable to space vehicles for which Aviv was grateful.

Sana was especially grateful to learn the buoys had been deployed, for meteorite damage to Cyprium Prospector was her greatest fear for her beloved Aviv. She had mentioned it to him only once in what seemed to be casual conversation during a romantic dinner several weeks prior to mission commencement. Aviv did a commendable job allaying much of her fear by describing the vessel's vast array of monitoring devices, and how Cyprium Prospector 's self sealing hull would respond to invasive breaches of almost any kind anticipated with space travel. It was more technical description than emotional assurance. He was merely answering a question, though it reassured her. That fear put to rest, Sana had become increasingly concerned with events on Earth and thoughts of what her husband might find upon his return.

Cyprium Prospector did not receive much communication regarding the events happening on planet Earth for reasons which were partly intentional and partly technical. GPATT didn't want any undue stress placed on the crew, and radio and television signals just weren't being directionally beamed into space because there was no profit in it. It was one thing for a stationary antenna to capture a signal from a geosynchronous orbiting satellite. It was quite another to beam signals toward a constantly moving target out in space, unless the signals were from GPATT. As such, the crew got its news in fragmented bits through infrequent personal messages from home, which arrived devoid of the sensational impact usually accompanied by the media's telling of events. So when the crew learned Iceland had become inundated with magma flows that had oozed through the crust, without any violent explosive renting popularly associated with volcanic activity, they were emotionally indifferent.

On a cold grey afternoon several months after the Beerenberg explosion and ensuing tsunami, now called the Jan Mayen Wave, a call for help came forth from the Republic of Iceland. This solitary island nation was in trouble. The entire population, some 320,000 people, needed to be evacuated. Eric Kimbrough and other members of the USGS Earthquake center had been monitoring increased quake activity at Iceland, and all along the ring of fire, with keen interest. And though they had never seen this kind of geologic behavior pattern before, they felt no particular alarm because the levels of magnitude registered just below the range for concern.

That same afternoon and several miles above the dam professor Olafur (Ollie) Ingolfson was conducting a field study with two grad students along the banks of the Glera. The Glera River in northern Iceland originates from mountain glaciers on the Trollaskagi Peninsula. Sometimes called the River of Glass, it courses its way through the Glera Valley from which it takes its name, and runs through the town of Akureyri and into the fjord Eyiafjorour on its way to the sea. The coast at the fjord's bottom is named Pollurinn and is known for calm winds and a good natural harbor. The Glera was dammed above the waterfall in 1920 to produce electricity. The dam was rebuilt some eighty years later, but the original power station did not survive. The river also used to separate Akureyri proper from Glera Village, but the two merged prior to the dam being built. Surrounded by mountains, the highest being Sulur at 3980 feet and Hlioarfjall at 3661 feet, Akureyri is Iceland's fourth largest municipality with a population of 17,000.

Ollie was a direct descendant of the Nordic chieftain Ingolfur Arnarson who is generally recognized as the first permanent Norwegian settler of Iceland. He established his home in Reykjavik during the late ninth century and his descendants have lived there since. Ollie moved from Reykjavik to Akureyri to take a professorship at RES – The School for Renewable Energy Science, a private graduate school which shared its facilities with the University of Akureyri. Ollie was in his late forties, six feet tall and in fair shape at 185 pounds. He had a wiry head of chestnut colored hair with sun-bleached blond ends, and a full beard to match.

They were ruggedly dressed for the assignment, yet they wore no caps, or gloves. The air was chill and there was some patchy snow on the ground, but in many places the earth was bare and barren, a scene unusual for the time of year.

Dagmar Gudrindottir and Billy Plummer were the two grad students who accompanied Ollie this particular day, and they were attracted to each other. Dagmar was a twenty-three year old blond-haired, blue-eyed native who had lived in Akureyri all her life. She wanted to help Iceland meet and maintain its energy needs in an environmentally friendly way by exploiting the abundant heat resource just below the island's surface. Billy was from Chicago. He was a twenty-four year old Irish Catholic, five feet eight inches tall, ambitious and smart.

Billy had served six months in the Marine Corps where he read about geo-thermal energy in a magazine. He loved the Corps, but was discharged when he was diagnosed with exercised-induced asthma. During college, he realized geothermal energy had tremendous lucrative potential. Billy wanted to make what he called 'real' money by using geo-thermal technology to produce heat in the Great Lakes area of the United States. That brought him to RES where he met Dagmar.

They were preparing a case study for using the river as a source for steam which could be generated geo-thermally above the dam. Iceland already used geothermal energy to heat nearly 90 percent of the nation's buildings. It made sense to consider the country's natural heat and water resources to melt snow and ice accumulation on a cross-country highway being planned, which would connect Reykjavik with Akureyri.

The Glera was about four hundred yards wide and thirty feet at its deepest point where professor Ingolfson stopped to take their first readings. A low lying mist was all about particularly over the water. Dagmar and Billy were walking together talking, while Professor Ollie stalked the river's edge intent on the task at hand.

"I've been meaning to ask you something." said Billy. "Why is everyone's last name different? Your last name is different from your parents', and their last names are both different."

"It is a bit tricky." Dagmar answered. "We use patronyms, sometimes matronyms. I'm named after my mother."

"What's a patronym?"

"Patronym means 'named after the father', matronym means 'named after the mother'. You take the first name of a parent and add 'son', or dottir to the end of it to get the new last name. I am named after my mother whose first name is Gudrin. Gudrindottir."

"Kind of hard to keep track of the relatives isn't it?"

"It can be, but we're used to it."

A sudden tremor caused the professor to lose his footing and tumble into the shallows. Dagmar and Billy steadied themselves as they held onto their equipment. Though it only lasted three seconds, the noise it produced was unnerving.

"Holy shit!" cried Billy.

Dagmar and Ollie seem unconcerned. Ollie recovered, stood up, but made no move to hurry back to the top of the bank.

"This water is warm." Ollie said with curious surprise. Most people would have been irritated at the discomfort which followed falling in the drink and getting their clothes soaked. But dedicated scientists are usually not like most people.

"That was an earthquake, right?"

"Yes." Dagmar smiled

Another smaller tremor shook the ground with the rumble of what could have been mistaken to be thunder off in the distance.

"Does that happen a lot?" Billy asked noticeably concerned.

"Not a lot, but often. You get used to it." Dagmar answered. "Relax, it's alright."

"What do you mean, 'warm' professor?" Billy asked. He turned and walked to the water's edge and squatted placing his entire hand into the river.

"Hey, you could take a bath in this. Is this normal?"

"No, it's not." answered Ollie in a serious tone.

"That's not good?" Billy questioned.

Ollie didn't answer. He stood up and looked upstream then downstream. There was now a visible current in the river where before, there was none. The dam was usually responsible for that.

Dagmar pointed toward the water. "Look!" she cried as a small log floated quickly by.

"The dam." Ollie said flatly.

"Maybe they opened the flood gates." Billy offered.

"None of them were open when we came up here. To release pressure, or lower the water level they usually open only one, or two gates. They would have had to open all twelve of them for the water to suddenly be moving that fast."

The ground shook and rumbled again. Though they said nothing, each was wondering if the dam had broken. The rumbling began to grow with intensity. Suddenly, the water level in the middle of the river began to drop. The ground beneath it was caving in. Huge clouds of steam were being discharged and moving upstream as though a locomotive was charging along the river bottom. The now constantly shaking ground was not so violent that they were unable to keep their feet, but it had become obvious the shaking wasn't going to stop. They ran to the top of the bank. What they saw struck them with fear and panic. A large long tentacle of molten magma had appeared and cut off their retreat. They were caught between it and the Glera. Ollie looked around quickly. Smoke and steam were filling the sky to the East, West and South. He surmised the magma may not be a local phenomenon. They would have to go North to Akureyri on foot and stay along the riverbank if they were to escape.

Iceland had always been volcanically active and on a fairly large scale, which accounted for the inhospitable variation in its topography. But months of seemingly minor earthquakes increasing in frequency had been the unrecognized harbingers of doom. Numerous steadily moving magma flows were suddenly emerging throughout the island and advancing across the landscape obliterating everything in their paths. The quakes had created fissures through which the magma was being pushed like toothpaste from a tube.

Earthquakes weren't the only precursors something was gathering force. Thousands of harp seals had suddenly left the security of land only to be seen in certain coastal waters in numbers never before observed. They were just milling about several hundred yards offshore. Something was amiss. Icelanders knew this could be a dangerous place for seals to tarry, but tarry they did, nonetheless. Not long after the seals entered the water, the island's nearly 350 bird species took flight apparently not wanting to land. Dogs began to howl and cats became restless. And then it started.

The ground began to rumble faintly at first. The vibration and noise grew until it approximated standing next to a rolling train of endless freight cars thundering their way to some unknown destination. Reports were dispatched from points all over the island that black and red hot molten magma was springing up seemingly everywhere. It wasn't just racing down the street, or marching in like an invading army from over the mountain plateaus. The fiery ooze was mysteriously appearing almost underfoot. Smoke and steam enveloped the island and turned day into twilight. The population panicked. They had always had a keen awareness of the destructive potential Mother Nature could unleash from below the ground. They also believed they were prepared for it. But nothing could have prepared them for what was happening now.

Ollie, Dagmar and Billy ran as much of the way as they could, but it was tough going due to the rocky shoreline. They followed Ollie's lead along the riverbank until they reached the University, shaken and out of breath. The parking lot was nearly empty. Dagmar's car had remained unmolested so, they piled in quickly and drove towards town. When they reached the dam there were several large cracks from which the river was gushing. Akureyri was flooding along the river's edge. The magma had not yet assaulted the township, but it was only a matter of time before the western half would be erased from existence.

Dagmar stopped the car to gaze at the dam. At that point, Billy took the lead. He knew their only sure chance of survival was by plane, or boat, and boats were easy access for the moment. Once the townsfolk awakened to the realization they were in grave danger, escape would become impossible. They had to act now.

"If this is as bad as I think it is, there's only one way out, and that's by boat."

"We should get to higher ground." said Ollie.

"That's not going to protect us from the magma." Billy argued.

"You don't know that." cried Dagmar.

"You're right. I don't. So I am going with what I do know. So far, going North we haven't run into anymore magma. I intend to keep going North and get off this island. The best way to do that is by boat, and if we don't go now, we may never get another chance."

"What about the airport?" asked Dagmar.

"Not enough time, and it's too far away, and we don't even know if the airport is still there. And even if it is, it's probably already inundated. We've got to go, now!"

Ollie nodded in agreement. With that affirmation, Dagmar stomped on the accelerator. Fearing the town was flooded along the river they took the Skardshlíd road above the dam to reach the Krossanessbraut Road which would take them close to the commercial docks.

They took a turn on Oseyri and sped into the boatyard where the Geisli, a 100 foot tug, was casting off its lines. Dagmar hollered and the boat waited long enough for them to jump onto the fantail. They would be numbered as three of the lucky ones who escaped the ruin which was crawling across the island.

Located along the Atlantic Ridge, Iceland was situated 175 nautical miles from Greenland, a land that was still a Province of Denmark, though ill equipped to mount a rescue operation of the size and immediacy needed by its island neighbor. Although Iceland's landmass was twenty one times smaller than Greenland, its population was five and half times greater. And due to the already tremendous strain on worldwide resources being used in the tsunami relief effort, any help coming from Greenland would be minimal.

Iceland was doomed. The island's twelve airports were quickly overrun with people only to discover the number of planes was devastatingly insufficient, or that the runways themselves were blocked with hot orange and black ooze. Akureyri Airport was the only airport spared by the onslaught of the magma, but it made no difference.

The spit of land on which it was located was suddenly swallowed up by an underwater fissure.

Boats were another resource in short supply, whose owners made quick use of to escape the spreading black death consuming the island. Sadly, only 29,000 people would be saved, and those primarily by boats and ships. The majority of the island's population would drown attempting to escape the onslaught which seeped unceasingly from below, and pursued them to the coast and into the sea. Many were cut off with no escape and were literally incinerated where they stood. Others would die from exposure believing higher ground would offer protection from the magma, but the highlands are a cold and uninhabitable combination of sand and mountains which lacked food, shelter and firewood.

For those stranded few who survived the magma, rescue was otherwise impossible due to inaccessibility of the uneven terrain. Communication with the outside world had been lost as the magma flows had destroyed telephone switching equipment and most of the communication towers. Within three days Iceland had become, with the exception of some of its higher elevations, a black smoldering mass.

~~~~

While reviewing the quake data with Eric, generated for what was being referred to as 'The Iceland Event', Emma realized her first significant breakthrough. It was time to return to Washington.

"Hello, Emma. It's good to see you." Dr. Wagner embraced Emma warmly. "So, what's the good news, if there can be any in light of recent events?"

"I know. Eric has been beating himself up over Iceland. Half the USGS is. But to tell you the truth, even if they had cried "wolf", I don't think anyone would have listened. Earthquakes don't always mean volcanic eruption."

"The USGS has been taking a beating, I agree with you. I'm not so sure any one can predict with accuracy *when* such cataclysmic events will occur, only that they *will*, and it doesn't take much expertise to say that. Unfortunately, answers are being demanded. It would please me if you had some."

"I don't have any answers, yet, but I do have some significant new information."

"Does this mean you have a theory?"

"It means I have some insight. Indulge me for a few moments. I think you will appreciate what I have to tell you."

"Please, proceed." he invited.

Emma placed the speed drive next to Dr. Wagner's computer and accessed the presentation she had prepared for him. She showed him various charts, graphs and maps.

"As you can see, there are numerous files here. Most of them are the data files which support what we are about to show you. Eric is the one who put this thing together. It's a very extensive database and program with some really great graphics. It contains my personal research data and all the earthquake and volcanic activity picked up on the global sensor network for the past five years, including the Iceland Event. I'm going to cut to the chase and give you the short version.

Before today, all of the geologic activity picked up on the sensor grid was not much more than a record of the activity. We knew when, we knew where, we knew duration, frequency and magnitude. And from this we have tried to predict events, tried to use the information as an early warning system. The problem is we have only ever had seconds of advanced notice. And in spite of our advances in technology, we haven't gained much ground. We haven't really learned to read Earth geology in order to predict the next big event with any precision. One reason is, with the exception of low level activity, the events have been pretty much haphazard. Oh, we know which areas are more active than others, and therefore, what areas are higher risks, but as to when and where an event might occur, has always been anybody's guess.

One of the things I asked Eric to do was try to predict the next big event, thinking that with the increase in geologic activity and the eruption of Beerenberg, we might be able to do just that. We had plenty of options to choose from, but we selected only four; location, frequency, magnitude and time. Sadly, we did not predict Iceland. But since then, a picture has emerged."

"What do you mean, picture?"

"Well, we've been manipulating our four variables for months. After Iceland we discovered, coincidentally I might add, a large portion of geologic activity was mapped in an annular area between the western edge of the Pacific plate and the eastern edges of the North and South American plates, as you can see in this map of the Earth's tectonic plates.

The data also indicates a sudden increase in activity, which correlates with the appearance of much of the unusual phenomena collected in my personal research, and..." Emma paused. "...the launch of Cyprium Prospector."

"What are you saying?" Wagner asked, realizing Emma just might be on to something. "None of this is random? Are you suggesting the possibility of a discriminate pattern?"

"I am." she answered, inwardly pleased at his comprehension of the summary being presented. "But just to you."

"Does the Cyprium Prospector have something to do with this?"

"I don't know, but it has become part of the equation. Whether it is an import part is unknown at this point."

Dr. Wagner's mind was racing trying to determine what might be happening. He calmed himself, reluctantly realizing he really couldn't determine anything. That is why he had hired Emma.

"This is excellent work." he praised her. "Of course you realize, it raises as many questions as it might answer. What else do you want to tell me?"

"I want to go back to the Moon."

"Interesting. I thought we were done there. Why the Moon?"

"Can't really say."

"Can't, or won't?" he asked pointedly.

"I'm looking for puzzle pieces."

"On the Moon?"

"I'm not sure I can explain it. Did you ever walk out of the house, or leave to go on a trip and feel as though you were forgetting something? It's kind of like that. Something is telling me to go back to the Moon, as though I missed something. It's a feeling that has been nagging me for quite a while. We gained some new perspective being on the OEPs. Maybe the same thing will happen if I go back to LP1 and Apollo Seventeen."

"All right, go back to the Moon. How do you want me to handle this?" he asked, gesturing toward her presentation.

"You may share the data with anyone you please, just don't mention the non random discriminate pattern stuff, and my name in the same sentence, unless whomever you show it to comes to the same conclusion first."

While Emma carried on with her research, environmentalists continued to try and explain the Beerenberg explosion, Jan Mayen Wave, the Iceland Event and other phenomenon as prophetic signs of impending doom and the result of global warming. The arguments were compelling. How else could one explain the ice melt in the northern hemisphere, the rise in sea levels, the recent nearly global bloom of plant growth with its almost as sudden disappearance, the increase in ocean and crustal temperatures, the vanishing of many of Earth's fisheries, massive wild and domestic herd collapses, an explosion of insect, frog and small mammal populations and the ever receding sunlight, which was giving way to more and more clouds, just to name some of the phenomenon?

Tremendous strides had been made over recent years to reduce 'greenhouse' emissions. Pollution levels had dropped sharply. The current difficulty was that there was plenty of blame to go around, yet no real solution because beyond the global warming explanation, no one could elucidate what was happening to Mother Earth.

Global infrastructure had been deteriorating and most of the world had fallen into one downward spiraling economic depression. Public pressure on the world's governments to act was immense, but the situation would soon pass beyond their ability to effect much change. Food and energy could no longer meet demand, and in fact, their production was in sharp decline. Traditional fertile growing areas and energy reserves were shrinking and would soon be inaccessible, or gone due to the results of global events and increased mantle temperatures. Greenery was dying and water was advancing.

The Earth was fast losing its ability to sustain human life on the scale that was needed, and neither people, nor governments seemed able to stop it. And yet, not everyone was buying the global warming argument as the end all explanation, especially Emma. Even she was unsure finding another cause would be timely enough to make a difference, assuming there was one to be found.

When Emma returned from Washington, Adam was unexpectedly at the apartment waiting for her. The mission he had thought would take him back into space for a week had been scrubbed because of national transportation issues caused by the coastal flooding, which by now had permanently altered the coastlines of the United States. Even river systems were affected as they had become less able to dump their excess into the now rising seas. Inland flooding had caused levees to break, bridges to collapse and roadways to wash away. Travel had become extremely difficult not only for automobiles, but also planes, trains and boats as well.

"This is a nice surprise." she said lyrically discovering he was home.

"The mission got cancelled. Transportation problems."

"That's not a surprise, but seeing you is." she cooed as they embraced and kissed. "It took me three days to make what should have been a one night trip, at most."

"So, how was Washington?"

"I'm going back."

"Back? You just got home."

"I mean to the Moon."

Adam gave her a curious look. "What's going on?"

"Not really sure, yet, and anything I tell you is classified."

"O-kay." he said hesitantly. "That sounds serious. You're beginning to worry me."

Emma said nothing because she really didn't know what to tell him, other than she was worried too.

"Listen, if you can't tell me, I understand. Should I be worried?"

"Dear, with what's been happening around the world, we all need to be worried."

"That's a bit vague, honey. Are you talking about Iceland?"

"Iceland, Beerenberg, Norway, everything!" she shouted, and then she started to cry.

Holding her in his arms he tried to comfort her.

"Hey, hey, what's all this?" he said soothingly. "The world is not going to end, at least not for another week." he added trying to make light of the recent dreadful events. "Look, I know things have gotten tough all over, but we're still here, we're still rockin' and rollin', the country will still go on. You're letting all this stuff stress you out. I know, it's a lot to be stressed over, but this isn't like you."

"I'm afraid, Adam. I don't want anything to be wrong, but something is very wrong. I feel it and I think I'm going to be the one who discovers what it is."

"Emma" he said pushing her away gently, yet holding her at arms length, "haven't we already established what is wrong; global warming? I mean come on, even you've said..."

"I know what I've said, and I've maintained all along I thought something else was happening as well." she rebuked him.

"Hey, look, I'm on your side."

"Right, and you just think the little girl is tired and emotional."

"Yes, I do, but I also have a great deal of respect for your work, and your opinion so, sue me if I'm trying to be comforting. It's not like I see you every day, and you really don't tell me what you're up to."

"That's because...I really don't know..."

"What you're looking for?" he said finishing her sentence. "I know, I've heard the speech."

"Well, I don't!" she countered. "And I can tell you this, what I do know frightens me."

"Then tell me."

"We've been over this."

"Okay. You're afraid because you think you're on the verge of uncovering some awful truth."

"Yes, but that's not the only reason I'm afraid. Look around!"

"Okay, I get that, but for argument's sake, let's say you do. Let's say you make the most terrible discovery of the millennium. Now what?"

"Exactly the point, I don't know what."

"Did you ever think for a moment, if you don't make that discovery, by the time anyone realizes what is really wrong, it might be too late to do anything about it?"

Emma considered Adam's statement for a moment and said, "I had better get back to work."

~~~~

Within three weeks Emma was back on LP1. She had been on the platform for nearly ten days, but had yet to descend to the Moon. She had been spending her time diligently reviewing her own solar global warming theory data, trying to tie it to events on Earth in the hope of discovery. She was perplexed, but motivated by what Adam had said to her. Although, now that she was back on LP1 and could go down to the lunar surface, the 'feeling' she had compelling her to return to the Moon was gone. She was at an impasse. There was nothing left to do, but pay a visit to the Apollo Seventeen Colony and settle some unfinished business, and that required a visit to Major Woo's office.

"Miss Cross, it is nice to see you. I heard you were here. I just got back myself."

"You just got back?"

"You didn't think they left us up here forever, did you?" he teased. "We rotate off and on the platform. It keeps us fit, and sane."

"Right."

"I presume you need a ride."

"Yes, I'd like to go down to the colony."

"I'll make arrangements with Lieutenant Traigne, same set up as before."

"What happened to Lieutenant Jefferson?"

"He's on rotation and not due to return for three more weeks. I must say, I didn't expect to see you again."

"I certainly did not expect to be coming back."

"What's the mission?"

"Research." she said plainly

Major Woo sat back quietly behind his desk expecting further clarification from Emma. Sensing this, Emma added sheepishly, "It's classified."

"Miss Cross, I need to know what your mission is, if you want me to help you."

"Didn't you get a copy of my orders?"

"Yes, I did, but they don't really explain why you are here."

"Major, I really don't have a mission, as such, not like the last time. I'm conducting research, which at the moment is classified. I can tell you I am exploring an idea, kind of a geologic 'what if ' scenario, that if became real, would be subject to national security, world security for that matter."

Major Woo didn't seem to be buying her explanation. Just like before, Emma thought. The major is not very trusting. It must come with the job.

"Major, I'm a geologist, not a GPATT spy, if that's your concern."

"I apologize, Miss Cross. I just don't like not knowing everything that's going on within my command. Of course, I will cooperate in any way I can to assist you."

"Thank you, Major. Tell you what, if I find the 'man in the moon', you'll be the first to know."

The quarters Emma was assigned to were the same as before, and with the exception of Major Woo, there were all new faces on both LP1 and at the Apollo Seventeen colony. Once she was settled in she sought out the two cadre assigned to her for this mission, David Steele and Derek Chen. She found both of them in the command post waiting upon her arrival. As before, these two were polite, eager and young.

"Pleased to meet you, mam." they said almost in unison.

"Pleased to meet you, too, gentlemen." They all shook hands.

"We've been ordered to be at your complete disposal." offered Chen.

"That's great, but can we stop with the 'mam' stuff? I'm not that much older than you are, it's Emma. May I call you Dave, and Derek, is it?"

"Fine by me." clucked Dave. "Where to first?"

"That depends. I noticed there's a new craft down here. Looks like it flies."

"Yes, mam." Dave said eagerly. "I mean, yes, yes it does. It's called an MA-SM-6 Grasshopper."

"Can you fly it?"

"Yes, mam." answered Chen quickly realizing his error.

"You know, you're really going to have to work on that." Emma said to Derek with a disdainful jest. "Okay, great. I want to go up in that."

"But Lieutenant Traigne said you'd only be using the Rover." protested Dave weakly.

"File your flight plan and tell Lieutenant Traigne I need to use the Grasshopper. If he has any objections, ask him to see Major Woo."

The flight plan was filed and Lieutenant Traigne was in Major Woo's office fifteen minutes later.

"That's not a tour bus Major, it's a multi-million dollar piece of hardware and there's only one of them! And she's a civilian, not even military, and we're going to let her go for a joyride? It's not even a real mission!" Traigne complained.

When the rant ended, Major Woo appeared he might capitulate, or so the Lieutenant thought.

"Tom, I agree with you one hundred percent," Woo paused "but she's got pull. We've been ordered to give her our complete cooperation by the Director himself. He called me personally and said to give her whatever she wants. She's on a personal assignment for him so, that's exactly what we are going to do. He even repeated the 'whatever' part."

"The Director?"

"The Director." he answered unequivocally. "Just make sure your rocket jocks don't leave orbit, Director, or no. She's allowed low level reconnaissance, no higher than 600 feet, any requests beyond that she will have to discuss with me personally."

"Aye-aye, Sir." he said submissively.

GPATT required a certain preparatory protocol before the MA-SM-6 Grasshopper could lift off. That the Grasshopper was kept 'mission ready' twenty-four seven was unknown to Emma. For her so-called joyride, flight prep would take two full days. She suspected Lieutenant Traigne, perhaps even Major Woo might be behind what she thought was a delaying tactic. This meant she had time off without much to do, but read, relax, watch videos, TV, or whatever. The only drawback for Emma was she had to remain at the colony while she waited.

So, she got in some exercise and read some online magazines, which were still covering the Iceland catastrophe, the Beerenberg explosion and tsunami aftermath, and on a national note, the vegetation death of Yellowstone, Yosemite and Napa Valley.

During day two of flight prep, Emma strolled into one of the day rooms where a documentary video on the 'big bang' theory was playing. The scene being depicted was a digital representation of what was theorized to occur when celestial bodies are caught in the gravitational forces of larger bodies. She watched with interest for a while wondering if she hadn't seen this presentation before.

Emma pondered the colorful depiction for a moment and thought it astonishing, as well as arrogant, that man would go to such lengths to explain the origins of things which occurred well before his own introduction. She knew reverse engineering of the processes of nature could only take us so far. The rest was a guess based on scant evidence, conjecture, theory and interpolation. And after all of it, the very beginnings of things were never really visible to us, but we guessed anyway and proclaimed 'It must be so.' Mere theory had incongruously transformed into fact, and we patted ourselves on the back, and congratulated the fact finders in the process, and the church of public education said "Amen", and it was so.

She wondered where God was in their process. Didn't He count? What about Intelligent Design? Ah, there's the root of the problem, no room for a creator in science. Man can't quite explain the beginning of the universe, himself, or dinosaurs, but whatever the explanation, it certainly cannot involve a Supreme being. We just need more time and we'll figure it out, and God? He's not real, and even if he does exist, He's really just some cosmic force who couldn't possibly care what humans are up to. There's that Jesus character though. How do we explain Him away? Santa Clause and the Easter Bunny will eventually supplant Him, and then Jesus will be like Buddha, a myth, a really nice guy who did some good things, but not really God. So much for real history.

At the end of her daydream churn, Emma vaguely recalled a scripture passage from the Book of Romans. She couldn't remember it word for word, but she knew well the flavor of its content;

For the invisible things of God from the creation of the world are clearly seen, being understood by the things that are made, even his eternal power and Godhead; so that they are without excuse.

When they knew God, they glorified him not as God, neither were they thankful, but became vain in their imaginations, and their foolish hearts were darkened.

Professing themselves to be wise, they became fools, and they changed the glory of the incorruptible God into an image made like to corruptible man, birds, four-footed beasts, and creeping things.

"And mankind continues to repeat itself." Emma said half under her breath concluding her silent rant as she walked out of the room. And though her mind had moved on to engage in more worthy endeavor than to watch TV, the images from the TV screen haunted her consciousness.

Chapter Eleven

"Water its living strength first shows,
When obstacles its course oppose."
Johann Wolfgang von Goethe

The MA-SM 6 Grasshopper gently lifted off the lunar surface and made its way smoothly across the wide level Mare Serenitatis toward the northern edge of Mare Crisium where the landscape abruptly rises from the flat of the mare. It would make a low pass over the suspected constructs identified in photograph LS3-51-21.6, hover momentarily, and capture a visual record of the area.

"The boys will be disappointed." Emma said aloud of the several scientists who would be most interested in her findings regarding photograph LS3-51-21.6.

Her two escorts just looked at each other knowingly. The anomalies were readily recognizable geologic formations found throughout the known lunar landscape. In fact, up close the structures didn't resemble any of the shapes thought to be perceived within frame. There was a small dome, though, a semi-translucent glass bubble-like obtrusion that was probably formed when the Moon's surface was hot and pliable and likely as old as the landscape which held it.

The craft proceeded southeast making its way next to the drilling accident site. Emma had her nose nearly pressed to the glass of her window, absorbed with the aerial view of lunar topography which the Grasshopper afforded at its cruising altitude of 150 feet. When they reached the bore site, the craft set down on the perimeter and Emma reluctantly donned her spacesuit for another turn of the area.

She trudged about for half an hour frequently stopping to look down at something, or look around at the landscape, as if to get a bearing. Lost in thought, or busy examining something, she hardly spoke a word to her guide who patiently waited upon his charge to finish, so they could return to the relative comfort of the Grasshopper.

Back on board, Derek Chen helped Emma out of her spacesuit. "Where to next?" he inquired.

Emma responded with a question. "How high have we been flying?"

"Right around 150 feet." said David.

"Can we go higher?"

"Yes. We are authorized to 600 feet. But that is our limit." he warned.

"Could we just go up slowly and fly in a circle a few times, so I can take a look around? After that we can head back." Emma added.

"We sure can." answered David.

The Moon was in its First Quarter phase. This meant that from Earth the right half of the lunar surface was illuminated by the sun, including part of that half popularly referred to as the dark side. As the MA-SM 6 rose slowly circling the bore site, Emma carefully studied the ground searching for clues. David smoothly piloted the craft higher, gradually widening the counterclockwise circle he had been requested to fly. The Grasshopper had reached an altitude of approximately 400 feet as the craft entered its third turn. Something caught Emma's eye which wasn't within the perimeter of the accident site. She asked David to fly due East and pointed to where she wanted him to proceed.

"Wow." David half exclaimed. "That's a lot different from what we're used to seeing."

The grasshopper's passengers peered out the windows in awe of the unusual lunar landscape below. They were looking at huge cracks in the surface, previously undetected, which proceeded in an east by northeast direction around the dark side of the Moon.

Not far from the bore site, and just behind a short, but very long ridge, Emma discovered the key she had long searched for which would unlock the mysteries behind the strange phenomenon that had been occurring on Earth. This key would bring the global warming debate to a halt, and open a door revealing an imminent threat to the tenuous future of life on Earth.

"Wonder what caused that?" Derek asked. "Looks like it goes on for miles."

Emma recognized the fissures; countless fumaroles from which steam had spewed forth for months, in a band that had grown 100 miles at its widest point and stretched for nearly a thousand miles from the bore point. Her accident investigation report would need to be revised to say the least.

~~~~

Constantly closing on its approach to Earth, Cyprium Prospector was unavoidably receiving an increase in alarming reports regarding conditions back home. Reality of the devastation could be contained no longer. Earth was in trouble. In her communiqués to Aviv, Sana briefly described the cataclysmic events which had occurred and the chaos that ensued. To Sana, it seemed the planet was dying and its inhabitants along with it.

Earth was in fact, rapidly losing its ability to sustain life. For years there had been the familiar calls of alarm from numerous scientific and environmental groups, but few seemed to actually take notice until after the Jan Mayen wave disaster. This one event placed such a strain on world resources, had nothing been wrong with the planet, it was foreseeable those resources could and would recover. Something was wrong, however, and resources were not recovering.

The increase in sea level had created back-flooding of formerly good agricultural land particularly in the United States. Fresh water had become brackish as it mixed with salty sea water. And though the water volume of Earth's surface had increased, rain was enigmatically often truant over much of the remaining land masses.

Food crops were becoming harder to sustain, ocean fisheries were disappearing and remaining domestic animal food stocks were starving from the inability to get feed. This strained the human food chain which added mounting pressures on the world's societies. Events had cascaded so quickly, there was little time to plan, or prepare. Famine was now global.

Sana was concerned about what might happen between now and the time Aviv would arrive back on Earth. The public was so consumed with world events, Cyprium Prospector's epic mission was all but forgotten. Chaos was about to be crowned king. The world was on the verge of collapse and nothing could be done to stop it.

Having returned from space, Emma was showing video and still images of her discovery just beyond the lunar drill site, to Eric at the earthquake center.

"You are the first person I've shared this with." she said leaning over his shoulder as he examined several of the photographs.

"What about your GPATT buddies?"

"Oh, some have seen the photos, but they're meaningless to them."

"How about Dr. Wagner?"

"I haven't contacted him yet. I wanted you to see them before I do that. What do you think?"

"What am I looking at?"

"You are looking at the never before seen and newest geologic formations on the Moon. Not only that, there is nothing like it anywhere on the Moon's surface."

"So, what caused this?"

"Steam."

The core sample drill team had been unwittingly drilling an eruptive fumarole, an opening in the crust which emits steam and gas often associated with volcanic activity. On Earth fumaroles occur along cracks and fissures where magma, or hot rock interacts with groundwater, similar to a hot spring, though the water usually boils away before it reaches the surface. During core sampling operations the Moon's molten core, heretofore believed to be solid, was introduced to unrecognized subterranean veins of ice, believed to be nonexistent, which were heated to the point where huge volumes of water vapor were caused to be released into space. An odd piece to the puzzle was that molten material, if it existed, should have been located pretty much within dead center of the Moon. It wasn't. Personally for Emma, the new formations, mostly large cracks, were a huge find, the literal smoking gun for the presence of subterranean water on the Moon. She felt vindicated, but not completely satisfied. This wasn't the mystery she was hoping to solve. Something was telling her this discovery had another meaning, and she needed to find out what it was.

"That's a lot of steam." exclaimed Eric.

"You'd better believe it. It took a lot of water to do that."

"That's one heck of a find, Emma." he added concentrating on the images before him. Emma realized his comment wasn't meant as a compliment.

"What are you thinking?"

"I was just wondering how much water it took to do all that. Ice is approximately 92 percent of the equivalent weight of water. A gallon weighs a bit over 8 pounds. One foot of ice, one cubic foot, would be about 62 pounds, so a block of ice two feet square, or 8 cubic feet would weigh, let's see, eight times two, plus eight times sixty, that's roughly 500 pounds. Damn, that's a lot of ice."

Taking a moment to process Eric's calculation and comment, Emma's eyes suddenly went wide. "That's it!" she exclaimed.

"What's it?" Eric said looking at Emma curiously.

"The effect cascaded releasing so much water...that's how all those cracks were formed." she gasped looking at one of the photographs. "That has to be it!"

"What? What has to be what?"

"I can't believe no one has thought of that."

"Thought of what, for crying out loud?!"

Emma looked Eric in the eye. "You just said 'That's a lot of ice.' Where did it go? It was turned to steam and evaporated. All that ice...all that weight."

"Yeah. The weight of all the ice and water evaporating would be huge." Eric responded, as though it was a no brainer.

"Think about that. A sudden loss of weight like that would do what?" Answering her own question, Emma continued "Cause a change in the mass and density of the moon." Eric was still processing. "It shifted."

"What shifted?"

"The Moon's orbit. The loss of all that water has resulted in a shifting of its elliptical orbit bringing it closer to earth."

"What are you talking? The Moon is moving away from Earth."

Emma quickly responded. "One of the first things the space agency did when Apollo 11 astronauts reached the Moon was to set up a laser reflector that would allow scientists on Earth to measure the distance from the Earth to the Moon. They found that the distance between the two increases approximately 4 centimeters per year. We can verify it."

"What the heck are you talking about? Oh my God! You're saying the loss of lunar mass from the ice turning to steam changed the Moon's orbit and increased the pull of gravity causing it to be forced closer to Earth?"

"Yes, and way faster than 4cm per year."

"So, the Moon is going to crash into the Earth?"

"No, I doubt that, maybe, I don't know. I need to check with the space agency first, and to do that I have to talk to Dr. Wagner."

Emma grabbed the telephone and dialed.

"Emma, I understand you have made a new discovery. I was wondering when you were going to call me. Congratulations!"

"Dr. Wagner, I need to verify something with the space agency. Can you help me?"

"What do you need?" he said equivocally.

"I'd like to know the measured distance between the Earth and Moon."

"That's easy, 864,000 miles."

"Thanks, but I need to know the exact distance today."

"May I ask why you want this?"

"I think I may have an explanation for what is going on, but I'll need that data to support my theory."

"That would be good news."

"Whether it is good news, or not may depend on your point of view, and Dr. Wagner

time is of the essence."

"Understood. You'll have the information shortly, Emma."

Emma thanked the Director of GPATT and hung up.

"Okay, what's your theory?" Eric asked.

"Not until I hear from Dr. Wagner."

Twenty minutes after Dr. Wagner received the request to measure the distance between the Earth and the Moon, Emma's phone rang.

"Emma Cross."

"Hi Emma, it's Ken Wagner."

"What did you find out?" she asked clenching her teeth.

"There has been a six percent cumulative change in the distance between the Earth and Moon over the past three years and it is accelerating."

"Six percent, in which direction?"

"Closer."

Emma was silent.

Dr. Wagner broke the silence. "How did you know to ask the question?"

"Ice."

"Not sure I follow." he said.

"The lunar subsurface ice melted, turned to steam and evaporated into space. My guess is so much ice melted and evaporated, it changed the mass of the Moon, which impacted gravitational forces and significantly changed its orbit causing it to be pulled closer to the Earth. Ironically, even though the Moon is lighter, its pull on the Earth has been increasing. I believe now this is the cause of most, if not all of the unusual phenomenon. In fact, I believe it is pulling the Earth's crust apart. It tracks with the data and it all began soon after the core drilling accident on the Moon."

Dr. Wagner was silent for a long moment as he thoughtfully considered what he had just heard. "So, what's your prognosis?"

"It will continue to get worse at least until the Moon's orbit stabilizes, and don't ask me when that will happen because I don't know when, or if it will happen, and assuming it does happen, I can't say these events will stop, or even subside."

Again, Dr. Wagner was thoughtfully silent for a long moment, then the line went dead.

"Hello? Dr. Wagner ?"

Emma turned to Eric who was engrossed with his flat screen. "I think the line just went dead."

"Holy shit!" Eric responded.

"What happened?"

"Earthquake, pretty severe." Eric said studying the screen in front of him.

Emma turned around puzzled. I don't feel anything.

"Not here. Appalachian mountains, twenty-five miles west southwest of Front Royal, Virginia. Did you know the Appalachians extend from Alabama through Maine in the United States, and continue across the southeastern provinces of Canada into Newfoundland?"

"Front Royal, Virginia, that's Luray Caverns."

"Epicenter seems to be a few miles west of there. There are interesting ridge formations, thrust faults mostly, that run from Strasburg to Harrisonburg that kind of stand out by themselves on the eastside of the Shenandoah River."

"I am familiar with them."

"This is odd. These readings indicate the whole sixty-some odd miles of ridge is moving. I've never seen this kind of activity in the East before. The quake must have taken out some transmission lines."

"But I am using a cell phone."

"Which also requires repeater towers to transmit the signals coming over those mountains. Some of them must have collapsed as well. Might take them a while to reroute power and telephone lines."

Eric was only partially correct. Like a stone that cracks a car's windshield, the quake he was observing via his console was only the start of a fracture which would split the entire Appalachian Range in the East from Mobile, Alabama northward, through Chattanooga, Tennessee - Roanoke, Virginia - Cumberland, Maryland - Harrisburg, Pennsylvania - Rochester, NY and on into Lake Ontario. The crack would become a quarter mile wide chasm four thousand feet deep. Hundreds of towns along its line would be leveled, or just simply disappear. Lake Ontario would drain flooding large portions of New

York, Pennsylvania, New Jersey, Delaware, Maryland and Virginia. The flotsam would take out everything in its path; dams, bridges, buildings, power-lines. The Chesapeake Bay and DelMarVa peninsula would become completely swamped and become part of the Atlantic Ocean.

The crack shook the entire eastern seaboard bringing down buildings as far away as Baltimore, Washington DC and Richmond. The East Coast would be entirely cut off from the rest of the country. In another month the crack would begin to ooze magma along eighty percent of its length boiling off water in huge clouds of steam which would blanket the land east of the divide.

~~~~

Dr. Wagner and many of his GPATT colleagues were able to escape from Washington before it was entirely flooded. They relocated to Ronald Reagan Jump Port which would also soon become inundated. The White House and Federal government relocated to San Antonio, Texas where Emma's theory was presented to the President and his cabinet by Dr. Wagner.

"Mr. President, ladies and gentlemen. Much debate over the state of our planet has occurred, particularly within the last three years. I know the popular view has been we are experiencing predicted, as well as, unanticipated effects of global warming due to pollution. Certainly, it is difficult to argue otherwise, in light of events taking place all over the world. This view is easy to embrace. Pollution is admittedly bad for the environment. Everyone agrees to that.

What can we do about it? The fix is obvious, even to a young child; stop the pollution and the problem is solved. Recognizing this, we took steps to reduce pollution, and we made progress. It would seem, however, we collectively implemented our fix, too little, and too late. But I must tell you, there have been those of us, who even in light of what seemed obvious, were reluctant to fully embrace the popular explanation, that so called 'greenhouse gasses' are solely responsible for melting ice and the resultant rising of our oceans.

And so, for quite some time, a small group of scientists have been quietly pursuing the possibility other explanations might exist in the hope of arresting the devastation that continues to plague our planet.

Regretfully, I am not here to offer you hope, but I do believe we have an explanation of the cause for what has been happening to the Earth. The explanation is 'global warming', but pollution was not the cause. It was the catalyst.

When we began to embrace the fact that pollution had to be abated, we developed new strategies and new technologies to produce clean cheaper energy for the ever growing demand. The need for copper to implement these technologies exploded to the point where we would, in five, or six more decades, run out of copper. That time arrived, and so we undertook the monumental project of mining this metal on another planet and launched Cyprium Prospector to Mars, which by the way is on its way home with an 80 percent capacity payload. Its mission has been a huge success.

Part of the project included developing a permanent colony on the Moon for the purpose of harvesting its resources and expanding man's habitat beyond the confines of Earth. In the process, as you are all well aware, three people were killed. In the shadow of that unfortunate accident, a great discovery was made. There is water on the Moon and in significant quantity. That discovery, however, was overshadowed by the launching of Cyprium Prospector, and before long our attention was turned toward the slowly growing catastrophes being inflicted upon all life on Earth.

You should recall, Dr. Emma Cross is credited for discovering that the Moon had a molten core and significant amounts of subsurface water ice. The discovery was a result of her investigation of the lunar drilling accident. The finding of her initial study, you should also recall, suggested that a contributing factor to global warming came from an increase in solar energy. As part of a separate study, Dr Cross was also cataloguing anomalous natural phenomenon occurring worldwide, when I subsequently asked her to attempt to find the cause for these events.

As I stated earlier, those of us who believed in the existence of possible other explanations, widened the view of our investigative lenses and further employed Dr. Cross to examine anything and everything that gave her pause. As a result, Dr. Cross along with Dr. Eric Kimbrough of the USGS, have made another significant discovery which solidly supports a new theory for the global warming elements assaulting our landmasses.

We all know steam was released after the drilling accident. What we did not realize was just how much was released. To further develop the research she was engaged in, Dr. Cross asked permission to do some field work on the Moon. While cruising over the lunar surface in an MA-SM-6 Grasshopper, Dr. Cross made a fantastic discovery a short distance east of the lunar drilling site, which by the way is technically on the back side of the Moon because it is just beyond visual range of what we can see of the Moon's surface from Earth.

Flying at approximately four hundred feet, and beyond a low lying ridge, Dr. Cross observed cracks in the lunar surface in an area estimated to be one hundred miles wide at the widest and a thousand miles long, cracks through which an inestimable amount of steam escaped, steam that came from huge deposits of subterranean ice."

Dr. Wagner paused to let that previously unknown piece of information sink in for effect.

"Ice is approximately ninety-two percent of the equivalent weight of water. A gallon of water weighs roughly eight and a half pounds. One cubic foot of ice, a block one foot long, one foot wide by one foot high would weigh nearly sixty-two and a half pounds. Now imagine in your minds for a moment, an average size refrigerator, the kind most of us have in our homes. If that refrigerator was a block of ice it would weigh 1500 pounds, or three quarters of a ton. Now we don't know exactly how much ice was melted into steam. Suffice it to say, we do know that it was a lot. So much so, that Dr. Cross has theorized the gravitational relationship between the Earth and the Moon has changed. A calculation of the current distance between the two has revealed the Moon is drifting closer to Earth and has been for some time." Everyone gasped.

"Dr. Cross believes, and so do I, that these changes in gravitational forces are causing the Earth's tectonic plates to behave violently, and the planet's molten core to be pulled up through the surface causing earthquakes, volcanic eruptions and an increase in crust temperatures, which is melting polar ice among other things."

"It is unclear at this time if, or when the Moon's orbit will stabilize, or how such behavior might further impact Earth. Members of the scientific community are at this moment engaged in calculating those answers, but if the Moon's orbit does not stabilize we can only fear the worst for all life on Earth."

~~~~

Governments are slow to react to change and rarely do they react with prudence, being too concerned with overreaction, cost, causing panic and getting reelected. They often become paralyzed, debating issues fearful their actions will be the wrong ones. It sometimes takes standing on the precipice to get leaders to act, and even then it is often slow and untimely. But that is where Earth's governments stood at this very moment. Because the rising of the sea was not an instantaneous event, but occurred gradually, if one could call over three years gradual, the United States government, among others, reacted slowly. It had been too busy with relief efforts and worldwide economic woes to pay close attention to its own coastline which was rapidly being reclaimed by the oceans. By the time the Appalachian Chasm appeared, the nations resources had been depleted by 80 percent. Everyone had been holding their collective breath thinking the fever that had gripped the planet would break, unaware it was only just heating up.

Someone had suggested now might be a good time to expand and supply the Lunar colony, Apollo Seventeen. It was an idea which quickly became the number one priority of GPATT and the Federal government.

Unfortunately, it would become an undertaking that would save few.

When parts of the coastline started to succumb to slowly rising water, it created an undercurrent of people moving away from those affected areas in an effort to get to higher ground. Subsequently, they were also moving to escape smoldering volcanoes and earthquakes, migrating to continental interiors believing them to be safer and having more readily available food supplies. Once they were in what they believed to be a safe zone, finding food became their primary motivation. Before long, a global migration of humanity began, particularly in countries bordering the Pacific basin.

The most significant aspect of the altered gravitational relationship between the Earth and Moon was that it had created a new kind of tide that acted on Earth's inner molten seas, which was increasingly pulling magma through Earth's crust at its vulnerable points, particularly along the *ring of fire*. The lush green tropical islands and atolls in the Pacific had been transformed into hot black desolate smoldering masses incapable of sustaining life. Guam, Palau, the Marianas, the Marshalls, Samoa, Fiji, the Solomons, New Caledonia, Micronesia, Hawaii, most of the Philippines, most of Japan, Indonesia and Malaysia were now nothing but burnt rock.

Having escaped their own devastation, migrants often arrived at a new destination only to find it too was burnt. In areas along the west coast of North and South America huge earthquakes rocked the land. People on both continents were trapped between the sea and high desolate mountains, but only if they were among the lucky few who survived the quakes. Global warming had truly arrived, though it came from heat generated far below the planet's crust. It did not result from man's pollution of the atmosphere, rather, it was the result of his effort to reduce it.

The *ring of fire* surrounding the Pacific basin was certainly the most geologically active area on the globe, although not exclusively. There were volcanoes in Africa, Asia, Antarctica, Europe and Australia as well, and many of them were beginning to erupt as the Moon swept ever closer to its beautiful blue neighbor. From the observatory on EP3, Emma and Eric had been able to observe volcanic plumes stretching from the Aleutians all the way down the coast of California, with some even developing in the eastern Rockies. EPs 1and 2 had also reported plumes in the Mediterranean, West Africa, and all over the Japanese and Indonesian island chains. They could also see the diminishing continental coastlines, but even they were becoming difficult to discern most days because of the cloud cover. As much of the world waited in fearful anticipation for the abatement of the rising seas, another more terrifying aspect of nature was about to assault the Earth.

Dr. Wagner had directed ESV sorties become a continuous operation of ferrying people and supplies to the orbiting platforms and the Moon for as long as it was possible. Those who were already in space stayed there, and though the effort to preserve human life was monumental, it was a mere drop in the bucket of humanity. The effort only transported 1200 souls into space before RJP was overwhelmed by the rising sea. There was hardly a coastline on the globe by then, that hadn't been overwhelmed, erased, or redrawn.

Emma, Eric and Dr. Wagner were three of the fortunate few to reach EP3, on what would be the last ESV to be launched from RJP. They weren't chosen for their expertise, discoveries, or pecking order. There was no lottery, no drawing, nor pre-selection process. It was fate, luck, karma, coincidence, Providence, chance. Irrespective of any label, they had been unknowingly swept along eddies and currents in time and space, where random circumstances cross-connect and produce an outcome. Theirs had deposited each of them in the last ESV to make the jump into space. They couldn't have controlled the situation had they been keenly aware of what was happening to them. They wouldn't even question it. Ninety minutes after their ESV lifted off, a huge tsunami wave crashed into the Texas-Louisiana coastline, generated by an earthquake that occurred along an underwater ridge at the northern edge of the Caribbean Plate, between the Yucatan Peninsula and Cuba, crushing any hope of further ESV launches into space.

Unaware Ronald Reagan Jump Port had been overwhelmed by water, Commander Adam Pickett boarded an empty ESV and prepared to disembark for Earth. In the back of his mind, as in the minds of all the pilots who were ferrying ESVs to and from the surface, he entertained the possibility he might not get off the ground for a return flight back to what was being viewed as, one of the safest places in the current crisis, an orbiting platform. At the moment, Adam was unsure of Emma's whereabouts, though, he felt confident she was still back on Earth. If he couldn't return to space, at least they would be together. Nevertheless, he too, was caught in those same eddies and currents of time and space.

Chapter Twelve

I looked at the earth, and it was empty and formless.
I looked at the heavens, and there was no light.
I looked at the mountains and hills, and they trembled and shook.
I looked, and all the people were gone.
All the birds of the sky had flown away.
I looked, and the fertile fields had become a wilderness.
The towns lay in ruins, crushed by the Lord's fierce anger.
Jeremiah 4:23-26

The view of Earth from EP3 was changing rapidly to something quite different from the first time Emma gazed upon her home from space. The beautiful blue and white ball was turning a brownish grey from thickening clouds and volcanic smoke. It was losing its celestial distinctiveness.

From space, under normal conditions, the Earth appears as a big blue marble. Third planet from the Sun, and the fifth-largest of eight planets in our Solar System, it is the largest of the four terrestrial planets Mercury, Venus, Earth and Mars. Terrestrial planets are primarily composed of silicate rocks, substantially different from gas giants, which may or may not have solid surfaces. Only one terrestrial planet, Earth, is known to have an active hydrosphere (surface water), and the only known place in the universe where life exists. And now that life was being threatened.

The final assault upon the Earth, resulting from the degrading gravitational influence of the Moon, would be the most violent and the most deadly; erupting volcanoes. Aside from the obvious immediate devastation caused by one erupting volcano, the ash clouds produced from so many volcanoes erupting was diminishing sunlight over most of the planet. The scene on Earth had become prehistoric. In conjunction with diminished sunlight, the ash covered plants and animals alike, bringing a slow death to almost everything it fell upon. The ash would asphyxiate the majority of most oxygen breathing species, although some would miraculously survive subject to their individual tolerance for the amount and duration the dust remained in the atmosphere. Water creatures would also be impacted as the falling ash would choke rivers lakes and seas. People, less self sufficient now than at any other time in history, would die because of a lack of food and fresh water. Mankind had suddenly found itself on the verge of extinction as one of Earth's inhabitants.

~~~~

Cyprium Prospector was fast approaching its home planet and in a few days it would take up station close to EP3. From its forward observatory, the crew could tell they were almost home. They could see both the Earth and the Moon forever bound to each other as they danced around the sun. But as Cyprium Prospector drew nearer to the end of its mission, it became evident the lovely planet they left behind, with its wispy white clouds, colorful land masses and blue oceans, had changed into something alien and ugly to them. Sana had been careful in her messages to Aviv not to alarm him to events happening on Earth, but Aviv knew something was terribly wrong. His main concern was for her safety, and until he was assured of that, he worried.

Coincidentally, or Providentially, however one preferred to view it, Sana would be one of humanity's survivors. She had been on leave visiting family in

Charlotte, North Carolina awaiting an ESV sortie which would take her back into space for her next tour of duty. When the time came, she boarded a Delta Airlines Boeing 787 at the Charlotte Douglas International Airport which would fly her to Dallas. From there she would transfer to a Beech Commuter 1900 turboprop for the leg to Corpus Christi, and then on by car to Ronald Reagan Jump Port. The jetliner taxied to runway 18L, received clearance from the tower and began to rumble down the concrete airstrip. Sana had always enjoyed takeoffs. They were akin to an amusement ride with the increase in engine noise, fast acceleration and then the smooth unmistakable feeling of flight.

Sana had a window seat and was intently watching the ground speed by so she could visually confirm the exact moment her plane left the ground. Believing the moment had arrived she held her breath when suddenly, the plane began to drift sideways and shudder, as though it had encountered a series of wide speed bumps. She had never experienced anything like it before. The aircraft's attitude was starting to angle upward when the last bump was felt, then abruptly they were airborne. The plane banked right as it began its climb, continuing the ascent on to Dallas as if nothing unusual had occurred. She wouldn't find out until after the plane landed a giant fissure had been ripped open along the entire Appalachian mountain chain, tremors from which, only moments sooner, would have held her plane to the Earth like a falcon's tether, then crash it on the runway.

Safely back on EP3, Sana had been monitoring a CAT 5 hurricane battering the southern United States. Weather had become even more of a factor with global temps increasing and seas rising. Hurricanes and tropical depressions had increased threefold and maintained their energy over landmasses longer, especially in the eastern U.S., now that the coastline had been reconfigured. She knew she wasn't supposed to send messages to Cyprium Prospector, which weren't all that secure to begin with, that might distress its crew, but the situation on Earth was way beyond her worrying about that now. She would inform Aviv. Cyprium Prospector was close enough that there was no longer any lag-time between radio transmissions. She transmitted a letter asking him to contact her by radio telephone, but only after he had finished reading it.

My Beloved Aviv,
You probably have a better understanding of what has been happening on Earth than your shipmates, but you do not know the whole truth. My heart aches that I must tell you. I truly fear that which you are returning to. GPATT is preparing a message with some video to send to you and the crew, as they have finally recognized it is time for you to be fully informed. First, let me assure you I am safe on EP3, and we will be together soon. But it is doubtful anyone will be able to return to Earth's surface for a long time, if ever. You remember the drilling accident on the Moon? It was recently discovered much more steam was released than previously imagined. So much so, it caused the Moon's orbit to decay bringing it closer to Earth and it continues even now. As the Moon comes closer, the gravitational pull on the Earth grows, bringing its molten core to the surface. Polar ice has melted and the sea has risen changing coastlines. Even our beloved Eilat has been claimed by the sea. The magma has covered many islands completely. Earthquakes and tsunamis have been continual and volcanic eruptions are occurring in many places.

It is believed the ash from the eruptions will cause an extinction level event, even with the assumption the Moon's orbit stabilizes and does not crash into the Earth. In the United States a huge chasm has formed along the Appalachian Mountains extending into Canada. Tens of millions are dead, governments are collapsing, food and water are running out. Communications are very limited and it is quite impossible to contact friends, or family. I fear for them greatly, and for us, for it seems indeed, the end has come, and we shall die in space. At least you will be with me. I long for you to be here for I am so afraid. We are being told RJP has been claimed by the water and no more ESVs can be launched. Hurry my beloved, for I cannot bear what the future holds for us without you.
Sana

To Aviv, Sana's letter sounded of the apocalypse, which he quickly realized had been brought about by an insatiability for the ore that now filled the holds of his ship.

"A copper apocalypse." he said to himself, as the grim images depicted in Sana's letter continued to replay over and over in his mind.

~~~~

"EP3 Control, this is the ESV Patriot ready to depart."

"Roger that, Patriot. Please stand by."

"Patriot, standing by." Commander Pickett responded

After several minutes Adam became impatient and was about to inquire as to the delay, when his radio came to life. "Patriot, this is Control. Stand down. Your mission has been aborted. I say again, Stand down."

"What's the problem, Control."

"Orders from the Director, Commander. RJP is no longer in operation."

When the last ESV reached EP3, Dr. Wagner ordered the immediate rationing of all food and drink on the orbiting platforms, Apollo Seventeen and Cyprium Prospector. He was relieved he did not have to send a personal message to the Mars outpost explaining the situation on Earth, or that they were on their own, because no one was left behind. Colonization was to commence with the next mission. This was only a test run in that regard.

Adam had been waiting when Emma disembarked. "I wasn't sure I would ever see you again." she said embracing him.

"Wasn't sure myself." he sighed with relief.

"What do you mean? Why wouldn't you see me?" Emma looked into his eyes trying to decipher his comment.

"Well, when RJP went down, they cancelled the sorties up here."

"Went down?" she said alarmingly.

"Don't you know? A tsunami wave struck the coast of Texas. Your ESV was the last one to be launched."

"The last one? You mean there won't be any more flights? We can get back, can't we?"

"RJP has been destroyed. Technically, we can return to the surface, assuming there is something to return to, but that won't be for a long time, if ever."

Emma slept fitfully that night. She tried to imagine what the tsunami wave must have looked like as it overwhelmed the jump port. She wondered, did the wave merely flood the facility, or damage it violently? Either way, it was useless now. For the time being, she didn't feel trapped, or that the situation was hopeless because ESVs could still return to Earth. It hadn't struck her that she might never be able to return to the planet, though she was all too aware of what was happening below. For some reason, she had lost her fear that the Earth was doomed. In her mind, things were going to stabilize and the Earth would be spared. It was just a matter of when. She was in denial. Emma wasn't emotionally ready to accept that the world just might end, and in her lifetime.

The next day an aid walked into Dr. Wagner's makeshift office on EP3 and announced "Director, Commander of Cyprium Prospector would like to know where he should take up station."

"Why are you asking me? Ask operations." he responded without looking up.

"They are deferring to you, Sir."

"Who is in charge of this platform?"

"You are, Sir."

"No, I'm not." he said, annoyed at such a ridiculous comment. "Who is the operations manager?"

"Major Devlin."

"Then go ask him."

"Director, with everything that has happened, he took leave to see his family in Oregon. He was due back three days ago, but we've lost contact with him."

"Who is relieving Major Devlin?"

"His exec, one Lieutenant Ann Marie Meyers, capable, but ...." his voice trailed off.

"But what?"

"She's new, Sir."

"What's their ETA?"

"14:30 tomorrow."

"Find Captain Adam Pickett and ask him to report to me. Tell the CP to stand by."

"Aye, aye, Sir."

Dr. Wagner sat back in his chair and thought about what had just transpired. He was the Director of GPATT, yes, but he didn't run operations. He managed indirectly at a very high level. Yet, now it appeared he would be directly responsible for the approximately 1200 humans currently stranded in space, and quite possibly the last remnants of the human race. He wasn't ready to jump to that conclusion quite just yet. Incredibly, the government had remained viable, and the President and Congress were still able to call shots on Earth, at least for the United Sates, and as far as he was concerned, in space as well. But he did acknowledge to himself he was now in charge of operations, like it or not.

Adam entered the Director's office and reported as ordered. "Captain...Adam," Dr. Wagner corrected himself, recognizing a less formal climate was probably in order. "Adam, I'm placing you in charge of EP3 operations."

"Sir? Major Devlin is in charge of OPS." Adam responded, bewildered at the pronouncement.

"Major Devlin is...well, Major Devlin never returned from shore leave, and I don't know anyone else up here. You have experience, and you are involved with one of the brightest individuals I know. In the field that counts for something, and from what I am able to gather, no one currently in OPS on this platform has any actual flight experience so, you're it, Major. You've just been promoted. By the way, Cyprium Prospector is due to be on station at 14:30 tomorrow. They're asking where we want them to park."

"Aye, aye, Sir. Thank you, Sir." was all he could barely stammer out of his mouth, surprised, but pleased.

Adam wasn't necessarily thinking in the long term, but he had Cyprium Prospector take up station close enough to EP3, so that a flexible passageway could eventually be constructed between the two. In the short term, resources had to be conserved and close proximity between the them just made sense.

Over the next three months, electronic communication with Earth ceased. Anticipating the possibility of lost, or diminished radio communication, many world governments agreed to monitor specific, previously identified AM, FM and VHF frequencies to be used by both the public and military. GPATT was now monitoring those frequencies twenty-four hours a day from the orbiting platforms, which included a three minute live transmission on each of those frequencies every hour on the hour. No GPATT transmission from Earth, however, had been received by any of the three OEPs in the last ten days. It had been eight days since any official broadcast from anywhere had been heard, and three days since the last private transmission from a man named Phelps, which had come from somewhere in the Quachita National Forest in Arkansas. Claiming to be survival experts, Richard Phelps, his wife Dot and their tweeny (slightly larger than a traditional mini) Dachshund named Roo Roo, were reportedly 'holed up' on the south side of some bluff bordering Dutch Creek.

Adam was in the EP3 command center when the 3 o'clock broadcast was made on VHF channel 1, the same channel Phelps was using when they last heard from him. "Anything from Phelps?" he asked.

"No, sir. Not for three days now."

"Are you getting anything?"

"Once in a while we get something that sounds like a mike being keyed. Nobody says anything though. It's kinda creepy."

"Well, in case anyone asks, we're going to keep this up indefinitely. There just might be people still alive down there that can hear us, even though they may not be able to answer right now. It will at least give them hope and let them know they are not alone. Make your broadcast."

"Aye-aye, sir. Security, security, security. This is Orbiting Earth Platform number three broadcasting every our on the hour, hailing all stations on VHF channel 1. It is now fifteen hundred hours, three p.m. in the central time zone of the United States. If anyone can hear me, please respond. This channel will remain open." Adam waited as the message was repeated and greeted with eerie silence.

At the end of a fire road, on a ridge 1800 feet above Dutch Creek, some fifteen miles west of Danville, Arkansas, the 3 o'clock broadcast from EP3 played over a radio in an AeroStream camper stolen by a man and his wife. The man had anticipated the catastrophe which was approaching, and for two years had been secretly storing provisions and planning for apocalypse, the seed of which was planted by the extraterrestrial quest for copper. He had stolen the camper because things had gotten so bad there was no longer any way to buy it. Cars, trucks, RVs and boats just sat in lots deserted by their owners who were trying to prepare for their own survival. Phelps and his wife simply drove to the RV lot, found the keys, gassed up their pre-selected camper from two 50 gallon drums in the back of his pickup, and drove off. He claimed he had enough laid up to last them for two-maybe three years, if he stuck to a ration plan he saw in a survival magazine. In his last transmission he said the air was hot and thick with ash and dust, and when it rained, it was like warm dirty bathwater. He hadn't seen the sun for quite a while, but as long as they stayed in the camper they were snug as a bug. He added he was worried about the Moon crashing into Earth and the possibility of a volcano erupting too close.

Hearing the transmission from EP3, Phelps keyed the mike to respond. When he did, the power in his camper went dead.

Adam heard the interruption through the comm speaker.

"There! Just like that, Major. It sounds like someone is holding down the button on a microphone, but not talking."

"Maybe they can't talk, or maybe their mike is malfunctioning." said Adam. "I had a boat radio once that could receive five by five. When I keyed the mike you could hear the signal interrupt my friend's boat radio, you just couldn't hear my voice."

They listened a moment longer, then Adam added, "If you hear that again, try asking if anyone is there. Say that you can hear the mike being keyed, but you can't hear their voice. Ask them to key the mike twice. If you get a response we can establish a dialogue with them by asking yes, or no questions. Tell them to key once for 'no' and twice for 'yes'. Keep me posted."

Inside the AeroStream the lights suddenly went out. And though it was the middle of the afternoon, it was like twilight outside because of the volcanic smoke and ash which filled the air. Dot looked at her husband somewhat alarmed.

"Been waiting for that to happen." he said out loud, as he hung the mike to his radio on its clip.

"Why? Do you know what it is?" she asked hopefully.

"Not really. I just figured sooner, or later we could expect some sort of interruption with the power to occur. Generator probably stopped. I'll turn on the battery power and go have a look."

Phelps went to the power panel, flicked a switch and the lights came back on. He grabbed a flashlight, a small toolbox, donned his respirator and goggles, exited the AeroStream and walked the short distance to an 8'X10' shed that housed the generator. Actually, he had three generators, two were for backup. He checked the fuel tank first. It was empty. After ten minutes Phelps returned to the camper and turned off the battery power. The lights stayed on.

"What was it?" Dot asked.

"It was out of gas. Guess I forgot to check it last time I was out there. Now, let's try those fellows on the space station one more time." Pulling the mike from the clip he pressed the talk button. "This is Dick Phelps. Can anybody hear me?"

~~~~

The Moon's orbital decay miraculously stabilized by what was believed to be the gravitational pull of the Sun. That stability brought two new phenomena. The first was an increase in rotational speed. For the first time in eons the Moon would spin on its axis, albeit very slowly, and begin to show the Earth its other side.

The second phenomena was that the Moon was suddenly being pulled away from Earth at the same relative speed as its apparent one-time near-collision course with Earth. This change in orbital attitude, also believed to have been brought about by the pull of the sun, and the new increase in speed of the Moon's axial rotation was helping to ease the geologic inflammation of the planet's crustal layer. Volcanic activity and quakes gradually diminished and within twelve months the Earth's geologic commotion had returned to pre-lunar accident levels. Scientists who predicted stabilization would occur did not live to see it, though it did occur at a time when it seemed all recognizable life would be extinguished. But was it in time to stop extinction, or did it merely slow its progress for a while?

Months later, when it was realized stabilization had been achieved, only a partial sigh of relief was released because it could only be perceived as a calculation on paper, or some measurement made by a laser. A dirty looking cloud cover continued to obstruct the view of Earth's oceans and continents, and when the occasional peek-through was observed, the land masses were impossible to discern. Overlay imaging on a computer screen gave the only recognizable shapes to the Earth below, and even those had changed. No one could say when the picture would get better, but the remnant of humanity was hopeful and they began marking time as A.S. (anno stabilis) for after stabilization, instead of A.D. And still, the radio signals from Earth remained hauntingly silent.

~~~~

There was little democracy among the space inhabitants because the vast majority of them were GPATT, or U.S. military, trained professionals all, who were accustomed to following orders and a strict chain of command. The military style of government worked well because everyone accepted and understood it, and it existed in what they still considered to be a free society. They also knew it would serve to protect them and their resources, better than a democracy. Adherence to rules was important if they were to have any chance at survival. They trusted one other, and those who were in command, believing they should trust the chain of command, if they ever hoped to return to Earth.

Yet, it was trust and respect for each other that kept things orderly and running smoothly, not position, or military authority. Besides, everybody knew that if anyone committed an inappropriate act, one could expect an immediate stoning, metaphorically speaking, from all of the neighbors, and among professionals, such humiliation alone was worse than being arrested by a GPATT sheriff. Hence, law and order prevailed. There were squabbles and arguments and tempers occasionally flared. That kind of thing happens even in a professional setting, but there was no crime.

In the sixteen months that had passed since Emma's ESV docked with EP3, the residents of the four orbiting platforms, Cyprium Prospector and Apollo Seventeen Lunar Colony had been waiting, hoping, for some sign that the Earth was healing itself, signaling the time was approaching when they might be able to return to their beloved planet. Yet, for well over a year, the dirty-cotton look of the cloud formations surrounding Earth had not seemed to change. Almost imperceptibly, though, the cloud cover was brightening the way a morning sky gives its first indication dawn is about to break. Bit by bit, the dirt was being gently washed away. Below the clouds on the ground, however, the weather had turned from a wet, mucky, humid, sticky mess, into hot, dry, dust-filled siroccos. Measurably, the air was beginning to cool slightly, although, cool was relative to the current temperature. Earth was still plenty warm.

The space farers had long settled into a daily routine of living in microgravity, shuffling between their six habitats for work, recreation and a change of scenery. Relationships formed and life went on, always with talk and hope of returning to Earth. Some even decided to marry, including Dr. Wagner, Adam to Emma, Eric, and Aviv to Sana who were the first. And though they married, due to limited resources, pregnancy was not only prohibited, it was taboo.

Unfortunately, as time passed, their courage began to weaken under the always present specter of dwindling resources. Only a few knew exactly how long the remnant in space could actually survive. Yet, everyone knew their resources could sustain them only so long. Water and air were not a problem, for those two elements could be recycled indefinitely, and some food was being grown on all six habitats, but it was minimal.

And even if they had the resources, it was unknown how long the human body could tolerate reduced gravity, or if they could physically survive the trip home. That's where Aviv's expertise was crucial. It was always known exercise was important for living in space, but during Cyprium Prospector's mission, Aviv discovered a regimen to maintain strength, and he persuaded Dr. Wagner to implement his program throughout the six habitats. It delivered good results and had the added benefits of boosting morale.

Life in space was actually very fulfilling for most, because time was not idly spent. Everyone was either working on ways to improve and extend their stay in space, or they were researching how they would survive once they were back on terra firma. And because Emma was a geologist, and Eric was an earthquake specialist, they were constantly being asked about the conditions that could be expected on Earth when they returned.

The two had actually teamed up to study what areas might be viable for food production, and how that might be accomplished. Through their research, they learned there were approximately 1500 seed banks world-wide which held food crops. Their locations, capacities and general condition, however, were currently unknown. Relevant though this information was, humanity's real hope lay with the Svalbard Vault in Norway.

Aptly nick-named the 'doomsday vault', Svalbard is actually a seed bank which holds millions of plant seeds from all over the world inside a sandstone mountain, called 'plateau mountain', at the Svalbard Archipelago on Spitsbergen Island. Spitsbergen was considered ideal due to its lack of tectonic activity and its permafrost which aids seed preservation.

Ironically, the archipelago was rocked by a 6.2 magnitude earthquake in February of 2008, five days before the vault's official opening. Thankfully, no damage was reported. The vault itself is 390 feet inside the mountain and 430 feet above sea level providing easy access and ensuring a cold, dry storage of the seeds, even if the icecaps melted. Prior to its opening, a feasibility study determined the vault could preserve seeds from most major food crops for hundreds of years.

Excited by the Svalbard find, Emma and Eric also began looking for animal sperm and egg banks. They learned the government of Great Britain had established a facility for preserving farm animals from extinction. They just didn't know where it was, or how well it was protected from disasters.

In the seventeenth month A.S., EP3 radio operators began to hear static on VHF channel 16, immediately following the 9 p.m. broadcast. In that month, observers also began to see lightning flashes in the cloud cover indicative of thunderstorm activity. As first, neither seemed important to those monitoring the phenomenon, but on the third straight night, Major Pickett was summoned to the command center. Five people were huddled around the radio operator when Adam walked in.

"You guys look like you're watching a ball game. What's going on?"

"We've got static." the operator intoned.

"Yes, I understand lightning has been sighted."

"That's what we thought too, Sir. But this is the third straight night now, and each time it has occurred after the 21:00 hours broadcast. Seems to have stopped now, Sir, but I recorded it."

"Good. Make sure you continue to do that every time. Let's hear what you've got."

They listened, as the operator replayed the 9 o'clock transmission, quietly anticipating the sound of static.

In radio reception, noise, also called static, results when disturbing influences affect the signal. These influences are usually electronic and include transmitted signals, or interference from noise picked up by the receiver's antenna, either electromagnetic (electronic equipment), or atmospheric (lightning discharges).

Their quiet patience was rewarded with the familiar sound of static. "Sksss", and Sksss."

"That sounded deliberate." Adam said. "Is that the same as before?"

"I really can't say, Major. It's static."

Adam turned toward the watch commander. "Lieutenant, I'd like to know what the cause of that static is."

"Yes, Sir."

"Is it lightning? Is someone trying to send us a message, or is it coming from our own OEPs, or an ESV, or from Cyprium Prospector? Check with commander Tamari. Get some help with this. Find out."

"Aye, aye, Sir."

At the end of four days the investigators assigned to the 'static' enigma were able to rule out interference from an ESV, the Cyprium Prospector and the OEPs. They couldn't completely rule out lightning, but they were fairly confident lightning was not the source of the static heard each morning after the 9 o'clock broadcast. Word about the static spread quickly and before long, it was piped throughout the habitats. It was ghostly, at first, but as the frequency of the interference increased and expanded into other time slots, most started to believe there were survivors on the planet surface and they were signaling.

Several weeks had passed since the first static was heard on EP3. Now, the other OEPs were receiving static after various broadcast times as well. When holes started appearing in the cloud cover, it became obvious the static they had been hearing was an attempt by someone on the surface to communicate, for within the static could now be heard the sound of garbled, barely discernable, unintelligible (but human) voices!

Chapter Thirteen

*The phoenix hope, can wing her way through the desert skies,
and still defying fortune's spite; revive from ashes and rise.*
Miguel de Cervantes

Scientists enamored of extinction level events, who predicted volcanic ash and dust would clog Earth's skies for years, were wrong. Ash and dust did fill the sky in a blanket so thick at times and in places, it suffocated nearly every living breathing thing. Most of the standing vegetation on the Earth died from lack of sun and water. The food chain collapsed. Life on Earth teetered on the brink. They were right about those things happening, yet, they underestimated the wonderful and complex dynamics powering our atmosphere, giving it the ability to gain equilibrium and refresh itself much sooner than was foretold. This was probably due to calculations made based only on what they could observe; how hot dry ash behaves in a normal atmosphere. Under recent conditions, the ash and dust interacted with much larger quantities of moisture which carried the debris back to Earth more rapidly than imagined. And although it would ultimately make the difference between life and death for all living things, the surface of Earth was forever changed, terribly scarred and littered with the perpetual reminders of the devastation and death that had been inflicted upon it.

The cloud cover had completely stifled all radio communication for nearly two years. But as the debris thinned out, and holes began to appear in the sky, the ability to communicate by radio slowly and sporadically returned, assuming there was anyone around to listen.

One night at dinner Emma braved a question to Adam. "Has there been any breakthrough with the radio static?"

"No. Actually, it's diminished some."

"Can you see anything through the holes in the clouds yet?"

"A little bit."

"What can you tell?"

"It looks pretty bad. We haven't seen any green. It's mostly dark brownish gray, but the holes are still small and they don't stay open for very long, but I can't imagine it's very pretty down there."

"People are pretty excited about the holes."

"It's a change, that's for sure."

"Aren't you excited about them?"

"I was, until I heard that it's still liable to be some months before we will have any idea about whether, or not we can go back."

"Well, I'm optimistic. The atmosphere has started to clear sooner than anyone thought possible. That's encouraging in my book."

"I agree, but, I'm worried about what we will have to go back to."

"We know where to find vegetable seeds and maybe even animal eggs and zygotes cryogenically frozen. They could still be intact. We should be able to produce food. There's probably a lot of buildings still standing. At least I have some hope that I'm not going to die in space."

"There won't be any power. No electricity." Adam intoned.

"At least we'll be alive. What's the matter? You're usually the one who's upbeat."

"Yeah, I know. I'm just a little down. I miss being on solid ground."

"Well, I think we all should start gearing up for life on planet Earth again, whatever that means."

"Yeah, I guess you're right. We should have some plans in place for starting over, one of which is, how do we get everyone down?"

"What do you mean? We'll fly, of course." she said flatly

"That's not the issue."

"Then, what is the issue?"

"There are more people up here than there are ESVs to fly them back. Once an ESV leaves space, there's no way for it to get back, not anymore, now that RJP is gone."

Emma was suddenly sick to her stomach. The thought of being trapped in space was not something she had ever really considered. Adam's blunt assessment had given her a fear she had never known before.

~~~~

Of the radio frequencies being monitored by the orbiting platforms, 147.450 megahertz FM was dedicated for use by the world's militaries. It was on this frequency the first intelligible signal was heard from Earth since Richard Phelps' last transmission from his camper perched above Dutch Creek. EP3 was over Great Britain when a significant split in the cloud cover opened up directly beneath it. Unaware of the opening, the radio operator began to hear chatter between two people and recognized it as military traffic, but he suspected it was radio traffic on the platform until he heard the words 'USS Maryland'.

"It's a sub!" he shouted, grabbing his earpiece with his left hand and pushing tightly. He looked up at the surprised faces in the room with him. "It's a sub! Listen!" he said turning a switch to the speaker on his console. The group listened long enough to realize they were hearing voices from Earth, and that's when the yelling, shrieking and whooping started.

A conversation was taking place between an Ohio Class ballistic missile submarine, USS Maryland (SSBN-738), and a cruise ship. They were trying to work out a trade of some sort.

"Quiet! Quiet!" shouted the watch officer. "See if you can raise them, and somebody go get Major Pickett."

The operator took a deep breath and keyed his mike. "USS Maryland, USS Maryland. This is Orbiting Earth Platform 3, do you copy? Over." There was no response, but the conversation between the two ships suddenly stopped.

"Try it again." ordered the watch officer. The operator keyed his mike a second time. "Calling submarine, USS Maryland. This is Orbiting Earth Platform 3, do you copy? Over."

They waited a long moment when the speaker crackled. "Orbiting Platform 3, this is USS Maryland, we read you loud and clear. We've been wondering about you boys up there in space. Glad to see you're still alive. Over." The radio rooms on EP3 and the submarine both went wild with cheering.

News of the conversation, naturally, spread quickly. The entire contact only lasted a short 16 minutes before the cloud cover closed up and interrupted the signal, but not before enough information could be exchanged for the sub to learn that the EPs were broadcasting every hour, and for

EP3 to learn there were 18 nuclear subs still operating, four nuclear powered carriers, several cruise ships and a handful of shortwave radio operators, one of whom was Phelps. There were also people alive underground at NORAD, sometimes referred to as Cheyenne Mountain, and the Canadian Air Operations Control Centers in the underground complex at North Bay in Ontario, Canada, as well as radio signals from other military defense bunkers in several other countries.

~~~~

As the weeks went by, the cloud cover lessened to the point where the Earth was finally becoming visible again. Familiar weather patterns could be observed, along with a new phenomena; dust cyclones, or dusters. They were hurricanes of hot, dry wind and dust with even higher wind-speeds, but they could only be found in the northern hemisphere. Rotating in a clockwise direction, they moved west to east over North America, Africa and Asia dying out upon reaching the sea, or when blocked by a mountain range. One such storm was bearing down on the Quachita National Forest in Arkansas.

Dick Phelps thought he had covered all bases when he selected his compound site, but he couldn't have foreseen a duster. His place in the woods should have provided them with lush green cover, even during the winter months because it was located in a pine forest. But the vegetation was all gone now and his thick green stand of pines had been transformed into an ash covered forest of snags, tree trunks devoid of leaf, needle and branch. They were very much exposed to the huge dust storm about to slam into the compound, whose camper and buildings were not anchored down except by their own weight. Phelps had no way to anticipate its coming. The duster struck at 11 A.M. while Dick was doing what he routinely did everyday; make his own hourly broadcast to test the airwaves.

~~~~

The view of Earth from space had changed from what was stored in video, photographs and collective memory. All of the continents had new coastline configurations, some more severe than others, and most notably those along the Pacific Basin. North and South America had lost the largest percentage of surface mass of all the continents, as earthquakes and volcanoes ravaged their coastlines narrowing their widths by a third. Civilization along both coasts had disappeared, swallowed by the Earth, or claimed by water. The land-bridge between the two continents had become broken by earthquake and eruption. Island paradises were now either totally submerged, or had become rocky outcroppings. Evidence of civilization still remained in many places, although, the land was dead. The Earth's surface had become like a desert, it's seas like wash-water. Earth was no longer the blue planet. Commander Aviv Tamari commented that the land masses reminded him of Mars because "...now they were one color, barren and devoid of living things". Remarkably, the polar ice cap regions were relatively undamaged by volcanic activity, being only slightly tinged with dust and ash.

There were only three land areas on the globe that were not physically devastated from forces triggered by the gravitational change in relationship between the Moon and the Earth; Antarctica, extreme Northern Russia and the northern end of Greenland, although Greenland had lost most of its ice, and its land mass had shrunk from rising sea levels. These areas had been exposed to only limited seismic activity comparatively speaking, and they were on the borders of the prevailing air currents that conveyed the ash clouds. Geographic proximity, however, did not save the inhabitants. Earth had become a brownish gray planet with no other color variations except for shading. Those few thousand souls who survived the devastation had been living on their wits, discipline and food stuffs gathered and stored in anticipation of the worst.

The United States military, specifically the Navy, was the best equipped to endure a long term test of surviving an extinction level event. Submarines and aircraft carriers were floating self sustaining cities that had at least some experience living in isolation. Earth's cataclysmic harbingers forced governments to implement plans to ensure humanity's survival, which included preparing its naval vessels and crews to attempt living through an extinction level event. Some of those vessels succeeded, along with a few cruise ships which sadly, possessed only a small compliment of passengers. These ships had huge food storage capacities and could recycle, desalinize and purify water. And as long as they stayed close to the poles the air was breathable. The submarines and aircraft carriers were also nuclear and therefore had nearly limitless power reserves.

The clearing atmosphere and ever normalizing weather patterns were helping to scrub the Earth's surface in some areas, having the effect of removing ash from surface soil. Even so, the land was barren. Like so many

Noah's Arks, the ships and orbiting platforms searched constantly for living things, especially green ones. With resources nearly exhausted, the cleaner air had brought with it a new hope for survival, and those who remained alive were anxious to once again stand upon the land and start anew, a start which would present them with their greatest challenge yet; finding food and clean fresh water. The remnant in space had also decided it was time to return to the surface, signaling the closing stages for the lunar colony and orbiting platforms, as well as certain death for anyone who remained behind.

The Phelps were finally able to come out of their silver colored cocoon. The air had become clean again and rarely required using a respirator anymore, or even a dust mask. They had survived their one and only encounter with a duster, and the little compound miraculously escaped any significant damage to its stores. The AeroStream with its rounded corners actually saved it from being carried away. Several smaller propane tanks were missing and two of the larger ones were on their sides and of course there was debris everywhere. An extremely large branch had blown against the door requiring Phelps to climb out a window to remove it.

Since taking up residence, they were by contrast, significantly exposed to view now that the concealing vegetation was gone. The compound, particularly the AeroStream, was visible for quite some distance. They were vulnerable and there wasn't much they could do about it, except keep watch and hope any encounter with other humans, as unlikely as that was, would not turn violent. Nevertheless, Richard Phelps started wearing a .357 magnum and slinging his M4 carbine whenever he was outside the AeroStream.

~~~~

The governing board, established by Dr. Wagner on EP3, had known for some time a problem existed in regard to returning the space dwellers back to Earth. The math just didn't work out. There weren't enough ESVs. More precisely, there weren't enough seats aboard the ESVs to accommodate the number of people currently living in space. Food and water resources were running perilously low and the question of 'How long can we live up here?' was being asked with frequency and demanding an answer. The few engineers alive had been working on the problem, and it seemed no solution could be found for the three hundred plus people who had no transportation back to Earth.

Had Cyprium Prospector not been on station, things would have been far graver for everyone. The behemoth returned with unused resources which helped to sustain those stranded in space. CP also carried extra construction materials and all kinds of equipment that would be needed on the surface, once they returned. The second unanswered question facing the governing board concerned how to get people and equipment back to Earth without leaving anyone behind.

Cyprium Prospector had forty MOTs, and while they collectively accounted for 320 seats, the engineers were doubtful they could be used to carry the life aiding equipment that would be needed back to Earth, let alone a live consignment.

When Dr. Wagner entered the meeting room the participants immediately quieted and sat down. "Okay. We all know the numbers inform us there isn't enough transportation to take everyone back to Earth. We do know that we have considerable container space for returning in-animates, but we are not sure if we can secure the trip through the atmosphere, or the landing. And we are running out of time. That is what our calculations tell us based on current available knowledge. So, we are still faced with the same three major action items; one -getting everyone down, two – getting MOTs and PPOCs safely through the atmosphere, and three - landing safely on the surface, and ladies and gentlemen, we will overcome those hurdles. I don't want... I won't accept... any other outcome. In fact, we shall no longer speak of these challenges in negative terms, because I am elevating them to a most worthy position. From this moment on, they shall be referred to as our collective goals.

Now, I think we should have three teams working on these goals and their related issues. I also think we should tell everyone what our status is, and openly invite ideas and alternatives as to how we might accomplish our goals. And when we have achieved our goals, we will achieve our objective; a safe return to Earth for all. Commander Tamari? Aviv, would you take responsibility for item two? Major Pickett, would you take action item number three, and Bill, could you run with number one?"

"Doctor Wagner, when can we expect transport to the surface to commence?" The question came from Bill Suljak, a top engineer who had been assigned to the first action item. Bill had just turned sixty. He was six feet tall, slender build and had a full, but short head of salt and pepper hair. Bill firmly believed there was no means available in which everyone could be transported back to Earth. His years of experience were incontrovertibly telling him some would have to be left behind. But Bill was a pragmatist, which made it difficult for him to see other possibilities, and until, or unless someone could show him exactly how such a feat could be accomplished, it just couldn't be done. He also secretly believed he was more valuable than most, which in his mind guaranteed him a seat on one of the returning ESVs.

"That is something which should be part of the planning process." Wagner answered.

"Why can't we start now? I'd be happy to coordinate things on the surface."

"Thanks, Bill, but I don't think we are there yet." Dr. Wagner said pleasantly. Inwardly, he was angry at the suggestion, but hoped it didn't show.

"Don't you think it would be a good idea to send an advance team? I mean, we don't want to just start sending everyone down all at once. The landings are going to require some coordination on the ground." His statement elicited some affirmative grunting from several associates.

"That's a good idea, Bill. We will need some coordination effort for sure, but we are not there yet. Before we agree to let anyone return to the surface, a lot more work has to be done up here, and I for one, am not prepared to determine who should be the first down until we can ensure everyone is going, or we have a plan in place for the alternative." he said firmly.

"We already know everyone can't return so, let's get on with it."

"Unacceptable!" Wagner exploded, glaring at everyone in the room. "We are not leaving anyone up here until we've exhausted all of the ideas from every living person who has an idea about how we can get everybody, and I mean everybody, back to the surface! And if we are faced with such a horrible moment, though I don't believe we will, but if we are, who will decide, you Bill? Listen up people, no one is going anywhere until we have guaranteed everyone will go. If you are not committed to finding a resolution for everyone then we all are doomed. And if you are willing to allow even one person to be stranded up here, you had better think about that person being *you*. We have ships, material and a lot of smart people up here, about whom I'm confident can work this out."

Dr. Wagner looked back at the rebuked engineer, but said nothing. He was waiting for Suljak to accept, or reject his request to head up action item number one.

"I think I'd like to have another opportunity to review my findings, maybe get some input from areas I haven't considered. I'll take number one." Bill said humbly.

"Thanks Bill. Don't know who I'd rather have working that piece, other than you."

When the meeting was over Aviv waited. He wanted to speak to Dr. Wagner privately.

"You know the key to all this revolves around getting the MOTs modified." he stated calmly.

"That's why I picked you. Can it be done?"

"You can't change the physics, Ken. If I were you, I'd be working on a plan B."

"Already have a plan B. A lottery is the only fair way I know."

"Well, I'm not ready to give up just yet."

"Like I said, that's why I picked you."

"You also realize, that even if we do come up with a solution, we may not have enough time."

"It's what I fear most, and why any modification you come up with has to be something that can be made quickly. Cannibalize the CP, the platforms and Apollo

Seventeen, if need be. Take anything, do whatever, just make sure you get everyone back to Earth."

"And assuming we all get back?"

"I'm working on that, too."

~~~~

Specialist John Bustard was an easy going guy, the kind who could be described as a 'good old boy' in the positive sense of the phrase. He wasn't a slow mover, but he wasn't necessarily filled with a sense of urgency either. He was, however, thorough and responsive and when the request for confirmation went over to Cyprium Prospector, Larry was glad John was the one handling it because he knew it would be done right.

"Green! There's green on the infrared!" shouted Specialist Larry Peters who was monitoring one of the screens on EP2. "It just appeared out of nowhere!"

"No shit. Tell me something I don't know." responded his buddy and colleague Charlie Colburne.

"That's not what I mean."

"What the hell are you talking about? Red appears *green* under infrared. It's called false color imaging, duh, and practically the whole damn planet appears that way now."

"Well, excuse me mister smartass. Please, let me rephrase. What I should have said is, blue!"

"Bullshit!" Charlie coughed, thinking he was being pranked, but he leaned over and looked at the screen Larry had been monitoring anyway. "Where? I don't see any blue. You lying sack of ... holy mother of pearl! That's blue! That's really blue! Call CP, see if they can visually confirm."

Larry immediately made the call. "Cyprium Prospector this is EP2."

"Go ahead EP2."

"I need a visual confirmation on the surface. Over."

"Wait one. Over."

"Copy that."

Larry and Charlie waited for what seemed like five minutes. In reality, only sixty seconds had passed before Cyprium Prospector responded again. "EP2, this is Specialist Bustard. What can I do for ya?"

"John! This is Larry Peters! I need a visual confirmation on the surface."

"That's easy." he chuckled. "It's mostly brown."

"No man. I got some blue on the infrared. East Latitude 30 degrees - 47 minutes - 19 seconds! North Longitude 47 degrees - 40 minutes and 11 seconds! Can you confirm? Over." he shouted quickly.

"Wait a minute. Give me that again."

"30 degrees - 47 minutes - 20 seconds, 47 degrees - 40 minutes - 11 seconds! Over."

"You sure about this? Over."

"I'm looking right at it, but before I tell anyone I want you to confirm it. Over."

"Stand by EP2. We'll check it out. It will take a few minutes. Over."

"EP2, standing by."

~~~~

It was a bit after midnight when Adam entered their quarters. He had been working the second shift for his rotation this month. Emma was still up reading. "Why aren't you asleep, hon?" he asked sweetly.

"Oh, I guess I'm just a little excited."

"Yeah? About what?"

"Well, I understand we might be going back to Earth soon."

"*Might* is the operative word there. Dr. Wagner established three teams at the board meeting today. He asked me to head up one of them for the purpose of landing safely back on Earth."

"I didn't think that was a problem for ESVs."

"It isn't a problem for an ESV. An MOT and a cargo box is another story."

"What's the problem?"

"Heat shielding. MOTs were designed to ferry back and forth from Mars, not Earth. If we tried to land an MOT attached to a cargo box the whole thing would burn up on re-entry, and you know that we are counting on using them for the 320 seats they have."

"Oh, Adam! Does that mean people might be left behind?"

"If we can't shield the MOTs, I'm afraid so."

"How would they decide who has to stay behind?"

"I don't know. Maybe they'll draw straws, and maybe they'll ask for volunteers. If we could get RJP up and running again it would solve our problem, but time is critical. We're running out of food and water. Anyone who would have to stay behind... well, no one is talking about that at the moment. Dr. Wagner said he's not leaving anyone up here. He believes we have the material and the brainpower to figure it out in time.

He's also going to make an announcement asking everyone for ideas as to how we might get everybody back to Earth, how we keep from burning up on re-entry and how we can land safely. Of course, we are still working a whole list of other issues for when we do get back to the surface."

"I know. My group is working on selecting a list of landing sites. We'll have to stick close to the coastline, so the Navy can scope out our selections."

"Fortunately, the ESVs can land without a runway, but they will require some glide space. MOTs are another story. My guess is we may be dropping them into the sea, shallow water at least. We are also going to need a lot of the equipment so, the cargo boxes will present a challenge. They will need to be air and water tight. You might want to include that with your planning. Maybe the Navy boys will have an idea, or two. You should probably think about landing close to a city, you know there may be resources still around."

"Yep. That's what we thought, too."

"I'm sorry. I don't mean to tell you how to do your job."

"No. That's alright. Like Dr. Wagner said, we want to hear all the ideas." The conversation paused for a moment when Emma somberly asked Adam the very question he was wrestling with. "Adam, do you think we will get everyone down?"

The ESV pilot shook his head. "I don't know." he said flatly.

~~~~

The color blue on an infrared image indicates, on the human visual spectrum, the color green, which normally represents plant life. And though everyone was counting on the resiliency of plants, finding green in what appeared to be a barren waste was akin to the needle and haystack. But there it was in beautiful deep blue tones on the infrared image.   The current picture image was a significantly magnified view so, no one could tell the exact location without zooming out. After convincing himself it must be plant life, Larry decided to take a wider view to make sure it wasn't something artificial.

"Hey, that's the Persian Gulf."   Charlie piped, obviously pleased with his recognition of the area.

Larry looked up at Charlie and smiled. "Is that what it is? I was never much good at geography."

"The reason I know that is because my son had to do a project on the Garden of Eden and the four rivers around it. That's the Euphrates." he said pointing to the river adjacent to the blue spot on the screen.

"Yeah, that's right, the Tigris and Euphrates. That would be something if the first place we find green is where it all began, according to the Bible."

"That would be something, wouldn't it?"

Just then the radio came to life. "EP2 this is Cyprium Prospector. Over."

"This is EP2. Go ahead, John. Over."

"Hey Larry, got some good news for you boys. That's real vegetation down there. It's low growing and we haven't identified what it is yet, but it's probably something indigenous. Over."

When Larry heard "real vegetation" he whooped. "Thanks, John. That's all I needed to know. Over and out."

There was significant good news and a small measure of bad news with Larry's discovery. The good news; although in a very small area, plants were thriving. That meant water and fertile soil, or at least, soil and water with enough quality to support life. It also meant, hopefully, the Earth was rebounding. The vegetation turned out to be wild *phoenix dactylifera,* a type of date palm found in warm dry climates typical of areas along the Persian Gulf. Its name was apropos, as it had literally risen from the ash. It thrives in gorges, wet rocky escarpments and seepage areas alongside brackish springs. So, it was logical these palms should be found where they were. The bad news was that the fruit of this particular date palm is inedible, but their existence provided hope food could once again be cultivated.

Chapter Fourteen

No one knows what he can do, until he tries.
Publilius Syrus

Lottery. It was a word and a concept Dr. Wagner found nagging at his consciousness with increasing frequency. As director of GPATT and leader of the remnant of that organization, it was his responsibility to include in any re-entry plan the possibility of dealing with an inability to accommodate everyone. He could have delegated the assignment, though he wouldn't have felt right about it. The task belonged to him alone, and he did his best to be impersonal and practical, focusing on the larger picture; the best interest of the whole. He had to reason that way because leaving anyone behind, to him, was like having to cut your own arm, or leg off to save your body.

Lottery. Hope was dissolving. His mind was struggling with uncertainty now. *There just aren't enough seats, unless you include the MOTs, but they aren't shielded, and even if they were you cannot land them. They would have to be dropped into the sea. But even if you could drop them into the sea, how do you soften the impact, or prevent them from sinking? Could the subs reach them in time? There is so little time left. Do you select winners, or losers? Was that the best way? What is the fair way? Are there other selection methods? Drawing straws was a method, but how would that be accomplished among so many? No, that's impractical. Perhaps the least painful and most acceptable selection process would be to draw names randomly. Most of these people are professionals. They would understand and accept their lot with dignity. They wouldn't swoon, or lose control of themselves by crying out, or misbehaving poorly. They had too much self respect, and respect for the feelings of their colleagues. Perhaps I should announce the number of seats available and advance the idea of a random drawing, suggesting if there were other preferred selection methods, they could be voted on as well. That way it would be the people who selected the process, rather than having it imposed on them.*

Though he concluded his latter approach would be best, Dr. Wagner still did not like it. He wouldn't write the idea down, or even speak to anyone about it. He would simply wait until all hope was abandoned before taking action of any kind on that part of his plan.

The three action items proposed to the governing board were dependent on one another. Solving action item 2 (heat shielding for MOTs) would support the goal of item 3 (ensuring a safe landing) and unequivocally resolve item 1 (everyone returns to Earth). Solving action item number 3 (landing safely) supported items 1 and 2, but hinged on item 2 being solved. Item 2 was key because, if you couldn't provide heat shielding for the MOTs, the other two items could not be accomplished. That was precisely why Dr. Wagner assigned action item number 2 to Commander Tamari.

After months on Cyprium Prospector, Aviv had gained invaluable experience dealing with finding alternatives and utilizing acceptable substitutes. He was their best hope for solving the heat shielding problem. Dr. Wagner was also confident Adam's flight experience would help him find an acceptable solution to his landing assignment. Item 1 was a simple math problem with only two possible outcomes and really didn't need much further exploration, but Bill needed to be kept busy to keep him out of trouble.

Aviv knew the thermal protective shielding (TPS) material used on ESVs was not available in any quantity on the orbiting platforms. There were small amounts for repairs, yet not enough to shield even one MOT, though MOTs did have TPS, but only of a sufficiency that worked in the thinner atmosphere of Mars, not the denser oxygen rich air of Earth. That MOTs already had some shielding was a plus because it meant Aviv's degree of difficulty in finding supplemental shielding material was significantly lessened.

Adam had been working on the problem of landing a craft, other than an ESV, on Earth well before Dr. Wagner's assignment. Operating from the assumption MOTs had adequate TPS material for re-entering Earth's atmosphere, Adam had begun to explore scenarios which would minimally impact an MOT and a PPOC full of supplies and equipment. A PPOC was a large metal and carbon fiber box to which no wings, or landing gear could be affixed, whose shape and center of gravity were designed to fall through the atmosphere with one side always facing downward. By contrast, an MOT was shaped like a delta for gliding, had rocket power to assist with landing and it had a guidance system. And though it could glide part way through Earth's atmosphere, it had no landing gear like that of an ESV, for it was never designed to be brought back to Earth. The question Adam was attempting to solve involved how to get the two back to Earth without crashing, or sinking. A hard landing was acceptable, of course, as long as no one got hurt. One thing became clear. There would be no way they would be able to drop a PPOC safely back to Earth without chutes, even if it was shielded.

Free fall through the Earth's atmosphere occurs at 17,500 miles per hour. That speed generates a lot of heat, which is why TPS is absolutely necessary. Why does re-entry have to be so fast? Actually it doesn't. Technology just hadn't come up with a viable means to slow re-entry, other than an aeroshell which could glide, or fly part of the way, like the ESV. Even if a PPOC was encased entirely in TPS, it still has to be slowed down enough to protect its contents when it strikes Earth. The early space vehicles, pre space shuttle, used parachutes and water landings. And although water and hard landings were both included in design plans for PPOCs, there were no parachutes, or material to make them.

Once Cyprium Prospector had returned from its mission, parachutes were to be brought up from the surface in small pods which would be affixed to the containers and self deploy once the MOTs detached. Without parachutes it was impossible.

As it was, MOTs, which did have parachutes, would also have to make water landings requiring coordination with the subs, or possibly be made in the shallows close to shore. There was some risk. It wasn't the best solution, but it was an acceptable one in light of circumstances, until Adam learned that the MOTs had to have additional shielding in order to enter Earth's atmosphere. It was a devastating setback.

Time was fast approaching when a decision would have to be made and action taken to ensure the survival of the remnant living in space. It was also becoming painfully clear a solution may not be forthcoming. Aviv had failed in his attempt to produce an acceptable substitute for TPS. Available material just didn't possess the unique properties needed for heat protection and dispersion. Dr.

Wagner would now have to face what nearly everyone else had already determined was inevitable.

The governing board argued for a long time. All agreed on two things; it was time to prepare the ESVs for re-entry, and no one should be left behind. But without TPS, people would have to remain in space. It was an unpalatable prospect to everyone. In order to break their paralysis it was agreed they would ask the Navy to have one of its ships, or planes do some recon on the RJP, posthaste, to determine the possibility of reviving the facility enough to mount a rescue of anyone who would be stranded in space. The board would also decide how they would administer a lottery, if required. There would be no popular vote.

First and foremost, no one would be exempt, except for the ESV commanders as they would be the ones flying the aeroshells back to Earth. Secondly, the lottery would be computerized. A randomly selected 15 digit binary code of 0s and 1s would be produced for each person. Using 0 and 1 to produce a 15 digit number would produce over 32,000 possible combinations, way more than required, thereby ensuring randomness and preventing duplication. The numbers would be printed on individual slips with corresponding barcodes and shuffled in the BINGO drum borrowed from EP3. Each person would be given the opportunity to hand select one number from the drum which would be scanned and entered into a secure file with their name. Once all the numbers were drawn, a computer would randomly select a set of those numbers from that file equaling the number of available seats. Within the privacy of their own quarters, individuals could check their status by logging in to a special program on the COMMAND.net and entering their personal I.D.   The screen would display either 'ACCEPTED' or 'unable to process'.

There were, of course, other variations bandied about which would have been just as effective. And though in the end, this method was chosen as being the most fair, it did not completely settle the issue. Of the 'ACCEPTED' group, it was anticipated there would be those who would want to give up their seats to others for various reasons. Some might want to stay with a friend, or loved one who was not selected. Others might choose to volunteer to stay, opting to take their chances on a rescue mission. And what about those who were ACCEPTED, but wanted to give someone a chance at life by potentially sacrificing their own? This prompted a debate among the governing board over the ownership and rights of anyone whose number was 'ACCEPTED'. Did 'ACCEPTED' mean a person was expressly assigned a seat aboard an ESV? Should 'volunteers' have been removed from the list? Should anyone wanting to relinquish their seat, have their place reinserted for another random selection? Was the selection really theirs to do with what they wanted? The debate was decided by examining the definition, purpose and spirit of the word 'lottery'.

Research on the term told them a lottery was a kind of contest, a game, or activity that had an outcome. Tokens might be distributed, or sold, the winning tokens being secretly predetermined, or ultimately selected in a random drawing. A lottery could include a selection made by lot from a number of applicants, or competitors. It could be a method of raising money by selling numbered tickets and giving a proportion of the money raised to holders of numbers drawn at random. Players would select a small group of numbers out of a larger group printed on a ticket.

If a player's selection matched some, or all of the numbers drawn at random, the player would win. It was an activity, or endeavor, the outcome of which is regarded as a matter of fate, or luck.

It was ultimately agreed, reluctantly by some, 'ACCEPTED' would mean a seat on an ESV was conveyed to the individual to whom it had been communicated, and once conveyed it was theirs to keep, or relinquish as they desired, either to another person, or back into the pool to be randomly reassigned to someone whose status was 'unable to process'.

The next issue the board had to wrestle with concerned when to implement the lottery and what reaction could be expected by those who received the message 'unable to process'. Security suddenly became a major concern due to fear of sabotage, or violence, so it was decided a small armed force of 'ACCPETED' personnel would be established strictly as a protective measure. That responsibility fell to the ESV pilots. ESVs and MOTs would be locked down and certain areas became 'off limits' to everyone. Those small subtle acts heightened the fear and stress levels of nearly everyone.

~~~~

Dick Phelps burst into the AeroStream, killed power to the generator and shut the stove burners off. Then he grabbed the twelve gauge shotgun and began ramming shells into it. He handed it to his wife and grabbed some extra ammo for his rifle and revolver.

"Someone's coming." he announced.

"People? There are people alive?" she asked with hope and excitement in her voice.

"Men. Five of them."

"Where are they?"

"Down along the creek."

"Did you speak to them?" Dot asked.

"Are you crazy?"

"We should talk to them. Maybe they have some news." she urged.

"No!"

"Maybe they're just looking for other survivors."

"I don't think so." Phelps responded unequivocally as he loaded the weapons.

"What are you going to do?"

"We are going to defend this place."

"They could be just like us you know, Dick. We haven't seen anyone in over two years."

"Listen to me. If they were just like us, they wouldn't have split up into two teams. Two guys are coming up on the right and three are coming up on the left. They're armed and they are flanking us. That's not a tactically friendly maneuver. I want you to stay in here. If anybody tries to get in, shoot them. Use the shotgun if anybody approaches that door, and the pistol if anyone tries to come through the windows. "

"Dick?" Dot wanted to ask her husband if he was going to kill these men.

"And don't hesitate!" he commanded and then disappeared through the camper door.

Confident in Dot's ability to handle firearms, Richard Phelps had placed his wife inside the AeroStream's entry door with a 15 shot 9mm semi automatic pistol and a sawed off 12 gauge pump action shotgun. He hastily constructed a blind atop a storage container wearing his .357 magnum revolver and holding the M4 carbine. Roo Roo stayed with Dot.

The three men on the northeast side of the bluff arrived first. Only one was armed. He carried a bolt action 30-06 hunting rifle. That meant the other weapon Phelps had seen was being carried by one of the two men coming up the other side. They approached the camper cautiously and quietly.

"That's far enough." Phelps warned from behind the blind aiming his assault weapon at the man holding the rifle.

"We don't mean any harm, mister." the oldest said as they craned their necks to see where Phelps was concealing himself.

"Then why are you pointing that gun?"

The man slung the hunting rifle on his shoulder. "We just want to talk."

"Anyone else with you?"

"Just us." the man lied. "You by yourself?"

The three newcomers were frail, dirty and hungry. They had a wild look which also made them dangerous. How they had survived was anyone's guess. That they had survived spoke volumes about what they must have done, and were prepared to do to stay alive. One was in his late twenties and carried the rifle. The other two were older; forties and fifties. Because of the lie, Phelps knew there could be no good outcome from this encounter. The three men were beginning to suspect the same thing.

"Just us five, you mean." Phelps responded flatly. The three looked at each other realizing they had been caught in the deception. "Why don't we wait for the other two before we have anymore talk."

"We're starving, mister. You got anything you can spare?" the middle aged man asked.

From inside the camper door, Roo Roo observed the two new arrivals hide themselves behind the shed to Phelp's right and barked a warning.

"Is that a dog?" the older one asked with great surprise, glancing toward the camper door.

"They got a god-damned dog!" the youngest one exclaimed.

"You gotta have some extra food mister, if you ain't ette that dog yet." said the middle aged man.

"No food." he responded with finality.

When Roo Roo barked again, Phelps deduced the other two men had made it to the top of the bluff, but were keeping out of sight. The youngest of the three men also gave their presence away with a glance.

"Tell your friends to join us." Phelps ordered.

The men didn't move, or speak. The two in hiding didn't quite know what to do, except look at the other for some direction which never came. Phelps was no murderer. He didn't want to kill anybody, and he hoped he would never be put in the position of even having to hold a gun on a man. He and Dot had conversed on several occasions about the possibility of having to kill in order to protect, not only themselves, but their food, and protecting their food was the same thing. They had over two years to think about and discuss how they would respond to the very situation they found themselves in now. And even though Dot was willing to talk, she was also willing to pull the trigger, if it got to that.

Dick was already at that point. 'Have to take out the one with the rifle first.' he told himself drawing a bead on the man's chest. 'Have to hit him on the first shot, kill him with the second one if need be.'

As the newcomers didn't show themselves, Phelps hollered. "You boys got three seconds to come out!"

The men momentarily froze. The other weapon Phelps couldn't see was a shotgun held pointed at the ready. The five men were at a disadvantage, however, because they hadn't formulated much of a plan in the event they actually encountered someone. Phelps didn't exactly know what he was going to do next, either, but he figured at some point part of his plan would involve killing them all.

As the two concealed men were still trying to decide what they should do, the young man with the bolt action rifle decided to un-sling his weapon and aim it where Dick was hiding. Phelps dropped him with a shot to the chest. One down. The middle aged man ran toward the camper while the older man threw up his hands yelling not to shoot. The yelling only caused Phelps to fire upon him next. He let go with two quick shots; one to the abdomen and one to the neck. He bled to death in the dirt. Two down.

As the third man went running toward the camper, he was unaware that he was running toward his death, not away from it. He had intended to run behind the AeroStream not into it, but Dot didn't know that. As he closed upon the camper door Dot fired a load of steel BB shot into his upper right torso. Three down.

The man with the shotgun came out of hiding and fired a round toward where he thought Phelps was hiding, while the other man ran to his downed comrade to retrieve the bolt action rifle. Phelps reacted. He ducked and crawled to the other side of the storage container. Dot was too far away from the two armed men to have any impact with the 12 gauge, but she fired for effect anyway. This distracted them both long enough for her husband to target and kill the man with the shotgun. Four down.

The fifth man scurried behind the pickup truck, took aim and fired one shot through the camper door. Phelps became filled with rage causing him to make a mistake.

"Dot!" he shouted giving away his exact position.

No answer. His enemy, cocked and loaded, turned toward the sound and fired. The shot was off, but struck the wooden edge of the container exploding splinters into Dick's face, eye and neck. The eyeball wasn't damaged, but he was temporarily disoriented and seeing stars. The splinters in his face and neck burned. He blindly fired a shot in the direction of what he thought was the pickup hoping to keep his assailant pinned down until he could see again.

The man stayed behind the truck believing it offered him his best protection. With rifle at the ready he waited for Phelps to make a move from behind the container. It was the opportunity Phelps needed to clear his head. After several long moments he took one of his boots off and pushed it out from behind the container and into the open. The man stupidly took the bait and fired at the boot. When he did, Phelps stood up and fired three rounds before the man could operate the rifle bolt and reload. Five down.

Dick Phelps had been cool under fire. He possessed the 'killer instinct' which had enabled him to accomplish what he had done. But now he was shaken and began to vomit. When the heaving stopped, he ran to the camper and found his wife lying still on the floor. She was alive. After firing the shotgun she stood up to chamber a round, tripped, and fell smacking her head on a stationary seat bottom which knocked her out cold. She would have a goose egg on her head for quite a while.

Phelps wanted to pitch the five dead bodies over the edge of the bluff, but he knew he couldn't do that, as it could give his position away to anyone else who might follow. The best thing, he decided, was to drive the bodies several miles away and dump them, arranging them with their weapons in a fashion which would suggest they shot each other over some quarrel. If discovered, no one would be the wiser.

~~~~

Prior to implementation of the lottery, an official announcement was made outlining the major points of the selection method. It was communicated that other details still had yet to be ironed out before actual implementation, which was expected to commence in a few days, a long time in which to contemplate only two possible futures.

Commander Tamari had become depressed over his inability to solve the shielding problem. Sana recognized his somber mood. "What will we do, Aviv?"

"To what are you referring, Dear?" he responded with an upbeat tone.

"What happens if only one of us..."

"Now, now. Don't start on any flights of fantasy."

"I'm not. I just want to be prepared."

"Well, I will tell you this. I will not leave you here alone. On the other hand, if you are selected, I want you to go. I'll figure some way to get back in an MOT. There has to be something we can do to modify them."

"Very noble of you, but if you think I'm going back without you, you are mistaken."

"Sana, if only one of us gets selected, and hopefully at least one of us will, you must be the one to return for several reasons, the first of which is, I might be more effective if I didn't have to worry about getting you back, too. If neither of us gets selected, then it's a moot point. The second reason, assuming I do not return, you can still bear children."

"Aviv!"

"I hope to God it does not happen that way," he exclaimed throwing up his hands "but survival of the human race will depend on who is able to bear children. There aren't that many of us left."

"Thank you very much. Now I feel like some sort of livestock."

"Sana. You are my wife, and I love you, and I do not want to share you with anyone. Just hope we stay together. Let's stop talking about this."

"How do we stop talking about it? Everyone is talking about it! Over 300 people are going to be stranded up here!"

"Thanks. I don't feel bad enough I have failed to find a way to save them, and you have to remind me how many."

"Aviv, you did not fail them." she said soothingly. "This is not your fault. You didn't cause this to happen. Keep looking, maybe you…"

"I've been looking! What do you think I've been doing?! I've looked everywhere and there's no solution!" he said angrily.

Calmly, Sana responded. "Didn't you just tell me there has to be a way to modify the MOTs, you just need to find it?"

"I meant maybe one, or two, not forty of them."

Sana embraced him. "Aviv, we will do whatever, together. I won't be afraid if we are together. And I don't want to be on Earth, if you are not there, too." They kissed, and then made love. If Aviv did have to stay behind, he wanted to make sure Sana's first child was his.

In the Pickett quarters, Emma was questioning Adam about the security detail he was about to pull and with a loaded weapon. "I don't like this. We've been up here for nearly two years and never once have we seen a gun, or posted guards. All of a sudden we can no longer be trusted?"

"Emma, it's not like that."

"Then you explain it to me. I trust these people with my life."

"Under normal circumstances, I do, too."

"Carrying guns and posting guards is not normal. Don't you see, it changes the status quo?"

"Dear, the status quo changed the moment the lottery was announced. Carrying a gun for self defense and enforcement of the rules benefits everyone. Look, this is just a precaution. No one is even supposed to see a gun."

"I see one."

"Come on, Emma."

"No, you come on."

"Look, we're about to tell some 300 souls we're going for a ride, they can't come, and we may, or may not be back for them. Translation, they're probably going to die in space and in a very short time. Now, do you really think they are all just going to sit still for that? I hope they do. But people under pressure and anxiety do crazy things. An ounce of prevention is worth a pound of cure. Trust these people? I trust them alright, I trust them to be human, and in my book that means anything is possible, and we should be ready for anything. Suppose someone gets it in their head that if everyone can't go, nobody goes, and that person attempts to enter a restricted area intent on killing us all, or destroying our only means of getting back to Earth, and the only way to stop them is to shoot them, but we can't shoot them because those of us on patrol don't have any weapons because they're all under lock and key? It's not guns that are bad, Emma, it's people. Besides, this is only a precaution. Things will be alright."

"Easy for you to say, you're a pilot." Emma started to cry.

"Hey, what's this?" he said, holding her by the shoulders. "The lottery hasn't started yet. You don't know what's going to happen. The odds are actually pretty good that we will be together. We're already ahead in the game. And know this, I won't leave you behind."

Emma laughed nervously. "How are you going to do that, with no way to come back?"

"Who says you have to stay behind anyway? But if that were the case, I'd find a way. I'm betting we can get RJP launch ready, and quick, too. If we have to leave anyone behind, Dr. Wagner is going to direct all ESVs to land as close to RJP as possible for the sole purpose of mounting a rescue operation. We'll get everyone down."

Emma stopped crying. "I hope you're right." she said, feeling encouraged by Adam's pep talk.

"Bet your ass I'm right. Now, I've got to go to work." Adam kissed her, and on his way through the door he said to himself, 'The glass is half full, the glass is half full'.

Work came to a standstill for most of the space dwellers. Everyone still reported to their duty stations, they were just too preoccupied to do anything other than talk, or worry silently about the lottery and its consequences. Some people were mad about the newly established security detail, while others thought it made good sense to protect the ESVs and other key areas. Ironically, it was actually a good thing for all because they were keeping an eye on each another.

The lottery began at 0900 on a Friday. Everyone had gathered on Cyprium Prospector to take his or her turn reaching into the Bingo drum and drawing a slip of paper which had a barcode and a corresponding series of 1s and 0s imprinted on it in a combination that made no recognizable sense. There was no drawing order. People just got in line whenever they wished. Dr. Wagner was the 117th person to draw. The process was orderly, as though they were going to cast a vote, or checkout groceries, or board a plane. All stood quietly in line until it was their turn to place their hand inside the drum and take any slip of paper they wanted.

Some plunged their hands deep inside, as though the action would secure them a better chance, while others delicately chose the first piece of paper their fingers touched. Next, they would hand the slip of paper to someone they probably knew, who would scan and confirm that the number they had drawn now corresponded with their name. All were hoping to pull a winner from the mesh cage, with the white letters outlined in red, that spelled, BINGO.

But the mood was not one of happy anticipation at winning a game of chance. It was quiet and somber. Reaching into the drum wasn't about winning, or losing, it was about living or dying, although at this point it wasn't about anything yet, because the computer would not make its random selection until everyone had taken a slip of paper from the cram inside the drum. The whole process was efficient, streamlined and impersonal the way it was designed to be, the way it had to be. No one hung around. They departed quietly as though having left the dentist office. Some returned to what had become his, or her routine. Others went straight to their quarters to wait for the announcement that selection was complete and their status could now be checked on the COMMAND.net. A few left to debate the fairness of life, having escaped extinction below, only to find themselves once again walking through the valley of the shadow of death. Some got drunk and some cried. Nearly all of them prayed.

At 15:00 hours (3 p.m.) that afternoon it was announced the numbers could be checked on the command net. Sana was ACCEPTED. Eric was ACCEPTED. Aviv, Emma and Dr. Wagner were 'unable to process'. Emma was devastated. She sat embraced in Adam's arms sobbing for over an hour before she would even say a word.

"I'll come back for you." Adam tried to be reassuring. "Forget that, I'm not going."

"You have to go." she said finally shutting off her tears.

"No, I don't. I want to stay with you for the rest of my life, however long that is."

Emma touched his face tenderly. "You can't. What about all those people depending on you to fly them back? You have to do it for them."

"Someone else can do it."

"There aren't any more pilots. Only you can do it. I'll be alright."

"I'll find a way to come back to you." Adam promised.

"You'd better."

Sana and Aviv started arguing at the news. It was an argument Aviv thought was settled. Sana wanted to give up her seat to a younger woman who did not get selected.

"I'm sure there are more than a few young girls who would be happy to take my place."

"You're going, and that is that."

"We could be rescued, you know."

"No!" Aviv said loudly believing he had the final word on the matter.

"Whatever you say, Dear." she answered, ending the argument, adding under her breath 'Is that your final answer?' Married, or not, Sana would make her own decision whether, or not to stay, not Aviv, and she felt quite content about her decision because she would be with Aviv, regardless of what was to come.

Dr. Wagner was unmoved. He would continue to proceed as he always had, quietly optimistic that they would be rescued, once RJP regained launch capabilities, and he would do everything within his power to make that happen.

Two days after lottery implementation, engineer Jason Shulze was talking to some of his colleagues about

SIRCA, questioning why the board had not considered it for the MOT shielding problem. He was familiar with TPS material, and felt strongly it should be considered, but he hadn't heard one way, or the other about it. His colleagues assured him, if SIRCA was what he claimed, the board had already considered it, and must have rejected it, or they would have heard about it by now. He was not assuaged by their reasoning so, they cajoled him into going to see the Director about it, straight away, which he did.

Dr. Wagner, who had an open door policy, was briefing Commander Tamari on the lottery implementation when Shulze knocked and walked in.

The two men looked up.

"Jason Shulze." he said nervously, extending his hand for a shake.

"What can I do for you?" the director asked.

"Dr. Wagner, has SIRCA been considered for the shielding problem, and if not, why not?"

The director looked at Aviv, then back at the questioner. Aviv shook his head. "We certainly would consider using SIRCA, if we had any."

"But we do have it. A lot of it."

"I'm sorry, but we don't. I've gone over the inventory listing for all the platforms, Apollo Seventeen and Cyprium Prospector numerous times. If we had any, it would have been incorporated into our plans sometime ago." answered Aviv.

"Commander, we have tons of the stuff. I've seen it. I can show it to you."

"Mr. Shulze, the only thing we have tons of is PPO and a significant quantity of S2F, and as much as I would like to use S2F as a heat shield...." Aviv didn't finish the sentence.

"Commander, how much S2F are you showing?"

Aviv looked at his inventory compilation. "Inventory shows 100 squares."

"Commander, S2F doesn't come in squares, but SIRCA does. Director, someone unfamiliar with SIRCA might easily confuse it with S2F because both materials utilize carbon fiber. If you don't show any SIRCA in inventory, someone missed it, or misidentified it in the inventory. I'm a thermal dynamics engineer. I know what the stuff looks like."

"Son, if that's true, you may have just saved us all."

After personally checking the S2F inventory, Aviv discovered someone had, in fact, incorrectly identified it. Cyprium Prospector indeed held a promising possible solution, though it was not without some risk. It was called SIRCA-Silicone Impregnated Reusable Ceramic Ablator. SIRCA was a monolithic insulating material incorporated with carbon fiber which provided thermal protection through ablation. It could be machined to custom shapes and applied directly to a spacecraft's hull without any additional coatings. And because it could be machined to precise shapes, it could be applied as tiles, leading edge sections, or whatever was required.

This particular TPS material had been developed at the space agency for use in an aeroshell's Backshell Interface Plate. The BIP as it was called, was located at attachment points between an aeroshell's back-side, called the after-body. Someone apparently foresaw a need for the material and loaded it on Cyprium Prospector prior to the Mars mission. There was more than enough SIRCA to cover the front leading surfaces of all 40 MOTs. So where was the risk using this TPS material in the re-entry plan? SIRCA had been demonstrated effective only in BIP applications, but it had yet to be proven as front leading surface, or fore-body TPS material of the kind used on ESVs.

Word spread quickly that a TPS material had been found, and that the likelihood of it meeting requirements was high. Hope soared, and tears of despair among the space dwellers changed to tears of joy and hope. Theoretically, SIRCA, added to the existing MOT protection, should be more efficient than the heat shielding found on an ESV. Even with what appeared to be the best of news, Aviv recognized that a test flight would have to be done. There was really no way to test how SIRCA would hold up during re-entry other than to attach the material to an MOT and fly one through the atmosphere. That called for volunteers. A pilot and co-pilot would have to fly an MOT retrofitted with SIRCA on a potential suicide flight for hook up with USS Maryland. If re-entry was successful, the lottery would be suspended.

Fully aware the space inhabitants would need a landing base and an operations center, USS Maryland embarked on finding a place which would meet their needs. After much consideration it was suggested Royal Naval Air Station Culdrose, not RJP, would be scouted to serve as the operations base for ESV landings and MOT extractions.

Located on Great Britain's southernmost peninsula, in County Cornwall on the Lizard Peninsula, RNAS Culdrose had traditionally held three major roles: serving the Fleet Air Arm's Sea King and Merlin helicopter squadrons; providing search and rescue for the South West region; and to train specialists for the Royal Navy. USS Maryland selected the RNAS site due to its proximity to the facility, its logistical component and potential for resources. It was also relatively close to Svalbard Seed Vault in Norway, which would be essential to their survival.

A small contingent landed on the beach at Carminlowe Creek and proceeded to walk approximately two miles to the airstrip. The submarines had been sending their crews on forays inland for sometime looking for food and clean fresh water, and they had met with some success. Canned and dry packaged food was plentiful, if you knew where to look, so was bottled water. Their primary problem was negotiating the ash which was like mud in some areas, especially when it rained, dry dusty and cement-like in other areas. The ash was everywhere. It was a sepia tone world except for the blue sky that had begun to appear with increasing regularity. No one knew how long the water would remain brown, but it too was getting clearer.

The twelve man scouting party followed a shallow depression which used to be a combination hedgerow and tree line ending at the main entrance to the base. The terrain made a gradual, but noticeable rise in elevation inland until they could see the tops of ash covered buildings surrounded by a razor-wire topped perimeter fence.

It was difficult going through the ash, similar to trudging through soft dry sand. The land was barren, devoid of growing things, yet the reminder of a greener time still remained in the stands of bare tree trunks and shrubbery that pushed through the monotone covered surface. It was also deathly quiet. No planes flew overhead, no cars, trucks, or buses drove along roadways, no dogs barked, or birds chirped. There were no signs of life anywhere, only skeletons poking through the ash.

Some were clothed, some were not, some were animal, yet, all were sun-bleached white and dust covered. It was surreal to say the least.

The buildings and runways of the base appeared to be intact. Numerous aircraft were in closed hangars and in pristine condition, along with a few pieces of heavy equipment which could be used to clear the runways. It was a promising find, and before long, the main runway was ready for the first ESV to touchdown. But before that could happen, an MOT had to make a successful water landing. Dr. Wagner and the board had not yet suspended the lottery, nor would they begin landing ESVs until a successful landing had occurred.

The flight path of the MOT would take it one full turn around the Earth and conclude in the water between the Isles of Scilly in the Atlantic and the Cornwall peninsula. Such a precise landing was a calculation of educated guessing at its best. But if the flight was successful, it would be relatively simple to follow. The real unknown, if there was only one, was the MOT pilots themselves. They had jet-fighter, or fighter/bomber experience, and they had flown in Mars' atmosphere and gravity, but none of them had ever made a re-entry flight back into Earth's atmosphere.

It was a fair day, weather-wise, when the test MOT departed Cyprium Prospector and headed for Earth. The craft entered the atmosphere a bit sooner than calculated, requiring some adjustment to its planned flight path. The MOT also made its re-entry with hotter exterior temperatures than anticipated, but the SIRCA held fast and did its job. The vehicle had a very touchy stick in the thicker atmosphere of Earth, forcing the pilot to make small, but frequent course adjustments. Once in Earth's atmosphere, the MOT became a fast glider.

The pilot had no trouble flying the craft to the extraction point a few miles from USS Maryland. The co-pilot had been reporting all was well with the flight, until it came time to deploy the parachutes. That was all that was known. The pilot had not said what was wrong, or what he suspected was wrong, just that he could not get the parachutes to deploy. The crew of the sub watched in horror as the MOT slammed into the sea. It was a devastating setback. There would be nothing to inspect, or recover because the MOT had crashed in water too deep for the sub to affect recovery. There was a positive in all this, though; it was quickly realized an MOT could practically drop on a dime, which meant shallow water recovery could become a reality.

The space dwellers went to work immediately to try and determine why the parachutes hadn't deployed. Admittedly, no one had tested the mechanism prior to the flight so, they were unsure whether, or not it had anything to do with the crash. Yet, in examining the other MOTs, nothing could be found to suggest mechanism failure.

Thermal dynamics engineer, Jason Shulze, the same engineer who unveiled the TPS material discrepancy, postulated a theory, absent any other recognizable cause for the failure which might have made sense.

"We've ruled out everything else." he said matter-of-factly.

"Everything we can think of." corrected Bill Suljak, "Not everything."

"Right. So what is the only other possible explanation that no one has mentioned?"

"It burned up?" quizzed Bill sarcastically.

"We already know that it didn't do that." avowed one of the engineers.

"Yes! But that has to be it. Not the MOT itself, of course, but look at the placement of the chute pod. The MOT wasn't designed to fly through Earth's atmosphere so, designers weren't worried as much about re-entry heat. I'm betting the SIRCA is doing its job, but the hull shape below the pod doesn't provide enough blow-by to protect the sides of the pod. The chute container is totally unshielded and must have sustained excessive heat damage on re-entry causing the failure."

His theory made sense. Before the next set of volunteers strapped themselves into the next test MOT, they wanted a demonstration of the chutes deploying in the launch bay on Cyprium Prospector. Accompanied by a rather large crowd, the pilot and co-pilot were graciously accommodated with a flawless demonstration to everyone's satisfaction and relief. The chute pod, now covered with SIRCA operated flawlessly. The second test flight was a triumph, so much so, it was determined they could land the remaining MOTs quite close to a very nice stretch of beach just east of RNAS.

When the time came, Adam had the honor of piloting the first ESV to touch down at Royal Naval Air Station Culdrose. He was nervous at the controls and unsure of his flying skills. It had been two years since he last sat in the cockpit of an ESV. Emma, Aviv, Sana, Eric and his bride were among the passengers of that historic flight. These were familiar, but heady moments. Re-entry was uneventful and the landing was performed well. The passengers cheered then they cried, and when there were no more tears, they sat in silence for a long time, prayerful, thankful, thoughtful. When strength and composure returned to them, each quietly rose and walked to the exit where they slid down a safety ramp into a daylight unlike any they had ever experienced. They knew it was Earth, yet it was alien to them. There were no crowds to greet them, no relatives, no marching bands, no politicians giving speeches, only a few U.S. Navy types who were there to observe and record. An eerie silence blanketed the abandoned air station, accompanied by a slight breeze full of heat and humidity. It was a barren monotone landscape void of life.

That night, their first back on Earth in what seemed like ages, the waning moon didn't look any different from what they had remembered, though it was closer to Earth than ever before. Their senses were reeling. Earth's gravity, which they had not experienced in quite some time, had exhausted them. The heat and humidity weren't helping, either, but they weren't sure if that was normal for the region, or a result of the cataclysm. They assumed the latter. For the moment, they were alive, this small remnant of civilization. They would be on a new quest now, survival. Humanity had become an endangered species. And though far different from the one of which Shakespeare wrote, when the Earth was still green, this too, would be a brave new world.